BOMBAY

stories

BOMBAY *stories*

SAADAT HASAN

MANTO

Translated by

MATT REECK AND AFTAB AHMAD

PENGUIN BOOKS

An imprint of Penguin Random House

PENGUIN BOOKS

USA | Canada | UK | Ireland | Australia
New Zealand | India | South Africa | China | Singapore

Penguin Books is part of the Penguin Random House group of companies whose addresses can be found at global.penguinrandomhouse.com

Published by Penguin Random House India Pvt. Ltd
4th Floor, Capital Tower 1, MG Road,
Gurugram 122 002, Haryana, India

First published in hardback by Random House India 2012
This paperback edition published 2014
This edition published by Penguin Random House India 2020

10 9 8 7 6 5

ISBN 9788184006414

For sale in the Indian Subcontinent only

Typeset in Sabon by R. Ajith Kumar
Printed at Manipal Technologies Limited, India

CONTENTS

INTRODUCTION

SAADAT HASAN MANTO — HIS LIFE

Saadat Hasan Manto was born on May 11, 1912 in the small town of Samrala near Ludhiana, a major industrial city in the current-day Indian state of the Punjab.[1] He claimed allegiance not only to his native Punjab but also to his ancestors' home in Kashmir.[2] While raised speaking Punjabi,[3] he was also proud of the remnants of Kashmiri culture that his family maintained—food customs, as well as intermarriage with families of Kashmiri origin—and throughout his life he assigned special importance to others who had Kashmiri roots.[4] In a tongue-in-cheek letter addressed to Pundit Jawaharlal Nehru, he went so far

1 Wadhawan, Jagdish Chander. *Manto Naama: The Life of Saadat Hasan Manto*. Trans. Jai Ratan. New Delhi: Roli, 1998, 14.

2 His family migrated into the Indian plains at some point near the beginning of the nineteenth century (Wadhawan, 13).

3 Flemming, Leslie A. *Another Lonely Voice*. Berkeley, CA: Center for South and Southeast Asia Studies, UC Berkeley, 1979, 4. Or Hasan, Khalid. 'Saadat Hasan Manto: Not of Blessed Memory.' *Annual of Urdu Studies* 4, (1984): 85.

4 Hasan, 85–95.

as to suggest that being beautiful was the second meaning of being Kashmiri.[5]

Manto's father, Maulvi Ghulam Hasan, was a lawyer from a family of lawyers.[6] He married twice, and Manto was the last of twelve siblings and the only son from his father's second marriage.[7] Hasan transferred to Amritsar some time after Manto's birth, and Manto grew up there in Lawyers' Lane, the area of town where lawyers resided.[8] He was a strict disciplinarian with whom the teenage Manto had a somewhat contentious relationship. Manto liked to portray his parents as opposites, with his father's coldness offset by his mother's warmth,[9] and while Manto never wrote much about his father, he did recount in the sketch 'Two Encounters with Agha Hashr' an incident in which his father swooped down upon the informal drama club that several high school friends and he had put together, broke the harmonium and tabla the boys had been using for musical accompaniment, and made it absolutely clear that he considered such activities an utter waste of time.[10]

5 Manto, Saadat Hasan. 'Pundit Manto's First Letter to Pundit Nehru (That Has Become the Foreword to a Novel)' ['*Pandit nehru ke nam pandit manto ka pahla khat (jo is kitab ka dibachah ban gaya)*']. *Untitled. (Baghair unwan ke.)* Lahore: Zafar Brothers, 1956. Republished in *Manto Baqiyat*. Lahore: Sang-e-Meel, 2004. 411.

6 Flemming, 2.

7 Ibid., 2.

8 Ibid., 14.

9 Ibid., 3.

10 Manto, Saadat Hasan. 'Two Encounters with Agha Hashr'. ('*Agha hashr se do mulaqaten*'.) *Bald Angels*. (*Ganje farishte.)* Lahore: Gosha-e-Abad, 1955. Re-published in *Mantonuma*. Lahore: Sang-e-Meel, 2003, 31.

While Manto's three elder half-brothers followed in the family tradition and became lawyers,[11] Manto didn't have the temperament to become a lawyer, and his school career as such was marked more by failure than success. In the Indian educational system, students must pass a final high school examination to be eligible for college, which Manto failed in his first two attempts because of poor scores in, of all subjects, Urdu.[12] After barely passing in his third effort, he entered the Hindu Sabha College in Amritsar in 1931.[13] At the end of his first year, he failed the annual year-end tests, and after failing again the subsequent year, he dropped out.[14] To complicate matters further, his father died on February 25, 1932.[15]

During these years, Manto did have the good fortune to meet Abdul Bari Alig, an editor of the Amritsar newspaper *Equality*.[16] Bari Sahib served as a writing mentor for the young Manto. Under Bari Sahib's tutelage, Manto translated Victor Hugo's novella *The Last Day of a Condemned Man*,[17] and the resulting book was published in Lahore in 1933.[18] This first translation was followed

---

11 Flemming, 2.

12 Ibid., 4.

13 Ibid., 4.

14 Ibid., 4.

15 Ibid., 3.

16 In Urdu, '*Musawat*'.

17 Hugo's *Le dernier jour d'un condamné* was first published in 1829. The fourth edition, published in 1832, was prefaced by a short drama, which served as Hugo's literary response to the criticism and controversy the novella had elicited. Manto translated both the dramatic foreword and the novella.

18 Wadhawan writes that Manto finished translating Hugo's novella in a mere fifteen days. Were this true, Manto's effort here would

by three more projects. With the help of Bari Sahib,[19] he and his friend Hasan Abbas translated Oscar Wilde's play *Vera, or the Nihilists*,[20] a melodrama about the despotism of the Russian monarchy and the efforts of a group of revolutionaries to overthrow the old order. After that he would go on to publish two collections of translated Russian short stories—*Russian Short Stories* and *Gorky's Stories*, a collection of Maxim Gorky's short fiction.[21] These earliest literary efforts showed Manto's ideological fervour and passion for social justice. They also revealed his tendency toward iconoclasm. Bari Sahib also introduced Manto to Communism. Manto later admitted that when

---

be characteristic of the fast work rate he demonstrated later. But Wadhawan does not cite any sources for us to verify whether this detail is factual or rather, stands as another example of how literary scholars have mythologized Manto as a sort of *enfant terrible* and Romantic genius. For an interesting look at how Manto has been used by literary scholars both in America and in South Asia, read Richard Delacy's 'Sa'adat Hasan Manto: The Making of an Urdu Literary Icon'. MA Thesis. Monash University (Clayton, Australia), 1998.

19 See 'Bari Sahib'. *Bald Angels*. Re-published in *Mantonuma*, 71.

20 *Vera, or the Nihilists*, Wilde's first play, was first produced in New York in 1882.

21 Wadhawan suggests that Manto knew Russian, French, and English but does not provide evidence to corroborate this (*Manto Naama*, 178). Alain Désoulières writes that Manto translated the Russian and French texts through English translations ('Vie et œuvre de Saadat Hasan Manto (1912–55).' *Toba Tek Singh et autres nouvelles*, Saadat Hasan Manto. Trans. Alain Désoulières. Paris: Buchet-Chastel, 2008, 11–12.) Lastly, in his essay 'Babu Rao Patel', Manto confesses that his English was mediocre: while it was good enough for basic comprehension, he found translating the English of Babu Rao Patel, the editor of a Bombay magazine *Film India*, very difficult ('Bari Sahib', 213).

Bari Sahib wrote an essay 'From Hegel to Karl Marx' for his short-lived journal *Creation*,[22] he hadn't even heard the name Hegel and knew Marx only as someone Bari Sahib talked about as a friend of the working classes.[23] Yet Manto took it upon himself to learn more about the Communist cause, and later he put his learning to use when he wrote a thumbnail historical essay on the Bolshevik Revolution,[24] as well as his short story 'Rude', included in this volume. Manto's debt to Bari Sahib was immense. He gave him what every young writer needs, both good writing advice and publication,[25] and Manto noted sardonically that if he had not met Bari Sahib, he might have become not a writer but perhaps a criminal.[26]

Manto's second attempt at university began in July 1934.[27] This time he travelled far from home to enter the prestigious Aligarh Muslim University. His career there did not last long, although this time it was not due to poor study habits. After nine months, he was diagnosed with tuberculosis.[28] This diagnosis, which later turned out to be incorrect, was a heavy blow to his scholastic ambitions

22 In Urdu, '*Khalq*'.

23 'Bari Sahib', 73.

24 'Red Revolution'. ('*Surkh inqalab*'.) *Manto's Essays*. (*Manto ke mazameen*.) Lahore: Maktaba-e-Urdu, 1942. Re-published in *Mantonuma*, 685–94.

25 Bari Sahib published Manto's short story 'A Show' ('*Tamasha*') in the inaugural edition of *Creation*.

26 'Several Encounters with Akhtar Sheerani' ('*Akhtar sheerani se chand mulaqaten*'). *Bald Angels*. Lahore: Gosha-e-Adab, 1955. Re-published in *Mantonuma*, 46. See also 'Bari Sahib', 85.

27 Flemming, 6.

28 Ibid., 7.

since tuberculosis was then a deadly disease.[29] He left the university, borrowed money from his elder sister, and retreated into the mountains, spending three months in a sanitarium in the small northern town of Batot.[30] Whatever the original cause of the chest pains he had been suffering in Aligarh had been, his health improved somewhat in the high altitude of the mountains. He returned to Amritsar in late 1935 and faced yet another set of challenges; his mother was without money and he realized he would have to start earning his own living. The next year his life would change considerably when he accepted the offer of Nazir Ludhianvi to go to Bombay to edit his weekly film newspaper *The Painter*.[31]

Thus began the second era of Manto's young life. When he arrived in Bombay, he was twenty-four years old. Manto would live in Bombay twice: from 1936 to 1941; and then after a hiatus of one and a half years, from 1942 until his final move to Lahore in 1948. In hindsight, he would recognize that these Bombay years were the best and most enjoyable of his life; and yet while Manto lived there his frequent bouts of ill health[32] coupled with his temperamental personality meant that his time in Bombay

---

29 Chandavarkar, Rajnarayan. *Imperial Power and Popular Politics: Class, Resistance and the State in India, c. 1850–1950*. Cambridge: Cambridge University Press, 1998, 234.

30 Batot is in Jammu near the Kashmiri border. See Manto's 'My Wedding' ('*Meri shadi*') for a brief accounting of this stretch of Manto's poor health. [*Above, Below, and in Between*. (*Upar niche aur darmiyan*.) Lahore: Gosha-e-Adab, 1954. Re-published in *Mantorama*. Lahore: Sang-e-Meel, 2004, 276–92.]

31 In Urdu, '*Musawwir*'.

32 Wadhawan, 46.

was not at all free of disappointments, sadness, or angst.

Shortly after Manto went to Bombay, his mother moved there as well. She went to live with his only full sibling, his elder sister Iqbal, in the suburb of Mahim.[33] His mother was eager to see him married, and in 1938 Manto became engaged to his future wife, Safiya, the daughter of a Lahore family of Kashmiri descent.[34] Their wedding did not take place until April 26, 1939 since Manto continually procrastinated because of his inability to support her financially and the uncertainty he had about his ability to be a good husband.[35] But to his own surprise, Manto took to being a husband. In May 1940 Safiya gave birth to a son, Arif, and Manto's life as a father began, though this would be bitterly truncated when the toddler died the following April.[36]

Manto worked at the Clare Road offices of *The Painter*. Upon his arrival he slept in the office of the newspaper and continued to do so until he had enough money to rent a room in a squalid building nearby—a two-storey building with holes in its roof, forty narrow rooms, and only two bathrooms, neither of which had a door.[37] He lived in these conditions—which caused his mother to cry when she first came to his room—until ten days before Safiya was to move in with him, at which point he hurriedly rented a room

---

33 'My Wedding', 279.

34 Ibid., 281.

35 Ibid., 285.

36 Flemming, 14. Manto would go on to write the short story 'Khalid Dear' ('*Khalid mian*') in honour of his dead son. [*Empty Bottles, Empty Cartons*. (*Khali botalen khali dibbe*.) Lahore: Maktaba-e-Jadeed, 1950. Re-published in *Mantorama*, 72–81.]

37 'My Wedding', 277 and 285.

nearby.[38] In August 1940 Nazir Ludhianvi suddenly fired Manto from the newspaper,[39] and Manto then took up the editorship of Babu Rao Patel's film magazine *Caravan*. Not even seven months had passed, though, when he grew dissatisfied with that job and accepted a position at All India Radio in Delhi.

During these years, Manto not only worked at editing jobs but also wrote stories and radio plays.[40] He published his first full collection of short stories, *Sparks*, as well as *Short Stories*.[41] Just as importantly, Nazir Ludhianvi introduced him to the film world where Manto soon began to work as a scriptwriter.

Manto's first job in the film industry came at the Imperial Film Company, and his first film credits appeared in the 1937 film *Village Girl* whose script and dialogue he wrote.[42] As this was India's first colour feature-length film, the Imperial Film Company had spent a considerable sum of money buying the required colour-processing equipment. When the film failed to make an impact at the box office, the company's future fell into doubt. Nazir Ludhianvi intervened once again on Manto's behalf and got him a job at Film City, where his pay jumped from forty to one

38 The room represented a considerable upgrade as it cost thirty-five rupees per month as opposed to the previous room's nine rupees (Ibid., 278 and 287).

39 'Babu Rao Patel'. *Bald Angels*. Re-published in *Mantonuma*. 215.

40 Ibid., 216.

41 *Sparks*. (*Atish pare*.) Lahore: Urdu Book Stall, 1936. Re-published in *Mantorama*. And *Manto's Short Stories*. (*Manto ke afsane*.) Lahore: Maktaba-e-Urdu, 1940. Republished in *Mantorama*.

42 Rajadhyaksha, Ashish and Paul Willemen, ed. *Encyclopedia of Indian Cinema*. Oxford: Oxford University Press, 1999, 272.

hundred rupees a month.[43] Yet when Seth Ardeshir Irani, the owner of the Imperial Film Company, learned that Manto had joined another studio, a tug of war developed. He wanted Manto back, and at twice his original salary Manto rejoined the Imperial Film Company.[44] This reunion didn't last long, though, because almost as soon as Manto returned, the company became insolvent. Manto's work there ended with his having collected only eight months' worth of his year's pay.[45] Manto then joined Saroj Movietone in June 1938, and yet this company's finances were so thin that it also immediately threatened to go out of business. Seth Nanu Bhai Desai, the owner of the studio, secured new financial backing, and the studio was relaunched as Hindustan Movietone. Despite disputes with Seth Nanu Bhai over unpaid back wages, Manto would stay there until his abrupt departure for Delhi three years later.[46] During his tenure there, Manto wrote the story for his second film *Mud*, a film that was later wisely renamed *My Hometown*.

Manto left Bombay for Delhi in 1941, and we might ascribe his departure to general malaise. His firing from *The Painter*, his dissatisfaction with his job at *Caravan*, the memory of the sudden death in June 1940 of his mother,[47] his uncertain health, and the stresses of living in a big city without ever earning a stable income all combined to make the job at All India Radio sound appealing.

While in Delhi, Manto's life as a writer improved. All

43 'My Wedding', 278.
44 Ibid., 278.
45 'Babu Rao Patel', 214.
46 Ibid., 215. See also 'My Wedding', 288.
47 Flemming, 11.

India Radio was emerging as an outstanding literary venue, and Manto came into contact with many leading Urdu writers of the time. His job at the station was to produce radio plays, and he did this with great diligence, churning out plays in impressive numbers, and in his short time in Delhi he saw several collections of his radio plays published.[48] Other aspects of his writing life flourished as well. Along with a volume of essays, he published a short story collection called *Smoke*.[49] Unfortunately, Manto's expectation that his health would improve in Delhi was not borne out, and his contentious and often oversensitive reactions to his colleagues eventually tired everyone involved.[50] A series of events unfolded in his second summer in Delhi that would lead him back to Bombay: Nazir Ludhianvi once again offered Manto a position at *The Painter*, and Manto's good friend Krishan Chander, who had originally offered him the job at All India Radio, left the station. When Upendranath Ashk—

48 The first four volumes of his radio plays were the following: *Come On.* (*Ao.*) Lahore: Naya Idarah, 1940; *Three Women.* (*Tin auraten.*) Lahore: Maktaba-e-Urdu, 1942; *Funerals.* (*Janaze.*) Lahore: Zafar Brothers, 1942; and *Short Stories and Plays.* (*Afsane aur drame.*) Hyderabad: Sayyid Abdul Razzaq Tajir Kutab, 1943. Flemming provides these dates in *Another Lonely Voice*. The first two dates are corroborated by short forewords Manto wrote and dated, both of which are included in *Manto's Plays.* (*Manto drame.*) Lahore: Sang-e-Meel, 2003. 265 and 481. In private correspondence, Sang-e-Meel lists the publication date of *Funerals* to be 1955, evidently a later edition of the original work.

49 *Smoke.* (*Dhuan.*) Delhi: Saaqi Book Depot, 1941. Re-published in *Manto Kahaniyan*. Lahore: Sang-e-Meel, 2004.

50 Flemming, 14.

another noted Urdu writer with whom Manto shared an especially acrimonious relationship—took over Chander's job, Manto couldn't reconcile himself to the fact that Ashk would be editing his work. While the station readied to broadcast a version of Manto's play 'The Wanderer' that was edited by Ashk, Manto unceremoniously quit.[51]

Manto returned to Bombay. He resumed editing *The Painter*; and upon the intercession of Shahid Latif, an old friend from Aligarh and husband of the influential Urdu short story and film writer Ismat Chughtai, he began to work for Filmistan, a film company where over the next six years he would meet many of the most famous actors, actresses, directors, and personalities of the film world. The next significant event in his life—and in the lives of all those in the subcontinent—came at the stroke of midnight, August 15, 1947, when India and Pakistan came into being. Safiya and the couple's three daughters left for Lahore, but Manto stayed, joining Shahid Latif and the famous film actor Ashok Kumar in their attempt to revive one of the first great Indian film companies, Bombay Talkies.[52] But trouble turned up there as well, when Kumar passed over Manto's work, deciding instead to adapt an Ismat Chughtai short story into a film.[53] Manto had a hard time accepting this decision. The perceived affront, coupled with increasing Hindu–Muslim communal tensions, made it difficult for Manto to see a future for himself in the changing political climate of Bombay, so he set out

51 Ibid., 14.
52 Ibid., 16.
53 Ibid., 16.

for Pakistan. He travelled by boat to Karachi and arrived in Lahore on January 8, 1948.

Thus began the last and the hardest era of Manto's short life. The seven years he lived in Pakistan were characterized by indigence, severe alcoholism, and nostalgic reminiscences about the life he had known in Bombay. He never adjusted to his new environment. He wrote in the introduction to his volume of short stories *Cold Meat* (1950) about his sense of dislocation upon arriving at his new home:

> For three months I was confused. I couldn't figure out where I was. Was I in Bombay, at my friend Hasan Abbas's place in Karachi, or in Lahore, where the Qaid-e-Azam Fund was being built up through proceeds from dance and music concerts being put on in a handful of restaurants?
>
> For three months I couldn't make up my mind about anything. It seemed as if three movies were playing simultaneously on one screen. Sometimes I saw Bombay's shopping districts and alleyways, sometimes I saw the small trams of Karachi rushing past donkey-drawn carriages, and sometimes I saw Lahore's noisy restaurants. I couldn't figure out where I was. I would sit lost in thought all day.[54]

In Pakistan he drifted through his days without steady employment, trying to maintain his dedication to being

54 'The Trouble of the Shining Sun' ('*Zahamat-e-mihr-e-darakhshan*'). *Cold Meat*. (*Thanda gosht*.) Lahore: Maktaba-e-Jadeed, 1950. Republished in *Mantonamah*. Lahore: Sang-e-Meel, 351.

a serious writer but encumbered by poverty and a debilitating drinking habit. He adopted the habit of writing a story a day and going immediately to a magazine's office to demand payment, only to spend this money on alcohol.[55] He entered a mental institution in April 1952 in a belated attempt to cure his alcoholism, but this had no lasting results.[56] Wracked by his disease, depressed about the uncertain status of his reputation, and distressed by his failure to provide for his family, he died on January 18, 1955.

MANTO'S BOMBAY

Bombay was where the motion picture made its first appearance on the subcontinent when the French Lumière brothers' Cinématographe was shown on July 7, 1896 at the upscale Watson's Hotel.[57] The honour of having made the first Indian film goes to Hari Bhatvadekar whose two short films—one of a choreographed wrestling bout and another of a man training a monkey—were shown in late 1899.[58] Bombayites would have to wait more than thirteen years for the first feature-length Indian motion picture to be released, when D.G. Phalke unveiled the mythological film *Raja Harishchandra* in May 1913.[59] In order to complete his film, Phalke mortgaged his life insurance policy to

55 Wadhawan, 143.

56 Flemming, 18.

57 Rangoonwalla, Firoze. *A Pictorial History of Indian Cinema.* London: Hamlyn, 1979, 10.

58 Ibid., 11.

59 Ibid., 12.

afford travelling to London to buy equipment,[60] converted his kitchen into a makeshift laboratory,[61] and, according to Manto, even sold off his wife's jewellery.[62] He also faced the difficulty of finding a woman to play the role of King Harishchandra's wife, as all the women he asked refused due to the impropriety they felt that acting involved, and Phalke was forced to give the role to a man.[63] Phalke would go on to make twenty mythological films and ninety short films,[64] becoming the undisputed champion of the silent era and the consensus 'father' of Indian cinema.

The next landmark in the history of the Indian film industry came in 1931 when *Light of the World* became the country's first feature-length sound film.[65] The Imperial Film Studio—the first studio at which Manto worked after coming to Bombay—claimed credit for this film, and their 1937 film *Village Girl* was the first feature-length colour film in the subcontinent.[66] The 1930s saw the first studio competition arise. Not only did the Imperial Film Company figure prominently on the scene, but the Prabhat Film Company and Bombay Talkies also made names for

60 Joshi, Lalit Mohan, ed. *Popular Indian Cinema: Bollywood*. London: Dakini, 2002. 15.

61 Rajadhyaksha, Ashish. 'Indian Cinema: Origins to Independence'. *The Oxford History of World Cinema*. Geoffrey Nowell-Smith, ed. Oxford: Oxford University Press, 1996, 402.

62 Manto, Saadat Hasan. 'A Glance at the Indian Film Industry'. *Manto's Essays*. In *Mantonuma*, 592.

63 *Popular Indian Cinema: Bollywood*, 16.

64 Ibid., 16.

65 Rajadhyaksha, 403.

66 *Encyclopedia of Indian Cinema*, 109.

themselves.[67] Prabhat was established in 1929 in Kolhapur though the studio was moved four years later to nearby Pune. Set up by V. Shantaram, K.R. Dhaiber, S.B. Kulkarni, and S. Fatehlal, the studio had several hits in the thirties, including *The Churning of the Oceans* (1934) and *The Immortal Flame* (1936).[68] In addition to the progressive social content of their films, the studio was known for the technical qualities of its products. The four founding members, as Manto notes, 'all had the same desire, and that was to outstrip everyone else in matters of art and technique.'[69] Bombay Talkies came into being five years after Prabhat and featured the husband–wife pair of Himanshu Rai and the beautiful Devika Rani, the former working as producer/director and the latter starring in films,[70] including the popular *Untouchable Girl*.[71] Furthermore, their studio is noteworthy from a historical perspective, as it employed three men who would later come to rank among the forefront of actors in the entire history of Indian cinema: Ashok Kumar (then a laboratory assistant), Dilip Kumar (then and afterwards an actor), and Raj Kapoor (then a clapper).[72]

---

67 Other prominent companies included New Theatres in Kolkata (founded 1931), Minerva Movietone (founded 1936), the Ranjit Film Company (founded 1929), Wadia Movietone (founded 1933), and Sagar Film Company (founded 1930). (For more see *Popular Indian Cinema: Bollywood*, Chapter One, and references in *Encyclopedia of Indian Cinema*.)

68 In Hindi, '*Amritmanthan*' and '*Amar jyoti*', respectively.

69 'Babu Rao Patel', 210.

70 *Popular Indian Cinema: Bollywood*, 21.

71 In Hindi, '*Acchut kanya*'.

72 Ibid., 22.

The burgeoning film industry aside, Manto's Bombay was a city of economic opportunity, attracting people from all over India and indeed from around the world. The census of 1921 revealed that an amazing eighty-four per cent of its work force came from outside the city.[73] These workers were men from villages and towns, thinking they would come to the city for a while to earn money to send back home. Often, they decided to stay for good, sending for their families and other relatives to join them. These immigrants developed their own lifestyle, which has now long since become a part of the Bombay myth. The tightly confined chawls constructed by the textile mills to house their employees were their environs, and it was here that two of the typical characters of Bombay, the gangster and the prostitute, came about.

A chawl can best be described as tenement housing. The rooms were tiny and without running water. Common lavatories and washrooms were located at the end of corridors, or as in 'Ten Rupees', the buildings were entirely without such facilities. Access to the water taps was a serious issue, especially in the summer when the water supply often failed. Getting water was the cause of much worrying and worse, and the communal water taps brought people together who would have been better kept apart. Sarita, a teenage prostitute, is the main character in 'Ten Rupees'. Manto writes about the tense encounters that could take place around the taps: 'But when Tukaram harassed Sarita by the water spigot one early morning,

73 Adarkar, Neera and Meena Menon. *One Hundred Years, One Hundred Voices: The Millworkers of Girangaon: An Oral History.* Intro. Rajnarayan Chandavarkar. Calcutta: Seagull, 14.

Sarita's mother started screeching at Tukaram's wife, "Why can't you keep track of that dirty rat? I pray to God he goes blind for eyeing my little girl like that."'

People jammed into the chawls' rooms. The 1930s saw the textile mills begin multiple shifts, and workers often rotated in and out of the chawls' rooms just as they replaced each other at the factory. The men returned to the chawls to collapse upon their mats, their peers sleeping right next to them; when these men returned to the factory, others came to sleep in the spaces just vacated. In 1931 a full three quarters of Bombayites lived in such one-room accommodations.[74] But sharing such tight quarters didn't bring about a sense of solidarity within the ranks of the workers. Instead, indifference manifested itself, as Manto writes in 'Ten Rupees':

> Sarita's mother was always telling this story [of the death of her husband], but no one knew whether it was true. No one in the building felt any sympathy for her, perhaps because their lives were so difficult that they had no time to think about others. No one had any friends. Most of the men slept during the day and worked nights in the nearby factory. Everyone lived right on top of one another, and yet no one took any interest in anyone else.

The chawls' overcrowding made maintaining order difficult. The police by themselves could not—or chose not to—serve as the main law enforcers, and so a new figure

74 Ibid., 21–22.

emerged, the 'dada', the Bombay hoodlum cum agent of the peace. A dada was at once a benevolent figure and one to be feared. Manto gives us two portraits of dadas, the extended one of Mammad Bhai in 'Mammad Bhai' and a briefer look at Dada Karim in 'Hamid's Baby'. The dada would help those living in the area where he ruled, even if it meant committing a crime to exact revenge and re-establish order. He had a reputation for violence, and his persona was built up through anecdotes, real and mythic, which exemplified his physical prowess, cunning, and keen eye for justice. He knew everything about his people, and he was expected to protect them. Mammad Bhai is feared for his ability in martial arts and his habit of wearing a razor-sharp knife beneath his waistband. But he is also a benefactor, making sure the sick get cured and the poor don't get cheated, and protecting the women of the neighbourhood.

Bombay's working world was a male one. In 1864 there were about 600 women for 1,000 men, and by 1930 the proportion of women had declined even further.[75] If women worked, it was because their family was so poor that they needed the income, however slight. In 1931, only thirteen per cent of women claimed employment, even though around two-thirds were of working age.[76] Prostitution developed out of these conditions and did so on a scale unlike anywhere else in India, as the migration

75 Chandavarkar, Rajnarayan. *The Origins of Industrial Capitalism in India: Business strategies and the working classes in Bombay, 1900–1940*. Cambridge: Cambridge University Press, 1994, 34.

76 Ibid., 94. Chandravarkar cites that two-thirds of women living in Bombay in the inter-war years were of working age—defined as being between the ages of fifteen and fifty-eight.

of unaccompanied males to the city met with destitute women forced to earn money by any means possible. In 1921 there were an estimated 30,000 to 40,000 prostitutes in the city.[77] (Contemporary figures estimate there are now about 450,000 prostitutes, and yet these numbers are approximate and conceivably on the low side.[78]) Manto saw how the unique social conditions of the city bred prostitution, and the figure of the prostitute became of considerable interest to him. In *Bombay Stories*, prostitutes of one type or another are featured in just about every story.

Another striking feature of Bombay was its ethnic diversity. One gauge of this would be Manto's enumerations of the ethnicities represented by prostitutes: in 'Mammad Bhai' he claims that there were prostitutes 'of every sort—Jewish, Punjabi, Marathi, Kashmiri, Gujarati, Anglo-Indian, French, Chinese, Japanese.' In the same story Manto mentions Arab pearl merchants and Chinese restaurateurs.[79] Otherwise, in several stories there are Punjabis and Kashmiris; in 'Khushiya' the prostitute Kanta Kumari is from Mangalore, Karnataka. 'Smell' and 'Mummy' feature Anglo-Indians; 'The Insult' and 'Rude' mention people from south India. 'Ten Rupees'

77 Ibid., 97.

78 David, M.D. *Bombay: The City of Dreams*. Mumbai: Himalaya, 1995, 243.

79 You might not think of the Chinese in India, but some Chinese have lived in the country for hundreds of years. Kolkata has historically had the largest Chinese community, and the history of Chinese there goes back to 1778. The city became home to 10,000 Chinese during the inter-war years and later boasted of around 30,000 people of Chinese origin. (Biswas, Ranjita. 'Little China Stays Alive in Eastern India'. *Inter Press Service News Agency*, August 3, 2006.)

and 'Mummy' involve characters from Andhra Pradesh; Pathans from the Hindu Kush Mountains are mentioned in 'Janaki.' Mammad Bhai is from Rampur, Uttar Pradesh; and Sen, the murdered musician in 'Mummy', is Bengali.

Not only did people come from everywhere to live in Bombay, but people of all religions lived there together in relative harmony—from the Parsi descendants of Zoroastrian immigrants from Iran to Jews, Christians, Hindus, Sikhs, Jains, and Muslims; and this history of tolerance has a surprisingly long history. Christian history in Bombay began almost 500 years ago. The Portuguese were the first to come, and they worked up and down the western coast, with the Jesuits and the Franciscans competing for souls to convert. While the Jesuits were said to have won out in Dadar and Parel, the Franciscans fared better among the native fisher-folk in Mahim and Bombay.[80] The architectural patrimony of Christianity in Bombay is old as well, as St Michael's in Mahim, the oldest surviving church in the city, was built in 1534, the year the Portuguese acquired land from the Sultan of Gujarat.[81] By the time the British took over, there were already Christians in the native population, and in 1674 the East India Company asked the British government to send over some good unmarried Anglican girls since the Company's workers were breaking religious etiquette by marrying native Indian Catholics.[82]

---

80 David, 18.

81 Ibid., 19.

82 Ibid., 39. Percival Spear notes that the British were marrying both natives and Portuguese Roman Catholics (*The Nabobs: A Study of the Social Life of the English in Eighteenth Century India*. London: Oxford University Press, 1963, 13).

The history of the Parsi community is deep as well[83] for they came as soon as the British, and their contributions—first as cloth merchants, then as shipwrights,[84] and yet later as industrial barons and intellectuals—greatly aided the city on its rise to prominence. A Jewish community also existed in the city:[85] the 1941 census showed more than 10,000 Jews living there, and the vast majority of these were the Bene Israel.[86] Mozelle from the eponymous story in *Bombay Stories* is Jewish. Manto provides us with certain Indian Jewish stereotypes—namely, Mozelle's traditional dress and wooden Sandals—but her licentiousness is clearly a fictional detail. Among the other communities, the Muslims ruled the area before the Western colonial intrusions, and Hindus of diverse types have lived in the area since perhaps time immemorial.

In only the last twenty years, Mumbai has increasingly become associated with communal violence, chiefly after the 1993 bombings and riots that seared the city and left

83 The Parsi community erected the Tower of Silence on Malabar Hill in 1674 (David, 219).

84 Ibid., 2. Also, Spear writes, 'The Parsi shipbuilder rather than the English merchant was the true maker of Bombay' (*Nabobs*, 71).

85 India has been home to three distinct Jewish communities: the Cochin Jews of Kerala, the Bene Israel Jews of the Konkan coast south of Bombay, and the Baghdadi Jews, who fled persecution in Iraq during the eighteenth and nineteenth centuries to settle as immigrant communities in Mumbai and Kolkata. The Bene Israel Jews got their name from the Muslims of the Konkan coast who identified them with the Banu Israel named in the Koran. (Isenberg, Shirley Berry. *India's Bene Israel: A Comprehensive Inquiry and Sourcebook*. Berkeley, CA: Judah L. Magnes Museum, 1988, viii, 25 and 375.)

86 Ibid., 297.

1,400 dead in the aftermath of the destruction of the Babri Mosque in Ayodhya, Uttar Pradesh.[87] The first notable example of such violence came during an eight-day stretch in 1893 when riots broke out in reaction to Hindu–Muslim communal fighting in Saurashtra, Gujarat. Eighty people died (thirty-three Hindus, forty-six Muslims, and one Jew), and 700 people were wounded.[88]

Riots erupted again in 1929, and yet these riots were not set off by religious acrimony; they began as a clash between striking workers of General Motors and a group of Pathan musclemen.[89] Pathans were an intimidating physical lot—tall, broad-shouldered men wearing turbans and flowing gowns, their kurtas so long they nearly touched the ground. From the wild mountainous regions of the borderland between Afghanistan and Pakistan, they had well, deserved reputations for violence. In addition to working as henchmen for corporate powers, they also worked as small-time moneylenders. They arrived on payday at the factory gates to demand repayment on loans and were said to go so far as to demand sex from women who could not pay up.[90] (Pathans figure in *Bombay Stories* several times. In 'Mummy', there is mention of a 'bloodthirsty Pathan' pressuring Chaddah to pay back a loan, and in 'Why I

87 Thomas Blom Hansen notes that the official death count was 800 (official death counts in India tend to be low), but also that 150,000 Muslims fled the city as well as another 100,000 who sought shelter in predominantly Muslim neighbourhoods (*The Wages of Violence: Naming and Identity in Postcolonial Bombay*. Princeton: Princeton University Press, 2001, 122).

88 Adarkar and Menon, 114.

89 Ibid., 169.

90 Ibid., 110.

Don't Go to the Movies', Manto mentions the 'intimidating Pathan guard.') A group of forty such Pathans were called in to break the workers' strike. They descended upon the offices of the Girni Kamgar Union, the leading Communist labour union, but the violence soon got out of hand and turned along communal lines. In the clashes, 106 people died and over 600 were wounded,[91] and in time these riots became known as the Pathan Riots.

Manto claims that he was twice witness to Hindu–Muslim violence during his first stint in Bombay (1936–41),[92] and there is no reason to doubt him, as the years before independence saw increased violence of all sorts, including labour strikes in connection with the Quit India Movement. And yet it wasn't until the communal violence of 1946–47 that Muslims thought to live separately for their safety.[93] Manto left the city due in part to the growing tension that divided the city on religious lines, and yet even then the growing unease he felt was more a premonition for what the future would hold than it was a part of the city he knew and loved.

LITERARY CONTEXT

Salman Rushdie has described Manto as a writer of 'low-life' fictions,[94] and this phrase helps explain why Manto had problems with government censorship and, to an

91 *Time Magazine,* February 18, 1929.

92 '*Matters*'. ('*Baten*'.) *Manto's Essays.* In *Mantonuma*, 695.

93 Adarkar and Menon, 20.

94 Rushdie, Salman. 'Damme, This is the Oriental Scene for you!' *The New Yorker,* June 23–30, 1997: 51.

extent, with many of his fellow writers. Rushdie's comment points not only to the low social status of many—in fact the overwhelming majority—of Manto's characters, but it also suggests the uncertain morals that many of these characters display. It was due to this second point that Manto found himself in conflict with the leading literary movement of India and Pakistan of the twentieth century, the Progressive Writers' Movement.

The Progressive Writers' Movement began in 1933 with the publication of the collection of short stories *Burning Coals*,[95] as four young writers critical of the shape Indian literature was taking came together to argue for a new way of writing that was politically minded and sceptical of religion. The movement took its official identity the next year when two writers living in London, Sajjad Zahir and Mulk Raj Anand, founded the Progressive Writers' Association,[96] and when the All India Progressive Writers' Association was established in 1936.[97] Urdu writers joined the revolutionary spirit by initiating their own Urdu Progressive Writers' Association, along with starting up the journal *New Literature*[98] that would be the effective mouthpiece for their efforts. The UPWA's first manifesto announced their intention that 'we want the new literature of India to make its subject the fundamental problems of our life. These are the problems of hunger, poverty, social backwardness and slavery.' In April 1939 in the first issue of *New Literature*, they again stated their position: 'In

95 Flemming, 24. In Urdu, '*Angare*'.
96 Ibid., 25.
97 Ibid., 25.
98 In Urdu, '*Naya adab*'.

our opinion, progressive literature is literature that trains its eye upon the realities of life, reflects them, investigates them and leads the way toward a new and better life.'[99]

Manto is considered a peripheral member of this movement. He did focus on the lower strata of South Asian society, and he was friends with many writers of the movement, most notably Krishan Chander and Ismat Chughtai. Nonetheless, the elite of the movement, both in India and later in Pakistan, often disapproved of Manto's writing and sought to distance themselves from him. In the All India Urdu Congress in Hyderabad in 1944, Sajjad Zahir criticized Manto's story 'Smell' for being obscene and for not having the reformatory intent that modern fiction should have.[100] Literature was meant to be a vehicle for social uplift, and Manto's stories often fell short of the ideals of the more doctrinaire: he portrayed society's sordid aspects as they were and remained free from any ideological programme. Manto was too individualistic (and perhaps too egotistical) to belong to any movement that demanded absolute allegiance from its members; he was too interested in his own viewpoint to sacrifice anything for the good of any group. Manto made his own views known on the Progressive Writers' Movement, and he wrote about them with bitter irony and sarcasm. Two examples include his story 'Progressives',[101] a trenchant criticism of the movement's pertinacity, and his satirical essay

99 Azmi, Khalil ur-Rahman. *Urdu men taraqqi pasand adabi tahrik*. Aligarh: Anjuman Taraqqi Urdu (Hind), 1972, 46, 67.

100 Ibid., 26.

101 *Manto Kahaniyan*, 267–77.

'A Progressive Cemetery'[102] that makes fun of the label 'progressive' by placing it in the context of the supposed advancements taking place in a Bombay cemetery.

Indeed, perhaps the most consistent reaction to Manto's writing during his lifetime was censure. Manto stood accused of writing obscenities on five separate occasions. His first four trials took place in Lahore and the last in Karachi, and in each instance he was eventually acquitted. His first trial took place shortly after the story 'The Black Shalwar' was published in 1941.[103] His second such experience took place after he had resettled in Bombay. A CID agent arrived from Lahore to arrest Manto at ten at night in his apartment on January 8, 1945, again in connection with 'The Black Shalwar' but also for his story 'Smoke'.[104] Manto was subsequently released on bail and ordered to stand trial in Lahore.[105]

Manto stood trial for the third time for his story 'Smell' and his essay 'Modern Literature'.[106] In the manner typical of his trials, he was convicted in the lower court but then acquitted in the sessions court.[107] On May 3, 1945 Special Sessions' Judge M.R. Bhatiya wrote in his judgment that in '[the story] there was nothing to incite lustful feelings, and moreover in the testimony of the expert literary witnesses the story is progressive . . . and will have no harmful effect on people's morals.'[108] Manto's difficulties with censorship

102 *Mantonuma*, 723–31.
103 In Urdu, '*Kali shalwar*'.
104 In Urdu, '*Dhuan*'.
105 Wadhawan, 90.
106 In Urdu, '*bu*' and '*adab-e-jadid*', respectively.
107 Wadhawan, 100.
108 'The Trouble of the Shining Sun'. *Mantonamah*, 372.

continued after Partition as well. After the Lahore literary journal *Portraits*[109] published his canonical story 'Open Up', the Pakistani government stepped in to close down the journal's printing operations for six months.[110] Manto's story 'Cold Meat' then became the focus of a series of trials. Manto, along with Nasir Anwar, the owner and editor of *Eternity*,[111] the magazine that printed the story, faced an arduous course that lasted over a year. Manto faced a prison term of three months' heavy labour and a fine of 300 rupees (along with three weeks' additional heavy labour if he couldn't come up with the money to pay the fine),[112] but in the end Sessions Court Judge Inayatullah Khan came to the reasonable conclusion that 'Cold Meat' was 'not obscene nor overly objectionable.'[113] Manto would stand trial one last time in Karachi for his story 'Above, Below, and in Between', with the result this time being a small fine that Nasir Anwar willingly paid.[114] Unfortunately, Manto's troubles with the Pakistani government have continued into the present, and on the fiftieth anniversary of his death, he was still banned on Pakistani television and radio.[115]

Other than the government censors and Manto's fellow writers, it's not clear how many read his work. His stories

109 In Urdu, '*Naqush*'.
110 'The Trouble of the Shining Sun', 354–56.
111 In Urdu, '*Javed*'.
112 'The Trouble of the Shining Sun', 382.
113 Ibid., 402.
114 Wadhawan, 116.
115 'Manto's Fiftieth Death Anniversary Observed: Ban on Manto's Writings on TV and Radio Condemned'. The *Daily Times (Islamabad)* January 19, 2005.

were published in the leading Urdu literary magazines of his time, but these presumably had small subscriptions as they did not alleviate the poverty that Manto battled for most of his life. Manto began his autobiographical essay 'My Wedding' with a self-conscious appeal to readers, 'For those of you who want to peek into my life, I'm going to tell you about my wedding',[116] and yet the curious question arises as to who exactly he imagined was interested. (Then again, writers do convince themselves that someone is listening.) When Manto left his employment in the Bombay film industry and arrived in Pakistan, he suddenly found himself unable to earn money writing and unwilling to find a new way of generating an income. In his essay 'Bald Angels', Manto wrote:

> To tell you the truth I was so bitter about things that I wanted to get an allotment.[117] Then I could comfortably sit in the corner and let my writing go. Any thoughts I had, I'd let them pass. If I didn't get an allotment, then I'd go to work in the black market or make bootleg liquor. But I feared that if I ended up doing that, I'd drink all the booze myself—all my efforts would be wasted and I wouldn't earn anything at all.[118]

116 'My Wedding', 276.

117 The Pakistani government was awarding land and businesses to immigrants from India so that they could begin to build up their new lives.

118 'Bald Angels', 224.

BOMBAY STORIES

Manto's best known stories are those set in the Partition days—gory, chilling narratives, such as 'Open Up' and 'Cold Meat' as well as the psychological portrait of madness in 'Toba Tek Singh.' Yet his writing had other focal points and bore other geographies in mind, in particular those related to Bombay.

For a restless soul like Manto, home would never be an easy concept, but there is good evidence to suggest that he felt more at home in Bombay's cosmopolitan, topsy-turvy metropolis than anywhere else. After immigrating to Pakistan, he was filled with nostalgia for the life he had known in Bombay. In the postscript to his volume of short stories *Yazid* (1951),[119] he wrote about his feelings for the city, his 'other home':

> Today I am disconsolate. A strange brooding has come over me. It is the same sadness I experienced four or four and a half years ago when I bid farewell to my other home, Bombay. It was a blow to have to leave Bombay, where I had lived such a busy life. Bombay had taken me in, a wandering outcast thrown out by even his family.[120] She had told me, 'You can live here

119 Yazid was the Umayyad Caliph responsible for the killing of Husain ibn Ali, the grandson of the Prophet Muhammad, at the Battle of Karbala on October 10, 680 (Hodgson, Marshall G.S. *The Venture of Islam: Conscience and History in a World Civilization, Volume 1, The Classical Age of Islam*. 1958. Chicago: Chicago University Press, 1977, 219).

120 Manto's family never threw him out (though his brother-in-law did forbid him to visit his sister's house in Mahim), and so Manto

happily on two paise a day or on ten thousand rupees. Or if you want, you can be the saddest person in the world at either price. Here you can do whatever you want, and no one will think you're strange. Here no one will tell you what to do. You will have to do every difficult thing on your own, and you will have to make every important decision by yourself. I don't care if you live on the sidewalk or in a magnificent mansion. I don't care if you stay or go. I'll always be here.'

I was disconsolate after leaving Bombay. My good friends were there. I had gotten married there. My first child was born there, as was my second. There I had gone from earning a couple rupees a day to thousands—hundreds of thousands[121]—and there I had spent it all. I loved it, and I still do!

Bombay meant something to Manto beyond being merely a place he knew, a city in which he had lived. In this wistful invocation, he states his outright love for the city. He mentions two chief things. For one, years of personal history important to him took place there. Compared to his new life in Lahore, his time in Bombay had been full of crucial, exciting work to do, money to be earned, and people to meet. He valued how the city had made him who he was, how it had given him the opportunity to be a writer and to mix with the creative elite of his country. In hindsight, he must have felt as if he had been part of an enormous, vital enterprise.

---

must have been referring only to his father's stern and sometimes disapproving figure.

121 This is another example of Manto's tendency to exaggerate autobiographical details.

But he also praises the city in another way. He appreciated how it had accepted him although he had failed by the middle-class standards of Indian society. Interestingly, the city's acceptance was not obvious approbation but benign indifference.[122] But with indifference came anonymity and in turn the freedom to become who he wished to be. Self-reliance and personal fortitude were traits that Manto valued, and when he saw that the city espoused the same qualities, he must have felt within his rightful domain. Bombay, more than Delhi, and certainly more than provincial Lahore, was the city of license and liberty that Manto craved, the place where he might become his own man.

Bombay Stories is a collection of Manto's fiction set in part or entirely in that city, and a unique sense of place emerges through the narratives. In fact, a merging of place and character seems to occur for Manto, as for many after him—to write about Bombay means to write about a certain group of characters of a particular milieu. *Bombay Stories* represents the first and best literary evidence of Bombay's emergence as the modern city we now recognize it to be, and Manto's way of characterizing the city—populating it with a motley crew of prostitutes, pimps, writers, film stars, musicians, the debauched, and the rich—has become typical of a sub-genre of Indian fiction that I will loosely call 'Bombay fiction.' Whether

122 An interesting contrast to this passage from *Yazid* would be to look at this comment in relation to the Manto character's comment in 'Mammad Bhai'. There the fictional Manto finds fault with Bombay for these very traits: 'Like I said, who in Bombay cares about anyone? No one gives a damn if you live or die' (*Mantonamah*, 591).

through historical coincidence or literary prescience or both, Manto stands at the very beginning of this important Indian literary tradition.

Manto never compiled all his stories set in Bombay in one volume, so this collection of translations is both a sample of his work and represents a specific aspect of it. I have organized the stories chronologically. In fact he wrote the bulk of them after immigrating to Pakistan (eleven of the total fifteen), and this retrospective attention appears prominently in several stories. For instance, in 'Mammad Bhai' he writes, 'It was almost twenty years ago that I used to frequent those restaurants'; and in describing the title character, 'I don't remember what exactly he looked like, but after so many years I can still recall anticipating that he must be enormous, the kind of man Hercules bicycles would use as a model in their advertising.' Most of these stories were apparently written, at least in part, to assuage the pangs of nostalgia.

Lastly, if Manto is indeed the first representative of the contemporary Indian genre, then we might also consider how his prose includes literary devices that we now characterize as post-modern. Many of these stories feature narrative irruptions and self-reflexive commentary; he also obfuscates the clean genre limits of biography and fiction. While most writers of fiction covertly include details from their lives, Manto goes further, and in many stories he incorporates an eponymous Manto character—a character that roughly corresponds to the actual man. There are seven such stories in *Bombay Stories*, and practically every story in which his character appears does, in fact, give us some detail that is true to his life. In 'Babu Gopi Nath', we find the character,

Manto, working at a weekly newspaper in Bombay, just as the actual Manto did. In 'Janaki' we find him writing film scripts. In 'Mammad Bhai' he falls ill with malaria while living in a tiny room. 'Rude' tells us how he spent time working in Delhi, as well as revealing his fascination with the Communist Party. In 'Barren' he talks about how he would earn seven to ten rupees for each story he wrote, and in 'Mummy' he mentions the death of his son. While each story provides us with some accurate biographical information, other details are blatantly inaccurate. 'Rude' provides us with the best examples. In this story Manto is re-acquainted with a character named Nasir, an old friend from Aligarh Muslim University. Manto did reunite with an old friend after returning from his hiatus in Delhi, but this was Shahid Latif. Also we notice that Nasir is a foreman in a factory and husband to the famous Communist leader Izzat Jahan, and Shahid Latif was married to the writer Ismat Chughtai and worked in the film industry.

Authorial intrusions also complicate stories—especially those with an eponymous Manto character—as they highlight the stories' constructed and textual nature, often in a disingenuous or misleading way. In 'Siraj' and 'Barren', two stories that use an autobiographical conceit, Manto refers without prompting or an obvious narrative reason to the fact of his writing. Relevant passages in 'Siraj' are the following:

> But this is the impression of a short story writer who in describing a tiny facial mole can make it seem as large as the sang-e-aswad in Mecca.
>
> These details are enough. I don't want to tell you what I thought because it's not relevant to the story.

> The city had built tin shacks there for the poor, and I won't mention the nearby high-rises because they have nothing to do with this story, only that in this world there will always be the rich and the poor.
>
> I don't want to get into the details, but Siraj was with me at a hotel.

And from 'Barren':

> Anyway, enough of this. If I go on in such detail, I'll fill page after page and the story will get boring.
>
> But now I've started talking about my stories!

By bringing attention to his authorial consciousness, Manto focuses our attention briefly on exactly what he pretends to dismiss or belittle: 'Siraj' is about storytelling (both Manto's and Dhundhu's), and it is about the rich and the poor, just as 'Barren' is about the exchange of stories and lies between Manto and Naim. Perhaps in 'Barren' we have an analogy that explains Manto's fact-befuddling style: Naim writes to Manto at the story's end to confess that he made everything up, and yet he also avers that while objectively false, his stories felt true, and that through his lies he expressed a real part of himself. As self-conscious reflections on storytelling interrupt the authorial transparency of documentary realism, we see a style emerge that makes Manto progressive in a sense separate from what the term meant during his lifetime: he had outstripped the literary conventions of his time.

Matt Reeck

KHUSHIYA

KHUSHIYA was thinking.

He bought some black tobacco paan and sat down in his favourite place near the paan seller's stall. The raised stone platform there became his domain at eight thirty every night when the auto supply shop closed, clearing away its clutter of tyres and miscellaneous parts.

He was slowly chewing his paan and thinking. The paan mixed with his saliva to form a thick juice that oozed between his teeth and squirted throughout his mouth. He felt as though his teeth were grinding up his thoughts, which the paan juice then dissolved, and maybe this was why he was reluctant to spit.

Khushiya was swishing the paan juice around inside his mouth and thinking about what had happened to him just half an hour ago.

He had gone to the fifth alley in Khetwadi where Kanta, the new girl from Mangalore, lived in the corner. Khushiya had heard she was moving and so had gone to find out if this was true.

He knocked on Kanta's door, and a woman's voice called out from inside, 'Who is it?'

'It's me, Khushiya!'

A few minutes later the door was pushed open from

inside, and Khushiya entered. When Kanta closed the door behind him Khushiya turned to look, and yet he wasn't prepared for what he saw. Kanta was completely naked; I mean she had a towel wrapped around her but it wasn't hiding much—everything that she had to hide was on full display.

'So, what brings you here, Khushiya?' Kanta asked. 'I was just about to wash up. Sit down, sit down. You should've told the tea boy to bring up some tea. After all—you know, right?—that worthless Rama ran away.'

Khushiya was dumbfounded—he had never been so unexpectedly confronted with a naked woman. He was so flustered he couldn't figure out what to say, and he wanted to avert his eyes from the naked spectacle in front of him.

He rushed for words, 'Go, go on and wash up.' Then he regained his composure. 'But why did you open the door when you were naked? You should've told me. I would've come back. But go, go wash up.'

Kanta smiled. 'When you said it was you, I thought, what's the big deal? It's only my Khushiya, I'll let him in . . .'

Sitting on the platform, Khushiya could still see Kanta's smile. He could sense her naked body standing in front of him, and he felt as though it was melting right into his soul.

She had a beautiful body. It was the first time Khushiya realized that a whore, too, could be attractive. This surprised him, but he was even more amazed to see that Kanta was not at all ashamed of her nakedness. Why was that?

Kanta had already answered this. She had said, 'When you said it was you, I thought, what's the big deal? It's only my Khushiya, I'll let him in.'

What's the big deal?

Khushiya was Kanta's pimp. From that point of view, she was his, but that was no reason to be stark naked in front of him. That was something special. Khushiya tried to imagine what Kanta must have meant.

In his mind's eye, he was still looking at Kanta's naked body. It was as tight as hide stretched taut across a drumhead. He had looked her up and down, and yet she hadn't cared at all. Still in shock, he had let his eyes rove over her sexy body, but she didn't so much as bat an eyelash. She stood there as though bereft of any feeling, like a wanton stone statue!

Come on now—there was a man standing in front of her, a man who like all men are always undressing women, and after that imagining God knows what else! But she hadn't minded a bit, and her expression had betrayed no shame. She should have been a little ashamed! She should have blushed a little! Granted she was a whore, but even whores don't behave like that.

He had been a pimp for ten years and had learned all his prostitutes' secrets. He knew that the girl living at the end of Pydhoni shared her place with a young man she pretended was her brother, and that she had a broken record player on which she played for him the song 'Why, You Fool, Are You Always Falling in Love' from her *Untouchable Girl* record. He also knew that this girl was deeply in love with Ashok Kumar, and that countless hustlers had scammed her for sex by pretending to set up meetings between her and the actor. He also knew that the Punjabi girl who lived in Dawar wore a coat and pants only because one of her boyfriends had told her that her legs looked just like those of the actress in *Morocco*. She had seen this film many times, and when her friend told her that Marlene Dietrich wore pants to show off her beautiful legs (for which she had a large insurance policy), then she began to wear pants too, even though she could hardly fit her butt into them. He also knew the South Indian girl from Mazagaon liked to sleep with cute college boys because she was fixated on having a beautiful child despite the fact that this was impossible because she was infertile. And he knew that the skin of the black Madrasi woman who always wore diamond earrings would never get lighter and that she was wasting her money on whitening creams.

He knew everything about his girls, but he never suspected that one day Kanta Kumari (whose real name was so difficult, he could never remember it) would be standing in front of him naked. It was his life's greatest surprise.

Khushiya continued to think, and the paan juice had built up in his mouth so much so that he was having problems chewing the small bits of betel nut that passed between his teeth.

Drops of sweat appeared on his small forehead, like the drops of water that emerge from paneer when you gently squeeze the soft mass through cheesecloth. His masculine dignity had been affronted, and when he remembered Kanta's naked body, he felt humiliated.

Suddenly he said to himself, 'I've been disgraced! I mean a girl stands in front of you stark naked and says, "What's the big deal? It's just my Khushiya?" Hell, she treated me like I wasn't the real Khushiya but the cat that's always dozing off on her bed, right?'

Now he was sure he'd been insulted. He realized that he implicitly expected women, whores included, to take him for a man and so to dress modestly in his presence, as had been the tradition for so long. He had gone to Kanta's room to find out when and where she was moving and beyond that hadn't thought about what she would be doing when he got there. If he had tried, he wouldn't have been able to come up with much more than a few possibilities:

1) She would be lying on her bed with a cloth strip tied around her forehead to combat a headache.
2) She would be picking fleas out of her cat's fur.
3) She would be removing armpit hair by applying that foul-smelling powder he couldn't stand.
4) She would be on her bed with cards spread out, busy playing Patience.

But that was the limit of his imagination. She didn't live with anyone, and so he hadn't expected to find anyone else there. He had gone there on business, and suddenly Kanta—I mean the clothes-wearing Kanta whom he always saw dressed for the day—appeared before him completely naked, or just about. Faced with this spectacle, Khushiya felt as though he had a banana peel in his hand while the banana itself had fallen to the floor. No, he felt something else: he felt as though he himself had been stripped naked.

If it had come to just this, Khushiya could have gotten over his surprise—he could have thought of some excuse or another. But the problem was the slut had smiled and said, 'When you said it was Khushiya, I thought, what's the big deal? It's only my Khushiya, I'll let him in.' This was still eating him up. 'The bitch was smiling!' he kept muttering to himself. Her smile had seemed as naked as her body, but what a smile! He felt as though he had looked into her body—as though a carpenter had scraped off dissimulation and he had gazed into her being.

He thought back to his childhood and how a lady who lived next door would call to him, 'Khushiya, honey, run and fill up this bucket with some water.' He would fill up the bucket and return. Then from behind a dhoti's makeshift curtain she would say, 'Come and put it over here. My face is covered in soap, and I can't see a thing.' He would push aside the curtain and put the bucket down next to her. He would see her naked body covered in soapsuds, but he never got aroused.

'Come on, I was only a kid then—I was so innocent!' Khushiya thought. 'There's a huge difference between a boy and a man. Who worries about purdah with boys? But now I'm twenty-eight. Not even an old woman goes nude in front of a twenty-eight-year-old.'

What did Kanta think he was? Wasn't he still a young man filled with a young man's desires? Of course, seeing Kanta nude so unexpectedly had flustered him. But with stolen glances, hadn't he checked her out and found her womanly assets in good condition? What surprise was there that he thought Kanta was well worth ten rupees and that the bank clerk was an idiot, the one that walked away last Dassehra when he was refused a two-rupee discount? And above all, hadn't he felt a strange tension ripple through his muscles, a tension that made him want to stretch his limbs and yawn? Why didn't this sexy girl from Mangalore respect his manhood but considered him just

Khushiya and so let him see her naked body? He angrily spit the paan juice on the pavement, making a messy mosaic there. Then he rose and boarded a tram home.

At home he washed up and put on a new dhoti. In his building there was a hair salon, and he went in and combed his hair in front of the mirror. Then suddenly something occurred to him. He sat down in a chair and sharply told the barber he wanted a shave. It was the second time he had come in that day, and so the barber asked, 'But Khushiya, did you forget? I shaved you just this morning.' Khushiya ran a hand over his cheeks. 'There's still some stubble.'

He got a good shave and had powder applied to his face. Then he left the salon. There was a taxi stand right in front of the shop, and he drew the attention of a driver in the style of Bombay by saying, 'Chi, chi!' and signalling with his finger to the driver to bring the taxi around. When Khushiya was seated in the taxi, the driver turned around and asked, 'Where to, sir?'

These three words, especially the 'sir', pleased Khushiya. He smiled and in a friendly manner said, 'I'll tell you soon enough, but first go towards the Paseera House by Lamington Road, okay?'

The driver set the metre by pushing its red lever down. He started the engine, which rumbled to life, and then turned the taxi toward Lemington Road. They travelled along the road and had nearly reached its end when Khushiya said, 'Turn left.'

They turned left and before the driver could shift into a higher gear, Khushiya said, 'Please stop in front of that pole there.' The driver pulled up right next to the pole, and

Khushiya got out. He went up to a paan stall and bought a paan. He talked to a man standing next to the stall, and they both returned to the taxi. When the two were seated, Khushiya instructed the driver, 'Straight ahead!'

The route was rather long, but the driver went wherever Khushiya signalled. After passing through many crowded markets, the taxi entered a half-lit alley devoid of almost all traffic. Some people were lying on bedding in the street, and others were getting massages. The taxi passed these people and reached a bungalow-like wooden house. Khushiya said, 'Okay, stop here.' The taxi stopped, and Khushiya whispered to his companion, 'Go. I'll wait for you here.' The man gave Khushiya a bewildered glance and then left for the wooden house opposite.

Khushiya stayed seated. He crossed one leg over the other, took a bidi from his pocket and lit it. After several drags, he tossed it onto the street. He was anxious, and his heart was beating so strongly that he thought the taxi driver hadn't switched off the engine. He imagined the driver was running up the bill, and so he said sharply, 'If you keep the engine running like this, how many more rupees will you earn?'

The driver turned around. 'Sir, the engine's off.'

When Khushiya realized his mistake, his anxiety grew further. He said nothing but bit his lips. Suddenly he put on the black, boat-like hat he had been holding. He shook the driver's shoulder and said, 'Look, a girl's going to come out. As soon as she gets in, start the engine, okay? It's nothing to worry about—it's no monkey business.'

Two people emerged from the wooden house. Khushiya's friend led Kanta, who was wearing a bright sari.

Khushiya moved to the side of the taxi partially in shadows. Khushiya's friend opened the taxi's door. Kanta sat down, and this man closed the door behind her. Immediately she cried out in astonishment, 'Khushiya! You?'

'Yes—me.'

'But you got the money, right?'

In a husky voice Khushiya addressed the driver, 'Okay, Juhu Beach.'

The engine rattled into life, making whatever Kanta was saying inaudible. The taxi lurched forward, leaving Khushiya's friend standing startled in the middle of the street as the taxi disappeared down the half-lit alley.

And never again did anyone see Khushiya sitting on the stone platform in front of the auto supply store.

TEN RUPEES

SHE was at the corner of the alley playing with the girls, and her mother was looking for her in the chawl (a big building with many floors and many small rooms). Sarita's mother had asked Kishori to sit down, had ordered some coffee-mixed tea from the tea boy outside, and had already searched for her daughter throughout the chawl's three floors. But no one knew where Sarita had run off to. She had even gone over to the open toilet and had called for her, 'Hey, Sarita! Sarita!' But she was nowhere in the building, and it was just as her mother suspected—Sarita had gotten over her bout of dysentery (even though she hadn't taken her medicine), and without a care in the world she was now playing with the girls at the corner of the alley near the trash heap.

Sarita's mother was very worried. Kishori was sitting inside, and he had announced that three rich men were waiting in their car in the nearby market. But Sarita had disappeared. Sarita's mother knew that rich men with cars don't come around every day, and in fact, it was only thanks to Kishori that she got a good customer once or twice a month because otherwise rich men would never come to that dirty neighbourhood where the stench of rotting paan and burnt-out bidis made Kishori pucker his nose.

Really, how could rich men stand such a neighbourhood? But Kishori was clever, and so he never brought men up to the chawl but would make Sarita dress up before taking her out. He told the men, 'Sirs, things are very dicey these days. The police are always on the lookout to nab someone. They've already caught 200 girls. Even I am being tried in court. We all have to be very cautious.'

Sarita's mother was very angry. When she got to the bottom of the stairs, Ram Dai was sitting there cutting bidi leaves. 'Have you seen Sarita anywhere?' Sarita's mother asked her. 'I don't know where she's gone off to. If I find her, I'm going to beat her to a pulp. She's not a little girl any more, and yet she runs around all day with those good-for-nothing boys.'

Ram Dai continued cutting bidi leaves and didn't answer because Sarita's mother usually went around muttering like this. Every third or fourth day she had to go looking for Sarita and would repeat these very words to Ram Dai where she sat all day near the stairs with a basket in front of her as she tied red and white strings around the cigarettes.

In addition to this refrain, the women of the building were always hearing from Sarita's mother how she was going to marry Sarita off to a respectable man so that she might learn how to read and write a little, or how the city government had opened a school nearby where she was going to send Sarita because her father very much wanted her to know how to read and write. Then she would sigh deeply and launch into a recitation of her deceased husband's story, which all the building's women knew by heart. If you asked Ram Dai how Sarita's father (who had worked for the railway) reacted when his boss swore at him, then Ram Dai would immediately tell you that he got enraged and told off his boss, 'I'm not your servant but a servant of the government. You don't intimidate me. Look here, if you insult me again, I'm going to break your jaw.' Then it happened. His boss went ahead and insulted Sarita's father, and so Sarita's father punched him in the neck so hard that this man's hat fell to the floor and he almost collapsed. But he didn't. His boss was a big man—he stepped forward and with his army boot kicked Sarita's father in the stomach with such force that his spleen burst and he fell down right there near the railroad tracks and died. The government tried the man and ordered him to pay 500 rupees to Sarita's mother, but fate was unkind: Sarita's mother developed a love for gambling and in less than five months wasted all the money.

Sarita's mother was always telling this story, but no one knew whether it was true. No one in the building felt any sympathy for her, perhaps because their lives were so difficult that they had no time to think about others. No one had any friends. Most of the men slept during the day and worked nights in the nearby factory. Everyone lived right on top of one another, and yet no one took any interest in anyone else.

Almost everyone in the building knew that Sarita's mother was forcing her young daughter to be a prostitute, but because they weren't in the habit of concerning themselves with others, no one ever contradicted Sarita's mother when she would lie about how innocent her daughter was. Once when Tukaram harassed Sarita by the water spigot one early morning, Sarita's mother started screeching at Tukaram's wife, 'Why can't you keep track of that dirty rat? I pray to God he goes blind for eyeing my little girl like that. I'm telling you the truth, some day I'm going to smack him so hard he won't know up from down. If he wants to raise hell somewhere else, that's fine, but if he wants to live here, he's going to have to behave like a respectable person, got it?'

Hearing this, Tukaram's squint-eyed wife rushed out of her room tying on her sari. 'Watch out, you old witch, if you say anything else!' she said. 'Your little angel flirts with even hotel boys. You think we're all blind—you don't think we know about that fine character who comes to your place and why your little Sarita gets dressed up and goes out? You—going on about honour—you must be kidding! Go! Get out of here!'

Tukaram's wife was notorious for many things, but every single person in the building knew about her relationship with the kerosene seller, about how she would call him inside and close the door. Sarita's mother made it a point to mention this. In a spiteful voice, she harped, 'And your gigolo, the kerosene seller? You take him into your room for two hours just to sniff his kerosene?'

And yet Sarita's mother and Tukaram's wife wouldn't stay angry for long. One day Sarita's mother saw Tukaram's wife whispering sweet nothings to some man in the darkness of night, and the very next day when Tukaram's wife was coming back from Pydhoni, she saw Sarita seated with a 'gentleman friend' in a car, and so the two agreed that they were even and began talking to each other again.

'You didn't see Sarita anywhere, did you?' Sarita's mother asked Tukaram's wife. Tukaram's wife looked through her squinty eyes towards the alley's corner. 'She's playing with her friend over by the trash heap.' Then she whispered, 'Just a minute ago Kishori went upstairs, did you see him?'

Sarita's mother glanced right and left. Then she whispered, 'I just asked him to sit down, but Sarita's always disappearing right when she's needed. She doesn't ever think, she doesn't understand anything. All she wants to do is play all day.' Then she headed off towards the trash heap, and when she reached the concrete urinal, she went up to Sarita, who immediately stood up and a despondent expression spread over her face. Sarita's mother angrily grabbed her by the arm and said, 'Go home—get going! All you do is horse around, you good-for-nothing.' Then as they were on their way home, she whispered, 'Kishori's been waiting. He brought a rich man with a car. So listen. Hurry and run upstairs. Put on that blue georgette sari. And look, your hair's all messed up. Get ready quick, and I'll fix your hair.'

Sarita was very happy to hear that a rich man with a car had come. She didn't care about the man but she really liked car rides. When she was in a car speeding through the empty streets, the wind whipping over her face, she felt as though she had been transformed into a rampaging whirlwind.

Sarita must not have been any older than fifteen, but she acted like a thirteen-year-old. She hated spending time with women and having to talk to them. All day long she kept busy playing meaningless games with younger girls. For example, she really liked to draw chalk lines on the alley's black asphalt, and she would play this game with so much concentration that it seemed as though the world would end if those crooked lines weren't there. Or she would take an old gunnysack from their room and spend hours engrossed with her friends on the footpath—twisting it around, laying it on the pavement, sitting on it, and such childish things.

Sarita wasn't beautiful or fair-skinned. Her face was always glossy because of Bombay's humid climate, her thin lips looked like the brown skin of the chikku fruit and were always lightly quavering, and above her upper lip you could always find three or four glistening beads of sweat. And yet she was healthy. Although she lived in a dirty neighbourhood, her body was graceful and fit—in fact you could say that she embodied youth itself. She was short and a little chubby, but this chubbiness made her seem only healthier, and when she rushed about the streets, if her dirty dress should fly up, passing men would look at her young calves that gleamed like smooth teak. Her pores were like those of an orange, its skin filled with juice, which, if you applied the slightest pressure, would squirt up into your eyes. She was that fresh.

Sarita had good-looking arms as well. Even though she wore a poorly fitting blouse, the beauty of her shoulders was still visible. Her hair was long and thick and always smelled of coconut oil, and her braid snapped like a whip against her back. Sarita didn't like the length of her hair because her braid gave her problems when she played, and she had tried all sorts of ways to hold it in place.

Sarita was blissfully free from worry. She got two meals a day, and her mother did all the work at home. Sarita carried out only two duties: every morning she would fill up buckets of water and take them inside, and in the evening she would fill up the lamps with a drop or two of oil. This had been her strict routine for years, and so each evening, without thinking, she would reach for the tea saucer in which they kept their coins and grab one before taking the lamp down to buy oil.

Once in a while, about four or five times a month, Kishori would bring customers, and the men would take Sarita off to a hotel or some dark place, and she considered this good entertainment. She never bothered much about these nights, perhaps because she thought that some guy like Kishori must go to other girls' houses too. Perhaps she imagined that all girls had to go out with rich guys to Worli to sit on cold benches, or to the wet sand of Juhu Beach. Whatever happened to her must happen to everyone, right? One day when Kishori brought a regular john, Sarita said to her mother, 'Mom, Shanta's old enough now. Send her out with me, okay? This one always orders me eggs, and Shanta really likes eggs.' Her mother replied evasively, 'Okay, okay, I'll send her out once her mom comes back from Pune.' The next day Sarita saw Shanta coming back from the open toilet, and she told her the good news, 'When your mom comes back from Pune, everything's going to work out. You'll start coming with me to Worli.' Then Sarita told the story of what had happened one recent night, making it sound like a wonderful dream. Shanta was two years younger than Sarita, and after listening to Sarita's story, she felt a ripple of excitement course through her body. She wanted to hear even more, so she grabbed Sarita's arm and said, 'Come on, let's go outside.' They went down near the open toilet where Girdhari, the shopkeeper, had put out dirty pieces of coconut to dry on gunnysacks. There they gossiped for hours.

Behind a makeshift curtain, Sarita was putting on her blue georgette sari. The cloth gave her goose bumps, and the thought of the upcoming car ride excited her. She didn't stop to think about what the man would be like or where they would go, but as she quickly changed she hoped that the car ride wouldn't be so short that before she knew it, she would be standing in front of the door to some hotel room where once inside, the john would start drinking and she would begin to feel claustrophobic. She hated those suffocating rooms with their two iron beds on which she could never get a good sleep.

Smoothing out her sari's wrinkles, she let Kishori look at her for a second, then asked him, 'Kishori, how do I look? Is the sari okay from behind?' Without waiting for an answer, she went over to the broken wooden chest where she kept her Japanese powder and rouge. She set her rusted mirror up against the window's iron bars, and bending over a little to look at her reflection there, she put powder and purple-tinged rouge on her dusky cheeks. When she was ready, she smiled and looked at Kishori for his approval. Then she haphazardly covered her lips in lipstick. The sum effect was that she looked like one of those clay dolls that appear in toy sellers' stores over Diwali.

Sarita's mother came in, quickly fixed Sarita's hair, and said to her daughter, 'Look, my little girl, remember to talk like a grown-up, and do whatever he says. This man is very rich, okay? He even has his own car.' Then she turned to Kishori, 'Now, quickly, take her out. The poor man! Just think how long he's been waiting!'

Outside in the bazaar, there was a factory wall stretching into the distance on which a small sign read, 'NO URINATING'. Next to this sign there was a parked yellow car in which three young men from Hyderabad were sitting, each one covering his nose with a hanky. (They would have moved the car, but the wall went on for a long way and the stench of piss ran its entire length.) When the driver saw Kishori, he said to his friends, 'Hey, he's coming. Kishori. And . . . and . . . hey, this girl's really young! Guys, look—the one in the blue sari.'

When Kishori and Sarita came up to the car, the two men in the back seat picked up their hats and cleared space between them for Sarita. Kishori stepped forward, opened the back door and quickly pushed Sarita inside. Then he closed the door and said to the guy behind the wheel, 'Sorry it took so long. She had gone to see a friend. So . . . so . . .?'

The young man turned around to look at Sarita and then said to Kishori, 'Okay, then. But, look . . .' He stuck his head out of the window and whispered to Kishori, 'She won't put up a fuss, will she?'

Kishori put his hand on his heart. 'Sir, please trust me.'

The young man took two rupees out of his pocket and gave it to Kishori. 'Go enjoy yourselves,' Kishori said and waved goodbye. Then the driver started the car.

It was five in the evening, and traffic filled the Bombay streets—cars, trams, buses, and people were everywhere. Sarita didn't say anything as she sat scrunched between the two men. She squeezed her thighs together and rested her hands on her lap, and several times just as she had built up the courage to say something, she would suddenly stop. She wanted to tell the driver, 'Sir, please drive quickly. I'm about to suffocate back here.'

No one said anything for quite some time; the driver watched the road, and the men in the back seat were silent as they thought anxiously about how for the first time they were sitting so close to a young girl, one who was theirs, one with whom they could mess around without getting into any trouble.

The driver had been living in Bombay for two years and had picked up girls like Sarita both during the day and at night; he had had many prostitutes in his yellow car and so wasn't nervous in the least. His two friends had come from Hyderabad: Shahab wanted to experience all that the big city had to offer, and so Kifayat, the owner of the car, had bought Sarita through Kishori. Kifayat had said to his second friend, Anwar, 'You know, there'd be nothing wrong if you got one for yourself.' But Anwar thought it wrong and couldn't bring himself to consent. Kifayat had never seen Sarita before, and despite the novelty she presented, he wasn't interested in her just then, since he couldn't very well drive and look at her at the same time.

Once they left the city and entered the suburbs, Sarita sprang to life. The cool wind rushing over the speeding car soothed her, and she felt fresh and full of energy again. In fact, she could barely contain herself: she began to tap her feet, sway her arms, and drum her fingers as she glanced back and forth at the trees that streamed past the road.

Anwar and Shahab were becoming more relaxed, and Shahab felt he could do whatever he wanted with Sarita. He reached around her waist, and suddenly Sarita felt someone tickling her. She sprang away, wriggling close to Anwar, and her laughter trailed from the car's windows far into the distance. Again Shahab reached out for Sarita, and she doubled over, laughing so hard that she could hardly breathe, forcing Anwar to scrunch against the car door and try to maintain his composure.

Shahab was in ecstasy, and he said to Kifayat, 'By God, she's really spunky!' Then he pinched her thigh very hard, and Sarita reacted impulsively, twisting Anwar's ear for no reason other than he was closest. Everyone burst out laughing. Kifayat kept looking over his shoulder even though he could see everything in the rearview mirror. He sped up, trying to keep pace with the laughter in the back seat.

Sarita wanted to get out and sit on the car's hood next to its iron fixture shaped like a flying bird. She leaned forward, Shahab poked her, and Sarita threw her arms around Kifayat's neck in order to keep her balance. Without thinking, Kifayat kissed her hand, and Sarita's entire body tingled. She jumped over the seat to sit next to Kifayat where she began to play with his necktie. 'What's your name?' she asked.

'Me? I'm Kifayat.' Then he took out ten rupees from his pocket and gave it to her.

The money distracted Sarita, and she instantly forgot what Kifayat had said as she took the note and crammed it into her bra. She was a child—ignorant and happy. 'That was very nice of you,' she said. 'And your necktie's nice too.'

Sarita was in such a good mood that she liked everything she saw. She wanted to believe that even bad things could be redeemed, she wanted the car to continue speeding along, and she wanted everything to fall into the whirlwind.

Suddenly she wanted to sing. She stopped playing with Kifayat's tie and sang, 'It was you who taught me how to love/and woke my sleeping heart.'

After singing this film song for a while, Sarita suddenly turned around and said to Anwar, 'Why are you so quiet? Why don't you say something? Why don't you sing something?' Then she jumped into the back seat and began to run her fingers through Shahab's hair and said to him, 'Let's sing together. You remember that song Devika Rani sang, "I wish I could be a bird singing through the forests"? I really like Devika Rani.' Then she put her hands together, propped them beneath her chin, and batting her eyelashes began to tell the story, 'Ashok Kumar and Devika Rani were standing next to each other, and Devika Rani said, "I wish I could be a bird singing through the forests", and Ashok Kumar said . . .' Suddenly Sarita turned to Shahab, 'Sing along, okay?'

Sarita began to sing, 'I wish I could be a bird singing through the forests'. And in a coarse voice Shahab repeated the same.

Then they all began singing together. Kifayat began honking the horn to the song's rhythm, and Sarita followed the beat by clapping. Sarita's feminine voice mixed with Shahab's raspy one, as well as the horn's honking, the wind's rushing, and the engine's rumbling—it all sounded like the music of a small orchestra.

Sarita was happy—Shahab was happy—Kifayat was happy—and seeing them all happy made Anwar happy too, and yet he was embarrassed for having been so inhibited. He felt a tingling sensation in his arms, and his repressed emotions awoke: he stretched loudly, yawned, and then felt ready to join in the revelry.

As she sang, Sarita took Anwar's hat from his head, put it on and then jumped into the front seat to look at herself in the rearview mirror. Seeing Sarita wearing his hat, Anwar couldn't remember whether he had been wearing it from the beginning of the car ride. He felt disoriented.

Sarita slapped Kifayat's thigh and asked, 'If I put on your pants, and wore your shirt and tie, would I look like a well-dressed businessman?'

But this talk of cross-dressing upset Shahab, and he shook Anwar's arm, 'By God, you're such an idiot to have given her the hat!' Anwar took these words to heart. He thought for a moment that he really was an idiot.

'What's your name?' Kifayat asked Sarita.

'My name?' Sarita took the hat's elastic cord and strapped in beneath her chin. 'Sarita.'

'Sarita, you're not a woman but a firecracker,' Shahab said.

Anwar wanted to say something, but Sarita began to sing in a loud voice, 'I'm going to build my house in the City of Love and forget the rest of the world!'

Kifayat and Shahab felt transported, but Anwar still couldn't get over his nerves. Sarita kept singing, 'I'm going to build my house in the City of Love and forget the rest of the world . . .' and she stretched out the last word for as long as her breath lasted. Her long hair was blowing back and forth, and it looked like a column of thick smoke spreading in the breeze. She was happy.

Sarita was happy—Shahab was happy—Kifayat was happy—and Anwar once again tried to join in, but when the song ended, everyone felt as though a shower of rain had suddenly stopped.

Kifayat asked Sarita to sing another song.

'Yeah, one more,' Shahab encouraged her. 'If they could only hear us now!'

Sarita began to sing, 'Ali has come to my courtyard. I'm staggering from joy!' Hearing these lyrics, Kifayat began swerving the car from side to side. Then suddenly the winding road ended, and they found themselves near the sea. The sun was setting, and the breeze off the ocean was becoming colder by the minute.

Kifayat stopped the car. Sarita got out and set off running down the beach, and Kifayat and Shahab joined her. She ran upon the wet sand by the tall palm trees that rose along the ocean's open vista, and she wondered what it was she wanted—she wanted to fade into the horizon, dissolve into the water, and soar so high into the sky that the palm trees stood beneath her; she wanted to absorb the sand's moisture through her feet, and . . . and . . . the car, the speed, the lash of the rushing air . . . she felt transported.

The three young men from Hyderabad sat down on the wet sand and began to drink beer, but then Sarita grabbed a bottle from Kifayat and said, 'Wait, let me pour you some.'

Sarita poured so quickly that the beer's head rose over the glass's edge, and this pleased her extraordinarily. She dipped her finger into the beer and licked off the foam, but it was very bitter and she immediately puckered her lips. Kifayat and Shahab burst out laughing. When he couldn't stop, Kifayat had to look away to calm himself, and then he saw that Anwar too was laughing.

They had six bottles—some they poured quickly so that

the head overflowed their glasses and its foam disappeared into the sand, and some they actually managed to drink. Sarita kept singing, and once when Anwar looked at her, he imagined that she was made of beer. The damp sea breeze was glistening on her dark cheeks. She was very happy, and now Anwar was too. He wished that the ocean's water would change into beer, and then he would dive in with Sarita. Sarita picked up two empty bottles and banged them against each other. They clanged loudly, and she burst out laughing, and everyone followed suit.

'Let's go for a drive,' she suggested to Kifayat. They left the bottles right there on the wet sand and raced ahead to the car to their seats. Kifayat started the engine and off they went. Soon the wind was rushing over them and Sarita's long hair streamed up, over her head.

They began to sing. The car sped, lurching down the road, and Sarita kept singing where she sat in the back seat between Anwar, who was dozing, and Shahab. Mischievously, she started to run her fingers through Shahab's hair, yet the only effect of this was that it lulled him to sleep. Sarita turned back to look at Anwar, and when she saw that he was still sleeping, she jumped into the front seat and whispered to Kifayat, 'I've put your friends to sleep. Now it's your turn.'

Kifayat smiled. 'Then who'll drive?'

'The car will drive itself,' Sarita answered, smiling.

The two lost track of time as they talked with each other, and before they realized it, they found themselves back in the bazaar where Kishori had ushered Sarita into the car. When they got to the factory wall with the 'NO URINATING' sign, Sarita said, 'Okay, stop here.'

Kifayat stopped the car, and before he could say or do anything Sarita got out, waved goodbye and headed to her home. With his hands still on the wheel, Kifayat was replaying in his mind all that had just happened when Sarita stopped and turned around. She returned to the car, removed the ten-rupee note from her bra and dropped it onto the seat next to him. Startled, he looked at the note. 'What's this, Sarita?'

'This money—why should I take it?' she said before she turned and took off running. Kifayat stared in disbelief at the note, and when he turned to the back seat, his friends were fast asleep.

BARREN

WE met exactly two years ago today at Apollo Bunder. It was in the evening when the last rays of the sun had disappeared behind the ocean's distant waves, which looked like folds of thick cloth from the benches along the beach. On this side of the Gateway of India, I walked past the first bench where a man was getting his head massaged and sat down on the second. I looked out as far as I could see over the broad expanse of water. Far out, where the sea and the sky dissolved into each other, big waves were slowly rising. They looked like an enormous muddy carpet being rolled to the shore.

Light shone from the streetlamps along the beach, and its glimmering reflection formed thick lines across the water. Beneath the stone wall in front of me, the masts of sailboats were swaying lightly with their sails lashed to them. The sounds of the waves and the voices of the beach crowd merged into a humming sound that disappeared into the evening air. Once in a while the horn of a passing car would sound loudly, as though someone in the midst of listening to a very interesting story had said, 'Hmm'.

I enjoy smoking at times like these. I put my hand into my pocket and took out my pack of cigarettes, but I couldn't find any matches—who knew where I had lost them? I was just about to put the pack back into my pocket when someone nearby said, 'Please, here's a match.'

I turned around. A young man was standing behind the bench. People in Bombay usually have fair complexions, but his face was pale to a frightening degree. 'You're very kind,' I thanked him.

He gave me the matches, and I thanked him again and invited him to sit down. 'Please light your cigarette. I have to go,' he said.

Suddenly I realized he was lying. I could tell from his tone that he was in no hurry and had nowhere to go. You may wonder how I could detect this from his tone alone, but that was exactly how it seemed. I said again, 'What's the hurry? Please sit down.' I extended my cigarette pack towards him. 'Help yourself.'

He looked at the brand. 'Thanks, but I smoke only my brand.'

Believe me or not, but again I could have sworn he was lying. His tone betrayed him as before, so I took an interest in him. I resolved to get him to sit down and light a cigarette. I thought it wouldn't be difficult at all because from his two sentences I could tell that he was fooling himself. He wanted to sit down and have a smoke, but at the same time something made him hesitate. I clearly sensed this conflict in his voice, and believe me when I say that his very hold on life seemed uncertain as well.

His face was incredibly skinny. His nose, eyes, and mouth were so fine that it seemed as though someone had drawn them in and then washed them out with water. At times his lips seemed to fill out, but then this clarity would fade like an ember disappearing in ashes. His other features also behaved this way: his eyes were like big drops of muddy water over which his thin eyelashes drooped, and his hair was the black of burnt paper. You could make out the contour of his nose if you were nearby, but from a distance it flattened out. He slouched a little and this made him seem of average height, but when he would suddenly straighten his posture, he proved to be much taller. His clothes were ratty but not dirty. His coat's cuffs were worn and threadbare in places. The stitching of his collar was coming undone, and his shirt seemed as though it would not last one more washing. But even in these clothes, he was trying to carry himself with dignity. I say 'trying' because when I looked at him again, a wave of wretchedness swept over him, and it seemed he wanted to disappear from view.

I stood up, lit a cigarette, and once again extended my pack toward him. 'Please help yourself.'

I rolled it so that he couldn't refuse. He took out a cigarette, put it in his mouth and lit it. He started smoking but suddenly realized his mistake. He took the cigarette out of his mouth, and pretending to cough said, 'Cavenders don't suit me, their tobacco is so strong. They're too harsh for my throat.'

'Which cigarettes do you like?' I asked him.

'I . . . I . . .' he stuttered. 'Actually I don't smoke that much. Dr Arolkar forbade it. But if I smoke, I smoke 555s because their tobacco isn't that strong.'

Dr Arolkar was known all over Bombay because he charged ten rupees for a consultation, and the cigarette brand he mentioned was also very expensive. In one breath he had uttered two lies, neither of which I believed, but I didn't say anything. I'm telling you the truth when I say that I wanted to expose his deceit and make him feel ashamed so that he would beg for my forgiveness. But when I looked at him, I realized lying had become a part of his personality. Most people blush after they lie, but he didn't. He believed everything he said and lied with such sincerity that he didn't suffer even the smallest pinprick of conscience. Anyway, enough of this. If I go into such detail, I'll fill page after page and the story will get boring.

After a little polite banter, I brought the conversation around to what I wanted to talk about. I offered him another cigarette and started to praise the charming ocean scene. As I am a short story writer, I managed to describe the ocean, Apollo Bunder, and the crowds in such an interesting way that he didn't complain about his throat even after smoking six cigarettes. Suddenly, he asked me what my name was. When I told him, he shot up from the bench and said, 'You're Manto? I've read some of your stories. I didn't know you were Manto. I'm very happy to meet you. By God, very happy, indeed!'

I wanted to thank him, but he began again, 'Yes, I remember very well. Recently, I read a story of yours—what was it called? Anyway, it was about a girl who loves some guy, but this guy takes advantage of her and then disappears. Then there's another guy who loves this girl too, the guy telling the story. When he finds out about the girl's predicament, he goes to see her. He says, "Don't think about what's past. Build upon the memory of love and forge ahead. Put to use the joy you were able to find." But actually I don't remember that much about the story. Tell me, is it possible—no, it's not about what's possible—tell me, wasn't that you? I'm sorry, I have no right to ask you that. But in your story, aren't you the guy who meets the girl at the brothel but leaves when she falls asleep exhausted in the dull moonlight?' He suddenly stopped. 'I shouldn't have asked you that. No one wants to talk about personal matters.'

'I'll tell you,' I answered. 'But I feel awkward telling you everything when we've just met. What do you think?'

His excitement, which had grown as he talked to me about my story, suddenly died.

'You're exactly right,' he whispered. 'And yet how do you know this isn't our last meeting?'

'Well, it's true that Bombay is a huge city, but I have the feeling that we'll meet many times. Anyway, I'm unemployed—I mean I'm a story writer—and so you can find me right here at this time every night, unless of course, I'm sick. A lot of girls come here, and so I come here to fall in love. Love isn't a bad thing!'

'Love . . . love . . .' He wanted to say something but couldn't bring himself to begin. He fell quiet like a burning rope losing its last coil.

I had brought up love only as a joke, but in fact, the setting was so charming that it wouldn't have been half bad to fall in love. At dusk, when the streetlights flicker on and a cool breeze picks up, a romantic quality hangs in the air and instinctive you want a woman close to you.

Anyway, God only knows what story he was talking about. I don't remember all my stories, especially the romances. In real life I haven't been close to that many women, and if I write about them, it's either to earn quick money or to indulge in some fantasy. I never think much about these stories since they aren't serious. But I have met a special kind of woman about whom I have written some stories aside from the romances. In any event, the story he mentioned must have been a cheap romance I wrote to fulfill some desire. But now I've started talking about my stories!

When he repeated the word 'love,' I suddenly wanted to say something more about the subject. 'Yes, our ancestors divided love into many types. But love, whether in Multan or on Siberia's icy tundra, whether in the winter or the summer, whether among the rich or the poor, whether among the beautiful or the ugly, whether among the crude or the refined, love is always just love. There's no difference. Just as babies are always born in one and only one way, love too, comes about in only one way. There's no difference if you say that Mrs Sayyidah went to the hospital to have her baby or Rajkumari went into the jungle, if you say that a bhangan stirs love in Ghulam Muhammad or a queen inspires love in Natwar Lal. Many babies are born prematurely and so are weak, and love, too, remains weak if it is rushed. Sometimes childbirth is very painful, and sometimes falling in love causes great pain. Just as a woman may miscarry, love can die before it has had a chance to grow. Sometimes women are infertile, and from time to time you'll also find men incapable of loving. That isn't to say they don't want to love. No, not at all. They want to, but they don't know how to. Some women can't have babies, and some men can't inspire love because they lack something emotional. You can have miscarriages of love too.'

I was so excited by what I was saying that I forgot to check to see whether he was taking it in, and when I turned his way, he was looking out over the ocean's empty distance and he seemed lost in thought. I stopped.

When a car's horn honked loudly, he woke from his trance and absent-mindedly said, 'Yes, you're completely right!'

I wanted to challenge him, 'I'm completely right? Tell me what I just said.' But I didn't say anything and instead gave him time to break free from his weighty thoughts.

He remained absorbed in thought for a while. Then he said again, 'What you said is completely right, but . . . well, let's talk about something else.'

I really liked the line of thinking I'd chanced upon, and being too excited to stop I started up again, 'Well, I was suggesting that some men don't know how to love. I mean, they want to love but aren't able to act on their desire. I think this is because of some psychological problem. What do you think?'

His face became pallid, as though he had just seen a ghost. This change was so sudden that I became worried and asked, 'Are you okay? You look sick.'

'No, not at all, ' he said, but his distress only grew. 'I'm not sick at all. Why did you think that?'

'Anyone would say you're sick, if they saw you right now. You're turning terribly pale. I think you should go home. Come on, I'll walk with you.'

'No, I'll go alone, but I'm not sick. Sometimes my heart gives me some trouble—maybe it's that. I'll be fine in a minute, so please keep talking.'

I sat silently for a while, and it seemed he wasn't in the right state of mind to absorb my words. But then he insisted, and I started up again, 'I was asking what you think about men who can't love. I can't imagine what it must feel like to be them. When I think about a certain type of woman, one obsessed with having a child, one who tearfully beseeches God for just one child, and who, when nothing comes from her pleading, tries to remedy her infertility with charms and spells, and who takes ashes from the crematorium and stays up countless nights reciting mantras given to her by sadhus, all the while continuing to beg and present offerings to God; then I imagine men who can't love must feel the same. They truly deserve our sympathy, and in fact, I feel more sympathy for them than I do for the blind.'

Tears came to his eyes, and clearing his throat he stood up. He looked past me and said, 'Oh, it's getting late . . . I had something important to do. Time has really flown by as we sat here, chatting.'

I got up too. He turned around and quickly grasped my hand, and then without looking in my direction he said, 'Now I want to go.' Then he left.

We met again at Apollo Bunder. I don't usually go for walks, but this was still a month before my interest in Apollo Bunder died—that is, a month before I received a long, saccharine letter from an Agra poet who wrote in a bawdy manner about Apollo Bunder and the beautiful girls there, remarking how lucky I was to live in Bombay. Now whenever someone asks me to go there, I think of that letter and feel nauseated. But our second meeting took place when I still went in the evening to sit on the bench where masseurs were busy close by thumping sense back into their customers' heads.

Twilight had turned to night. The October heat lingered, and yet there was a light breeze. People were out walking, carrying themselves like weary travellers, and behind me the kerb was lined with parked cars. Almost all the benches were full. I sat down next to two garrulous men, a Gujarati and a Parsi, who had been sitting there for God knows how long. They were speaking Gujarati, but their accents were different, and the Parsi modulated his voice in a way so that when they started to talk fast, it sounded like a parrot and a mynah were fighting.

I got sick of their endless prattling and got up. I turned to walk in the direction of the Taj Mahal Hotel, and suddenly I saw him walking in my direction. I didn't know his name and so couldn't call out to him, but when he saw me, he stared at me as if he had found what he was looking for.

There weren't any empty benches, so I said, 'It's been quite a while since we met. There aren't any empty benches here, so let's go and sit in the restaurant over there.'

He made some desultory remarks, and we set off. After walking a bit , we got to the restaurant and sat down on its big cane chairs. We ordered some tea, and I offered him a cigarette. Coincidentally, that very day I had gone to Dr Arolkar who had told me to stop smoking, or if I couldn't manage that, then to smoke good cigarettes like 555s. According to the doctor's instructions, I had bought a pack just that evening. My friend looked carefully at it, then looked at me as if he wanted to say something and yet he said nothing.

I laughed. 'Don't think I bought these cigarettes just because of what you said. It's quite a coincidence that today I went to see Dr Arolkar for some chest pain I've been having. He told me I could smoke these cigarettes, but just a few.'

I looked at him as I spoke and saw that my words seemed to upset him. I quickly reached into my pocket and took out the prescription Dr Arolkar had written. I put it on the table and said, 'I can't read this, but it seems like Dr Arolkar has prescribed every possible vitamin.'

He stole glances at the prescription on which Dr Arolkar's name and address were written alongside the date, and the restlessness that had earlier shown on his face immediately disappeared. He smiled and said, 'Why is it that writers are often undernourished?'

'Because they don't get enough to eat. They work a lot, but don't get paid much.'

The tea came and we started to talk about different things.

Probably two and a half months had passed since our first meeting. His face had become even more pallid, and black circles had developed around his eyes. He seemed to be suffering from some chronic emotional problem because in the course of talking, he would stop and unintentionally sigh, and if he tried to laugh, no sound came out.

Suddenly I asked, 'Why are you sad?'

'Sad . . . sad . . .' he said, and a smile spread over his lips, the kind that the dying take pains to show when they want to prove they are unafraid of death. 'I'm not sad. You must be sad.'

Then he drained his tea in one gulp and stood up. 'Okay, then. I have to go. There's something important I have to do.'

I was sure he didn't have anything to do, but I didn't stop him from going. I had no chance to find out his name, but at least I learned that he had serious emotional problems. He was more than sad—he seemed to be suffering from depression—and yet he didn't want others to know about his sadness. He wanted to lead two lives: the one being that of outward reality and the other being in his head, and this second one consumed his every waking moment. That being said, he was unsuccessful in both lives, and I hadn't figured out why.

I ran into him for the third time at Apollo Bunder, and this time I invited him home. We didn't speak to each other on the way there, but that changed once we arrived. At first his face clouded with sadness, but then he chased it away and tried against his nature to impress me with lively conversation. This made me pity him even more: he was trying so hard to avoid reality, and yet, at times, this self-deception seemed to please him.

As we talked, he glanced at my table and saw a wooden picture frame there that held the photo of a young woman. He got up and approached it. 'Do you mind if I look at this picture?' he asked.

'Not at all.'

He gave the picture a cursory glance and went back to sit in his chair. 'She's a very pretty girl. I take it she's your . . .'

'No, that was a long time ago. I liked her, even loved her. But, sad to say, she didn't know, and I . . . I . . . no, well, her parents married her off. The picture is a souvenir of my first love that died before it really even began.'

'A souvenir of your love,' he repeated, passing his tongue over his dry lips. 'But you must have had other affairs. I mean you must have experienced real love too.'

I was about to say that I was one of those men like him who couldn't love. But then, who knows why, I stopped and without any reason told a lie, 'Yes, I've had my share. You must have had a lot of lovers too.'

He turned completely silent, as silent as the ocean's depths. He fell lost in thought, and when his silence began to depress me, I said, 'Hello, there! What are you thinking about?'

'I . . . I . . . nothing. I was just thinking about something.'

'You were remembering something? Something from a dream? An old wound?'

'A wound . . . an old . . . wound . . . not any wound. I have only one, and it's very deep, and very deadly. One is enough,' he said and then stood up to walk around the room. But as it was small and filled with chairs, a table, and a cot, there was no space, so he had to stop by the table. Now he looked very carefully at the picture and said, 'They look so similar—yours and mine. But her face wasn't so mischievous, and her eyes were large and knowing.' He sighed with disappointment and sat on a chair. 'It's impossible to understand death, especially when it happens to someone so young. There must be some power that opposes God, a power that's very jealous and wants no one to be happy. Anyway.'

'No, no, as you were saying,' I encouraged him. 'But, to be honest, I actually thought you'd never been in love.'

'Why? Just now you said I must have had many lovers,' he said and then looked questioningly at me. 'If I've never been in love, why am I always sad? If I've never been in love, why am I like I am? Why don't I take care of myself? Why do I feel like I'm melting away like a candle?'

These were rhetorical questions.

I said, 'I was lying when I said I thought you'd had many lovers, but you too lied when you said you weren't sad, that you weren't sick. It's not easy to know what others are feeling. There might be many other reasons for your sadness, but as long as you don't tell me, how can I know? No doubt you're getting weaker and weaker by the day, and obviously you've experienced something terrible, and . . . and . . . I feel sorry for you.'

'You feel sorry for me?' Tears welled in his eyes. Then he said, 'I don't need anyone's sympathy. Sympathy can't bring her back from the grave—the woman I loved. You haven't loved. I'm sure you've never loved because you have no scars. Look over here,' he said, pointing at himself. 'Every inch of my body is scarred by love. My existence is the wreck of that ship. How can I tell you anything? Why should I tell you when you won't understand? If someone tells you his mother has died, you can't feel what he must feel. My love—to you—to anyone else—will seem completely ordinary. No one can understand its effect on me. I was the one who loved, and I was the one everything happened to.'

He fell silent. Something must have caught in his throat, because he repeatedly tried to swallow.

'Did she take advantage of your trust? Or did something else happen?'

'Take advantage of me? She wasn't capable of taking advantage of anyone. For God's sake, please don't say that. She wasn't a woman but an angel. I curse death, which couldn't stand to see us happy! It swept her away under its wings forever. Aghh! This is too much! Why did you have to remind me of all this? Listen, I'll tell you a little of the story. She was the daughter of a rich and powerful man. I had already wasted all of my inheritance by the time I met her. I had absolutely nothing and had left my hometown and gone to Lucknow. I had a car, so I knew how to drive, which is why I decided to become a driver. My first job was with the Deputy Sahib, whose only child was this girl—' All of a sudden he stopped. After a while, he emerged from his reverie and asked, 'What was I saying?'

'You got a job at the Deputy Sahib's house.'

'Yes, Zahra was the Deputy Sahib's only child, and I drove her to school every morning at nine o'clock. She kept purdah, and yet you can't keep hidden from your driver for long, and I caught a glimpse of her on the very second day. She wasn't just beautiful. I mean there was something special about her beauty. She was a very serious girl, and her hair's centre parting gave her face a special kind of dignity. She . . . she . . . what should I say she was like? I don't have the words to describe her.'

At great length, he attempted to enumerate Zahra's virtues. He wanted to describe her in a way that would bring her to life, but he didn't succeed, and it seemed like his mind was too full of thoughts. From time to time his face became lively, but then he would be overcome by sadness and start sighing again. He told his story very slowly and as though he found pleasure in its painful recitation.

It went like this. He fell completely in love with Zahra. For several days he kept busy devising different strategies to catch a glimpse of her, but when he thought about his love with any seriousness, he realized how impossible it was. How can a driver love his master's daughter? When he thought about this bitter reality, he became very sad. But he gathered his courage and wrote a note to Zahra. He still remembered its lines:

> *Zahra,*
> *I know quite well I'm your servant and that your father pays me thirty rupees a month. But I love you. What should I do? What shouldn't I do? I need your advice.*

He slipped this note into one of her books. The next day as he took her to school, his hand trembled as he drove, and the steering wheel kept slipping from his grip. Thank God he didn't have an accident! He felt strange all day, and while he drove her back from school in the evening, Zahra ordered him to stop the car. He pulled over, and Zahra spoke very seriously, 'Look, Naim. Don't do this again. I haven't told my father about it—I mean the letter you slipped into my book. But if you do this again, I'll be forced to say something. Okay? Let's go. Start the car.'

He told himself he should quit his job and forget his love forever. But this was all in vain. A month passed without his resolutions were his dilemma being solved, and then he mustered the courage to write another note, which he stuck into one of Zahra's books just as before. He waited to see what would happen. He was sure he would be fired the next morning, but he wasn't. As he was driving Zahra home from school, she once again asked him to refrain from such behaviour, 'If you don't care about your honour, then at least think about mine.' When she spoke in this stern way, Naim lost all hope. Again he decided to quit his job and leave Lucknow forever. At the end of the month, he sat down in his room to write his last letter, and in the weak light of his lantern, he wrote:

> *Zahra,*
> *I've tried very hard to do as you wanted, but I can't control my feelings. This is my last letter. I'm leaving Lucknow tomorrow evening, and so you won't have to say anything to your father. Your silence will seal my fate. But don't think that I won't love you just because I live far away. Wherever I am, I will always love you. I'll always remember driving you to school and back, driving slowly so that the ride would be smooth for you, for how else could I express my love?*

He slipped this letter into one of Zahra's books. On the way to school she said nothing, and in the evening she said nothing as well. He lost all hope and went directly to his room. There he packed his few possessions and set them to the side, and in his lamp's weak light he sat down on the cot and fell into thinking about his hopeless love for Zahra.

He was miserable. He understood his position. He knew he was a servant and had no right to love his master's daughter. And yet he couldn't understand why he shouldn't love her—after all, he wasn't trying to take advantage of her. Around midnight, when he was still ruminating upon this, someone knocked at his door. His heart skipped a beat. Then he reasoned it must be the gardener. Someone had probably fallen ill at home, and he was coming to ask for help. But when he opened the door, it was Zahra. Yes,

Zahra—without a shawl, she was standing there in the cold December night! He couldn't find any words to say. For several minutes they stood there in funereal silence. At last Zahra opened her lips and in a quavering voice said, 'Naim, I've come. Now, tell me what you want. But before I enter your room, I want to ask a few questions.'

Naim remained silent.

'Do you really love me?' she asked.

Naim felt as though someone had just hit him. He blushed. 'Zahra, how can you ask me that question when answering it will only belittle my love? Can't you tell I love you?'

Zahra didn't say anything. Then she asked her second question, 'My father's rich, but I'm worth nothing. Whatever they say is mine isn't really mine but his. Would you love me even if I weren't rich?'

Naim was a very emotional man, and this question, too, stung him deeply. 'Zahra, for God's sake, please don't ask me questions whose answers you can find in trashy romance novels.'

Zahra entered his room, sat on his cot and said, 'I'm yours and will always be yours.'

Zahra kept her word. They left Lucknow for Delhi, got married, and found a small house.

The day when the Deputy Sahib came looking for them, Naim was at work. The Deputy Sahib scolded Zahra sharply, telling her she had destroyed his honour. He wanted her to leave Naim and forget everything that had happened, and he was even ready to pay Naim 2,000 to 3,000 rupees. But his strategy didn't work. Zahra said she would never leave Naim. She told her father, 'Dad, I'm very happy with Naim. You couldn't find a better husband for me. We don't want anything from you. If only you could give us your blessings, we'd be very grateful.'

Zahra's father became incensed. He threatened to have Naim thrown in jail, but Zahra asked, 'Dad, what crime has Naim committed? If you want to know the truth, we're both innocent. Anyway, we love each other and he's my husband. This isn't a crime, and I'm not a child.'

The Deputy Sahib was smart and quickly understood that if his daughter had consented to marry Naim then he couldn't bring any charges against her husband. He left Zahra once and for all. Then after a while, the Deputy Sahib tried to intimidate Naim through some people he knew and also tried to bribe him. But nothing worked.

The married couple was happy, even though Naim didn't earn much money and Zahra, who had never had to do anything for herself as a girl, had to wear cheap clothes and do housework. Zahra was happy that she had entered a new world, one in which Naim's love revealed itself anew each day. She was truly very happy, and Naim was too. But one day, as is God's will, Zahra had severe chest pains and before Naim could do anything she died. That is how Naim's world became shrouded in darkness forever.

It took him about four hours to get through his story, as he told it slowly and with evident relish. When he finished, the pallid hue on his face lifted, and his face glowed, as though someone had given him a blood transfusion. And yet his eyes were full of tears, and his throat was dry.

When he finished telling his story, he got up hurriedly, as though he had somewhere to go. 'It was really wrong of me to tell you this story. It was really wrong of me. Zahra's memory was not meant for anyone but me. But . . . but . . .' His voice quavered as he fought back tears, 'I'm living, and she . . . she . . .' He couldn't continue and so quickly shook my hand and left.

I never saw Naim again. I went to Apollo Bunder many times to find him but was never successful. After six or seven months, I got a letter from him, which I'll copy below.

Sahib!

You must remember the love story I recited at your house. It was completely false. All lies. There's no Zahra and no Naim. I'm real, but I'm not the Naim who loved Zahra. You once said there are people who can't love, and I'm one of those—someone who wasted his entire youth trying to love. Naim's love for Zahra was something I made up to amuse myself, just as Zahra's death was. I still don't understand why I killed her in my story, although it probably has to do with how everything I touch ends up cursed.

I don't know whether you believed my story. But I'll tell you something strange. I thought—I mean, while I told the story—I thought it was completely true! One hundred per cent true! I felt I had loved Zahra and she had truly died. You'll be even more surprised to hear that as days passed, the story seemed more and more real, and Zahra's laughter began to echo in my ears. I started to feel her warm breath. Each part of the story came to life, and thus I . . . I dug my own grave.

Even though she was imaginary, Zahra was more real than me. She died, and so I, too, should die. You will get this letter after my death. Goodbye. I'm sure I'll meet Zahra somewhere, but where?

I've written to you only because you're a writer. If you can make a story out of this, you're welcome to the seven or eight rupees. (You once told me you get seven to ten rupees for a story.) This is my gift to you.

Well, goodbye.

Yours,
'Naim'

Naim made up Zahra and then died. I've written this story and live on. This is my life's boon.

THE INSULT

AFTER an exhausting day, she lay down on her bed and immediately fell asleep. The official from the city's Sanitation Department whom she called 'Boss' had just fucked her and left for home in a drunken stupor. He could have stayed the night, but he professed great concern for his lawfully wedded wife who loved him very much.

The money she had earned from the official in exchange for her bodily labours was slowly slipping from the top of her tight, saliva-stained bra, and these coins clinked together in rhythm with her breathing, a sound that dissolved into that of her heart's irregular beating. In fact, it seemed as though the coins were melting right into her blood! Heat was spreading through her chest, caused in part by the brandy, a small bottle of which the official had brought, and in part by the beora, which they had drunk with water after the soda had run out.

She was lying face down on her long and broad teak bed. Her arms were bare up to her shoulders and spread out like a kite's bow. Her right armpit's shrivelled flesh was nearly blue from having been shaven over and over; it looked like a chunk of skin from a plucked hen had been grafted there.

Her room was small and messy and things were strewn about everywhere. Underneath her bed, her mangy dog had propped his head on top of three or four withered sandals and although asleep, was baring his teeth at some invisible something. The dog's fur was so patchy that if someone saw him from a distance, they would mistake him for the folded piece of sacking used to wipe the floor.

Her beauty products were stored in a small niche in the wall—rouge, lipstick, powder, a comb, and the iron pins she used to put up her hair in a bun. A cage hung nearby in which a green parrot slept, its face hidden in the feathers of its back. The cage was filled with pieces of raw guava and rotten orange peels, and around this foul-smelling fruit hovered small black flies and moths. There was a cane chair with a grease-stained back next to the bed, and to the right of this chair rested a beautiful stool on top of which was a portable gramophone made by His Master's Voice. A tattered black cloth was draped over the gramophone, and on the footstool and everywhere else in the room, rusty needles were littered. Four picture frames hung on the wall above this stool, and each held a man's photo.

At a short distance from the photos—I mean, just as you entered the room and in the corner on the left—there was a brightly coloured picture of Ganesha that she had probably ripped off a bolt of cloth and framed, and both fresh and withered flowers hung over its frame. In that incredibly oily niche, she kept a cup of lamp oil, and to its side was a small lamp, its flame standing erect like a flick of paint on a devotee's forehead in the room's torpid air. Burnt-out stumps of incense soiled the niche.

When she made the day's first money, she would hold it out before her, touch it to the statue of Ganesha, and then touch it to her forehead before stuffing it in her bra.

Her breasts were large, so there was no chance the money would fall out, but when Madho came on vacation from Pune, she had to hide some of it in the small hole beneath the foot of her bed that she had hollowed out just for this purpose. Her pimp, Ram Lal, had told her how to keep her money from Madho. When he heard that Madho came from Pune to sleep with her, he said, 'How long have you been seeing this bastard? What a strange love affair! The asshole doesn't spend anything but gets to sleep with you, and then he makes off with your money? There's something wrong with this picture. You must really like this guy. I've been a pimp for seven years, and I know all you girls have weaknesses.'

Ram Lal pimped all over Bombay—for 120 whores whose rates went from ten to a hundred rupees. He told Saugandhi, 'Bitch, don't waste your money like that. He'll strip your clothes right off your back, the motherfucker! Dig a little hole beneath the foot of your bed and hide all your money there. When he comes, say, "I swear, Madho, I haven't seen one dick all day! Order me a cup of tea and a pack of Aflatoon biscuits from the tea boy downstairs. My stomach's growling." Okay? Things are rough right now, honey. The Congress Party, the fuckers, have banned alcohol, and business is very slow. But at least you find a way to get liquor. I swear to God, when I see your empty bottles and smell the wine, I really want to be reborn a whore.'

Saugandhi liked her breasts more than any of her other physical attributes. Her friend Jamuna encouraged her, 'If you support those cannon balls with a bra, they'll stay firm forever.'

Saugandhi laughed. She replied, 'Jamuna, you think everyone's just like you. For ten rupees, men do whatever they want with you, and so you think this must be true for everyone. If any man ever touches me there, just see what happens!' Then she remembered something. 'Oh, let me tell you what happened yesterday. Ram Lal brought over a Punjabi at two in the morning, and they decided on thirty rupees for the night. After Ram Lal left, I turned off the light, and this guy got so scared! Jamuna, are you listening? I swear, as soon as the lights went out, he started shaking up and down! He was scared of the dark! I asked, "Hey, what're you waiting for? It's about to turn three. Your time's running out." He said, "Turn it on, turn it on." I asked, "What do you mean?" He said, "The electricity! The electricity!" I said, "What electricity?" He said, "The light! The light!" His shrill voice made me break out laughing. I said, "No way!" When I pinched his chubby thigh, he sprang to his feet and turned on the light. I quickly covered myself with the sheets and said, "Don't you have any shame, asshole?" When he returned to the bed, I rushed over to turn off the light. This made him anxious again. I swear it was a fun night—sometimes dark, sometimes light, sometimes light, sometimes dark. As soon as he heard the morning's first tram, he put on his clothes and left. The bastard must have won a bet or something. I mean, why else would he waste his money like that? Jamuna, you're so clueless. I know a lot of tricks for guys like that!'

Saugandhi really did know a lot of useful tactics, which she shared with one or two girlfriends. Her general advice went as follows, 'If he's good but doesn't talk much, then tease him a lot, try to irritate him, tickle him, play with him. If he has a beard, then run your fingers through it like a comb and twist a few hairs. If he has a big belly, pat it like a drum. Don't give him the chance to do what he wants. He'll leave happy and you'll be saved. Guys that never say anything are dangerous. They'll really hurt you if you let them!'

But Saugandhi wasn't as clever as she thought, and she had very few regulars. She was extremely emotional, so at the crucial moment, every ruse she knew would slip from her mind. Her stomach had many stretch marks from the time she had given birth, and the first time she had seen those lines, they reminded her of the lines her mangy dog made in the ground, pawing out of frustration whenever a bitch passed, ignoring him as she worried over her puppy.

Saugandhi lived mostly in her mind, but a kind word always made her body tingle with pleasure, and although she told herself that sex was worthless, her body liked it very much! She dreamed of being overcome by fatigue, the type of fatigue that would beat her to sleep, the type of sleep that falls upon you after being ground down all day—how delightful it would be! That type of unconsciousness that wraps around you after being utterly wrung dry of your last ounce of energy—what pleasure! Sometimes she wasn't sure if she existed, and sometimes she felt as though she was stuck in between, floating high in the sky with the wind encompassing her—the wind above her, below her, on the right, and on the left—nothing but the wind, suffocating and yet wonderful! As a child, when she played hide-and-seek, she would hide inside her mother's big trunk, and while waiting to be caught, she would become afraid of suffocating and her heart would race. How much she had liked that sensation!

Saugandhi wanted to spend her entire life inside a trunk like that while people looked for her in vain, though occasionally she would let them find her so that she, too, could go in search for someone. Her life for the last five years was just like hide-and-seek: sometimes she went looking for someone, and sometimes a man came for her. That was how her life passed. She was happy because she had to be. Every night she shared her wide, teak bed with a different man, and she knew countless ways to keep her johns in their place. While she had resolved many times not to accept their vulgar demands and to treat them indifferently, she would always get caught up in the moment and give in. She couldn't control her desire to be loved.

It seemed like every night some john would proclaim his love to her. Saugandhi knew they were lying, and yet her emotions would overwhelm her and she would imagine they really did. 'Love'. What a beautiful word! She wanted to smear it all over her body and massage it into her pores. She wanted to abandon herself to love. If love were a jar, she would press herself through its opening and close the lid above her. When she really wanted to make love, it didn't matter which man it was. She would take any man, sit him on her lap, pat his head, and sing a lullaby to put him to sleep.

She was so full of love that she could have loved any of her customers and moreover, could have kept this love alive forever. She had already sworn her love to the four men whose photos were hanging on the wall. She felt like a good person, but why weren't men good? She could never understand this, so once while looking into the mirror, she spontaneously said to herself, 'Saugandhi, time has not been kind to you!'

The time she had spent as a prostitute—the days and nights of the past five years—was all that mattered to her. She was not as happy as she had dreamed of being, and yet she was content. Anyway, it wasn't as if she were planning to build a palace. Money wasn't an issue. She usually charged ten rupees, from which Ram Lal took a two and a half rupee cut, and so she got seven and a half rupees a day, and that was enough. When Madho came from Pune to 'poke' her, as Ram Lal liked to put it, she handed over ten or fifteen rupees although she did this only because she had a crush on him. Ram Lal was right—there was something about Madho that Saugandhi liked.

Why don't I just go ahead and tell you everything.

When Saugandhi met Madho, he had said, 'You don't feel ashamed? Do you know what you're selling me? Why do you think I've come? *Chi, chi, chi.* Ten rupees, and like you say, two and a half are your pimp's. What's left, seven and a half, right—seven and a half? For seven and a half rupees you promise to give me something you can't give, and I've come for something I can't just take. I want a woman, but do you want a man? Any woman will do for me, but do you really like me? What's our relationship? It's nothing, nothing at all. Only these ten rupees—two and half are your pimp's and the rest you'll waste—they're all that connects us. You're eyeing it, and I'm eyeing it. Your heart says something, and my heart says something. Why shouldn't we make something together? I'm a head constable in Pune. I'll come once a month for three or four days. Stop doing this. I'll buy everything for you. What's this room's rent?'

Madho went on to say many more things, the sum of which had such a strong effect on Saugandhi that for several moments she felt like a head constable's wife. Madho tidied the room and took the initiative to tear up the pornographic photos at the head of her bed. Then he said, 'Saugandhi, dear, I won't let you put up pictures like that. And this water pitcher—look how dirty it is! And this—this rag, these rags—aghh!—what an awful smell! Throw them outside. And what have you done to your hair? And . . .' Saugandhi and Madho talked for three hours, and afterwards Saugandhi felt as though she had known him for years. No one ever paid any attention to the room's smelly rags, the dirty pitcher, or the pornographic photos. No one ever treated her room like a home, where domestic concerns were possible. Men came and left, without even noticing how filthy her bed was. No one said, 'Look how red your nose is today! I hope you don't catch a cold. Wait here. I'll go get some medicine.' Madho was really good. Everything he said was irreproachable. How incisively he had scolded her! She began to feel she really needed him and that was how their relationship began.

Madho came from Pune once a month and before going back always said, 'Look, Saugandhi, if you take up your old job, well, then our relationship is over. If you let even one man sleep here, I'll grab you by your hair and throw you out. Look, as soon as I get to Pune I'll send a money order for this month's expenses. Remind me, what's the rent here?'

But neither did Madho send any money nor did Saugandhi stop being a prostitute. Both knew very well what was going on. Saugandhi never asked Madho, 'What're you blathering on about? Have you ever given me anything?' And Madho never asked Saugandhi, 'Where did you get this money? I didn't give it to you.' Both were lying, and both were pretending. But Saugandhi was happy just as those who can't wear real gold become content with imitation trinkets.

Completely exhausted, Saugandhi had fallen fast asleep with the light on. It hung overhead, and its sharp light fell directly on her eyes but she didn't wake up.

There was a knock at the door. Who would come at two in the morning? The rapping penetrated Saugandhi's sleep only faintly, as a fly's buzzing would. The knocking intensified, and she lurched awake. Her mouth was full of bitter and viscous saliva, its taste a mixture of the previous night's liquor and the small bits of fish wedged between her teeth. She wiped off the smelly paste with the hem of her lungi and rubbed her eyes. She saw she was alone. She bent over to look underneath the bed—her dog was grimacing through his sleep, his mouth propped up on the dried-out sandals. Then she looked over at the parrot's cage and saw the parrot sleeping, its head lodged in the feathers of its back.

Someone was knocking. Saugandhi got up, her head throbbing. She scooped a ladleful of water from the pitcher and gargled. She guzzled another ladleful and went to the door to crack it open.

'Ram Lal?'

Ram Lal was tired of knocking. 'Are you dead or what?' he asked, furiously. 'I've been standing here knocking myself silly. Where were you?' Then he lowered his voice and asked, 'Is anyone inside?'

Saugandhi shook her head, so Ram Lal shouted, 'Then why didn't you open the door? Aghh! I've had enough of this. That must have been some sleep, huh? I'm never going to make it in this business if I have to beat my head against a wall for two hours just trying to get a girl out of bed. And why are you staring at me like that? Quick, take off that lungi and put on your flowery sari. Powder your face and come with me. There's a rich man waiting for you in his car. Hurry up!'

Saugandhi sat down in the easy chair, and Ram Lal came in and started combing his hair in front of the mirror. Saugandhi reached towards the stool, picked up a jar of balm, and opened its lid. 'Ram Lal, I'm not in the mood today.'

Ram Lal put the comb back in the niche and turned around. 'You should have said so first.'

Saugandhi rubbed balm across her forehead and temples. 'Not that, Ram Lal,' she said. 'It's not that. I just don't feel good. I drank a lot.'

Ram Lal's mouth began to water. 'If there's any left, hand it over! I want some too.'

Saugandhi put the jar of balm on the stool. 'Do you think I'd have this damn headache if I didn't drink it all? Look, Ram Lal, bring your guy up here.'

'No, no, he won't come. He's a gentleman. He was even anxious about his car being in the alley. Put on something and come with me. You'll start feeling better.'

All this trouble and just for seven and a half rupees. When Saugandhi had a bad headache, she usually wouldn't work, but now she really needed the money. The husband of a Madrasi woman who lived next door had been killed by a car. Now this woman had to return with her young daughter to Madras, but she didn't have enough money to cover the journey. She was worried to the point of distraction. Saugandhi had reassured her just the day before, 'Don't worry. My boyfriend's about to come from Pune. I'll get some money from him and buy your tickets.' Madho was indeed about to come, but Saugandhi would have to come up with the money on her own. With all this in mind, she got up, quickly changed into her flowery sari and put on some rouge. She drank one more ladleful of water and went out with Ram Lal.

The alley, larger than some small towns' markets, was completely silent. The light from the streetlights was weak, as their fixtures had been painted over due to the war. She could just see a car parked at the alley's far end, and the black car looked like a shadow in the mysterious silence of the night's last hours. Saugandhi felt as though her headache had spread across the entire scene, and even the wind seemed bitter, as though it too felt the after effects of the brandy and moonshine.

Ram Lal walked ahead and said something to the men in the car. Saugandhi reached the car, and Ram Lal moved aside and said, 'Look, here she is. She's a very good girl. She's just started working.' Then he turned to Saugandhi. 'Saugandhi, come over here. The boss wants to see you.'

Saugandhi lifted up the edge of her sari in her hand and stepped up to the car's door as the man shone a flashlight on her. The light dazzled Saugandhi's sleepy eyes. But then she heard the click of a button, the light went out, and the man said, 'Yuhkk!' Instantly, the engine jumped to life and the car took off down the alley.

Saugandhi did not have any time to react. She still felt the glare of the flashlight in her eyes and hadn't even been able to see the man's face. What had just happened? What was this 'yuhkk' echoing in her ears?

'I guess he didn't like you,' Ram Lal said. 'All right then, I'm leaving. I've wasted two hours for nothing.'

Saugandhi had to fight off a desire to do something violent. Where was that car? Where was that man? So that 'yuhkk' meant he didn't like me? That bas . . . .

She caught herself. The car was already gone, and its red tail-lights were fading into the darkness of the night's empty market. But this red-hot 'yuhkk' was piercing her chest! She wanted to shout out, 'Hey, you rich fuck, stop the car! Come back here for just a minute.' But fuck that asshole—he was already too far away!

She stood in the deserted market. Her flowery sari, which she wore on special occasions, was rippling in the breeze and seemed to be saying, 'Yuhkk, yuhkk.' How she hated that sound! She wanted to tear her sari apart and fling its scraps into the wind!

She recalled how she had put on lipstick and powdered her cheeks to make herself more attractive, and now she felt so ashamed by this that she began sweating. She rationalized her feelings, 'I didn't dress up for that pig! It's my habit—not just mine but everyone's. But at two in the morning, and Ram Lal, and this market, and that car, and the flashlight!' And as she thought all this, the streetlamps started flickering on all around her, and again she thought she could hear the rumbling of a car's engine.

She was sweating, and the balm on her forehead was seeping into her pores. Her body felt distant, and she felt as though her forehead didn't belong to her. A gust of wind blew across its sweaty surface, and she felt like someone had cut up a piece of satin and stuck it to her forehead. Her head was still throbbing, but the internal noise of her thoughts had drowned out the pain. Saugandhi wanted the pain to engulf her body—she wanted pain in her head, in her legs, in her stomach, and arms too, the kind of pain that made it impossible to think. Thinking this, she noticed a sensation in her heart. Was it pain? Her heart contracted and then returned to normal. What was that? Damn, that was it! That 'yuhkk' was messing with her heart!

Saugandhi turned towards home, then stopped to think. Ram Lal said the man thought I was ugly. But, no, Ram Lal didn't say that. His actual words were, 'I guess he didn't like you.' But maybe he . . . but maybe he . . . did dislike the way I look. But if he thought I was ugly, so what? I think a lot of men are ugly. The last new moon, that john was really bad. But did I scrunch up my nose in disgust? When he climbed on top of me, wasn't I revolted? Didn't I just stop myself from throwing up? But, Saugandhi, you didn't kick and scream. You didn't turn him away. This rich guy in the car spat in your face. 'Yuhkk!' What could this 'yuhkk' mean?

1) 'What a joke! This girl's so ugly even her mother can't bear looking at her.'
2) 'I wouldn't let this bitch shine my shoes.'
3) 'Ram Lal, where did you unearth this specimen?'

4) 'Ram Lal, you went out of your way to praise this girl? Ten rupees for this? A cow's asshole would be better.'

Saugandhi was seething from head to foot. She got angry at herself and then at Ram Lal, but she quickly exonerated them and began to think about the man. With every bone in her body, she wished to see that man once more. She wanted to redo the scene once more, just once more. It would happen like this. She would stroll up to the car, a hand would emerge with the flashlight, it would flash in her face, and she would hear that 'yuhkk.' But this time she would leap on him like a wild cat and furiously scratch at his face. With her long fingernails, she would tear into his cheeks. She would grab him by the hair, drag him outside, and pummel him without mercy. And when she got tired, she would cry.

She thought of adding the crying part only because three or four tears were already welling in her eyes—she felt that angry and helpless. She asked herself, 'Why are you crying? What's wrong with you?' Tears continued to swim in her eyes. She blinked and her eyelashes became wet, and Saugandhi stared through her tears in the direction where the man's car had gone.

Suddenly she heard a noise—*phar, phar, phar*. Where was it coming from? Saugandhi looked around but didn't see anyone. Then she realized what it was—it was her heart that was racing and not the sound of a car! What was going on? Why would it be going along fine and then suddenly begin to pound? It was like a needle catching on a worn-out record, and the music's natural flow, 'The night passed while I counted stars . . .' turning into a one-word echo, 'stars, stars, stars . . .'

The sky was filled with stars. Saugandhi looked up and exclaimed, 'How beautiful!' She wanted to think of something else, but their beauty only served as a nasty reminder and she thought to herself, 'Stars are beautiful, but you're ugly. Did you forget already how that man insulted you?'

But Saugandhi wasn't ugly. She remembered all the recent times she had looked in the mirror, and while there was no doubt she didn't look the same as she had five years earlier when she was living with her parents and free from all worry, in any event she wasn't ugly. In fact she was the type of woman that men stare at. She had all the bodily attributes that men want in a woman, and was young and had a good figure. Sometimes when bathing, she would see with pleasure how round and firm her thighs were. She was also polite, friendly, and compassionate, and so it was hard to imagine that she ever disappointed any of her customers.

She remembered the year before when she had been living in Gol Petha over the Christmas season. A young man had spent the night, and when he got up the next morning and went into the next room to take his coat off the hook, he discovered that his wallet was missing. Saugandhi's servant had stolen it. The poor soul was very upset. He had come on vacation from Hyderabad and didn't have enough money to get back. Saugandhi felt so sorry for him that she gave him his ten rupees back.

'What have I ever done wrong?' Saugandhi addressed everything around her—the darkened streetlights, the iron electricity poles, the pavement's rectangular stones, and the street's gravel. She looked at her surroundings and then lifted her gaze to the sky, but there was no answer.

She knew the answer herself. She wasn't bad at all but good, and yet she wanted someone to praise her, someone to put his hand on her shoulder and say, 'Saugandhi, who says you're bad? *That* person's the bad one!' No, there wasn't any special need for that. It would be enough if someone said, 'Saugandhi, you're really good!'

She thought about why she wanted someone to praise her, as she had never before felt such a strong need for this. Why did she turn even to inanimate objects, asking them to confirm her worth? And why did she feel in her body such an overwhelming desire to give comfort? Why did she want to take the world onto her lap? Why did she want to cling to the streetlamp, putting her hot cheeks against its cold iron?

Then for a moment she felt as though everything was looking at her with sympathy—the streetlamps and the electricity poles, the paving stones, everything! Even the star-filled sky that hung above her like a milky sheet in the growing light seemed to understand her, and Saugandhi in turn felt she could understand the stars' twinkling. But what was this confusion inside her? Why did she feel so unsettled? She wanted to get rid of the bad feelings boiling inside her, but how could she do this?

Saugandhi was standing next to the red mailbox at the alley's corner. Sharp gusts of wind buffeted it, and the iron tongue hanging inside its mouth rattled. Again Saugandhi looked in the direction the car had gone, but she didn't see anything. How much she wanted the car to come back just once, and . . . and. . . . But then she reasoned with herself, 'I don't care if it doesn't come back. In fact, good for it! Why should I worry myself to death over it? I'm going home and I'll sleep like a baby. What's the point of rehashing everything? Why should I worry over nothing? Let's go, Saugandhi, go home. Drink a ladleful of cold water, rub in a little balm, and go to bed. You'll sleep well, and tomorrow everything will be okay. Fuck him and his car!'

These thoughts assuaged some of Saugandhi's pain. She felt like she had emerged from a cold pond after bathing. Her body felt lighter, as she felt after praying. She began walking to her home, and was her spirits lifted, her steps seemed almost buoyant.

She had nearly reached her apartment when the memory of the man waylaid her again, filling her body with a throbbing pain. Her steps turned heavy, and she felt as though she was reliving the experience step by step—once again she left her room for the market, had a light shone in her face, and was insulted. She felt as though someone was pressing his thumb against her ribs, as you press your thumb into a sheep or goat to see if there is any meat beneath the hair. That rich fuck had . . . ! By God, Saugandhi wanted to curse him! And yet what would come from that? She thought, 'The real pleasure would come from branding his every inch with insults. The real pleasure would come from saying something to hurt him for the rest of his life. Or tearing off my clothes right in front of him, I would ask, "This is what you came for, right? Here, take it for free—take it. But not even your father could buy what I've inside me!"'

Saugandhi was thinking of different ways of taking revenge. If just once she ran into him again, she would do this . . . no, not this, but this . . . she would take her revenge like this . . . no, not like that . . . like . . . . But when Saugandhi realized she would never see him again, she resigned herself to cursing him beneath her breath, and not even with such a bad word, just something that would stick to his nose like a fly to sit there forever.

In this bewildered state, she reached her second-floor room. She took her key out of her bra and reached out to unlock her door, but the padlock was missing! Saugandhi pushed one of the door's panels inward, and this made a light creaking sound. Someone unlatched the chain from inside, and the door yawned open. Saugandhi entered.

Madho was chuckling. He shut the door and said to Saugandhi, 'Today you took what I said to heart—a walk in the morning is very good for your health! If you get up and take a walk like this every morning, all your sluggishness will go away, the pain in your waist too, the pain you've been complaining about so much. You must have walked all the way to Victoria Gardens and back, right?'

Saugandhi didn't answer, and Madho didn't press her. In fact, he never really meant that she should answer his questions, and he talked only because he had to.

Madho sat down on the cane chair with the stained back, crossed his legs, and stroked his moustache.

Saugandhi sat on the bed. 'I was just expecting you.'

Madho was startled. 'You were expecting me? How did you know I was coming?' Saugandhi relaxed her lips into a thin smile. 'I dreamt about you. I got up, but no one was there. So I decided to go for a stroll, and . . .'

This pleased Madho. 'And I came! Well, what do you know! Whoever said that people are connected by their hearts was exactly right. When was your dream?'

'At about four o'clock.'

Madho got up from the chair and sat next to Saugandhi. 'And I dreamt about you at exactly two o'clock. You were standing next to me in this very sari. What were you holding—what was it? Oh, yes, you were holding a little bag full of money. You gave this bag to me and said, "Madho, what're you worrying about? Take this bag. My money's your money, right?" Saugandhi, I swear, I got up immediately, bought a ticket and came here. What should I say? I'm in a lot of trouble! Out of the blue, someone filed a police report against me. If I give the inspector twenty rupees, he'll let me go. Aren't you tired? Lie down, and I'll massage your feet. If you're not used to walking, you're sure to get tired. Here, put your feet next to me and lie down.'

Saugandhi lay down. She folded her arms behind her head for a pillow and then in a cloying tone said, 'Madho, what bastard filed a report against you? If you think there's a chance you might go to jail, just tell me. If you give him twenty or thirty rupees—no, even fifty or a hundred—you won't regret it. If you get off, it's like saving yourself a fortune. Anyway, stop that, I'm not that tired. Stop and tell me everything. Just hearing the words "police report" made my heart start pounding. When will you go back?'

Madho smelled liquor on Saugandhi's breath. He thought this the opportune moment and so quickly said, 'I'll have to go back in the afternoon train. If the sub-inspector doesn't get fifty or a hundred by the evening, then . . . well, there's no need to give him a lot. I think fifty should be enough.'

'Fifty!' Saugandhi exclaimed.

She got up slowly and went up to the four photos on the wall. Madho's was the third from the left: he was seated on a chair with a floral-printed curtain behind him. He sat with his hands on his thighs, and in one hand he held a rose. On the stool next to him were two thick books. Everything in the photo was so conspicuous that they all seemed to be saying, 'We're having our picture taken! We're having our picture taken!' In the photo, Madho was wide-eyed, and the whole situation seemed to make him uncomfortable.

Saugandhi started cackling, a sharp laugh that pricked Madho like needles. He rose and approached her. 'Whose photo are you laughing at?' he asked.

Saugandhi pointed to the first photo from the left, that of the official from the city's Sanitation Department. 'His—this guy's,' she said. 'Look at his snout. He used to brag, "A queen once fell in love with me." Yuhkk! Can you imagine a queen loving this nose?'

Saugandhi ripped the frame from the wall with such force that the nail came out along with some plaster. This shocked Madho, and before he could recover, Saugandhi threw the frame out of the window. It fell two floors down and hit the ground with the sound of breaking glass.

'When his rag-picking queen comes by on her trash-collecting rounds, she can take him with her,' she mocked. Again Saugandhi erupted in bitter laughter. It rained from her lips like embers flying from a grindstone.

Madho forced himself to laugh.

Saugandhi ripped the second frame off the wall and threw it outside.

'What does this place mean to that bastard?' she asked. 'From now on ugly men are banned—isn't that right, Madho?'

Madho again forced himself to laugh.

With one hand, Saugandhi took down the picture of a man wearing a turban, and with her other hand she reached for Madho's photo. Madho shrank back as though she was reaching for him. Then Saugandhi ripped them off the wall, along with their frames and nails.

Saugandhi laughed loudly and then shouted, 'Yuhkk!' She threw both frames out the window, and after a moment, they heard the sound of shattering glass. Madho felt as though something inside him had broken. He forced himself to laugh.

'Yes, good job,' he said. 'I didn't like that photo, either.'

Saugandhi slowly approached him. 'You didn't like that photo?' she repeated. 'Why would you—is there anything likeable about you? You and your circus nose, you and your hairy forehead, you and your donkey nostrils, you and your twisted ears, you and your bad breath, you and your dirty body? You didn't like your photo? Yuhkk! It hid all of your blemishes. You know, these days you're supposed to be proud of your flaws!'

Madho shrank back further. When he reached the wall, he yelled, 'Look, Saugandhi, it seems like you've started working again. Now for the last time I'm going to say . . .'

Saugandhi interrupted him. 'If you start to work again,' she imitated him, 'well, then our relationship is over. If you let any guy sleep here, I'll grab you by your hair and throw you out. I'm going to send you a money order for this month's expenses as soon as I get to Pune. What's this room's rent?'

Madho was aghast.

'I'll tell you,' she answered herself. 'Fifteen rupees. Fifteen, and I charge ten. And, as you know, two and a half go to the pimp. The remaining seven and a half—seven and a half, right?—are mine. And for those seven and a half rupees, I promised to give you things I couldn't, and you came for things you couldn't take. What was our relationship? Nothing—just these ten rupees. We pretended, saying things like, "I need you and you need me." At first it was ten rupees, and today it's fifty, and you're eyeing it and I'm eyeing it. And what have you done to your hair?'

With one finger, Saugandhi flicked off Madho's hat. He didn't like this at all.

'Saugandhi!'

Saugandhi took out a handkerchief from Madho's pocket, smelled it, and threw it on the floor. 'This is a rag, a rag! Aghh, it smells awful! Pick it up and throw it outside.'

'Saugandhi!'

'No—fuck off with your "Saugandhi this and Saugandhi that"! Does your mother live here that she's going to give you fifty rupees? Or are you some young, handsome stud I've fallen in love with? You son of a bitch! Are you trying to impress me? Am I at your beck and call? You fucking bum, who do you think you are? I'm asking you, "Who the hell are you? A fucking burglar? Why exactly have you come here in the middle of the night? Should I call the police? Who cares if there's really a police report against you in Pune—maybe I'll file one against you here."'

Madho was terrified. 'Saugandhi, what's happened to you?'

'Go fuck your mother! Who are you to ask me that? Get out of here—or else!'

When Saugandhi's mangy dog heard her yelling, he rose agitatedly from beneath the bed, turned in Madho's direction, and began to bark. Saugandhi laughed loudly. Madho was scared. He bent down to pick up his hat, but Saugandhi yelled, 'Hey, don't touch that! You—get out of here. As soon as you get back, I'll parcel-post you your fucking hat.'

Then she laughed even louder. She sat down on the cane chair, and her dog chased Madho out of the room and barked him down the stairs.

When he came back, he was wagging his powerful tail. He sat next to Saugandhi's feet and shook his head, flapping his ears against his cheeks. Saugandhi suddenly felt the frightening stillness that surrounded her, something she had never before felt. It seemed as though a train full of passengers had emptied station by station and now stood desolate beneath the last tin awning. It was a painful hollowness. Saugandhi tried to dispel this feeling, but she couldn't. All at once a rush of thoughts passed through her mind, but it was as though her mind were a strainer and all her thoughts caught inside it.

For quite a while she stayed in the cane chair, but even after thinking things over, she couldn't find any way to soothe herself, so she picked up her mangy dog, put him on one side of her wide teak bed, lay down next to him and immediately fell asleep.

SMELL

IT was a monsoon day just like today. Outside the window the leaves of the peepal tree were glistening in the rain, just as they were now. On this very teak bed, now pushed back a little from where it used to rest next to the window, a ghatin girl was nuzzling against Randhir's side.

Outside the window, the leaves of the peepal tree were shimmering beneath the overcast night sky just as if they were flashy earrings, and inside the girl was trembling and holding on to Randhir. Earlier, after reading each and every section of an English newspaper (even its ads) throughout the day, Randhir had gone out onto his balcony to relax a little as evening approached. The girl, probably a worker at the neighbouring rope factory, was then standing under the tamarind tree to escape the rain. Randhir had cleared his throat to get her attention and then signalled with his hand for her to come up.

He had been very lonely for a number of days. On account of the war, almost all the Christian girls in Bombay, ones he was used to getting cheap, had been conscripted into the Women's Auxiliary Forces. Many had opened 'dancing' schools in the Fort where only British soldiers were allowed. Randhir was depressed. He could no longer get these Christian girls. Even though he was more cultured and attractive than the soldiers, he wasn't allowed into the Fort's whorehouses, simply because he wasn't white.

Before the war he had slept with many Christian girls, both in Nagpada and in the area around the Taj Hotel. He knew he was far more familiar with the intricacies of such relationships than the Christian boys with whom the girls pretended to be in love, only to lure one of those fools into marriage.

To be honest, Randhir had called the girl up to his room just to take revenge on Hazel for her new and arrogant indifference to him. Hazel lived in the apartment beneath his, and each morning she would put on her uniform, place her khaki hat crosswise over her military-style haircut, and go outside to strut down the pavement as though she expected everyone in front of her to fall to the ground, sacrificing their bodies to provide her with a carpet to walk across.

Randhir wondered why he was so obsessed with those Christian girls. Of course they were good at showing off all their assets, they talked about their periods without hesitating at all, they talked about their past love affairs, and they loved dance music so much that they started tapping their feet whenever they heard it. This is all true enough, and yet other women could be like that too.

When Randhir motioned for the girl to come up, he didn't imagine that he would go to bed with her. But when she entered his room, he saw her soaked clothes. He feared that she might get pneumonia, so he said, 'Take those off. You'll catch cold.'

She understood, and her eyes flashed with shame. When Randhir took off his white dhoti and offered it to her, she hesitated a moment and then unwrapped her dirty kashta sari, placed it to the side and quickly flung the dhoti over her lap. Then she began trying to remove her skin-tight bra that was tied together in a knot stuck between her cleavage.

She kept trying to loosen the knot with the aid of her nails but the rain had tightened it. When she got tired of this and admitted defeat, she turned to Randhir and said in Marathi, 'What can I do? It's stuck.'

Randhir went to sit by her and try his luck with the knot. After vainly trying for some time, he grabbed one edge of her bra's neckline in one hand, its other edge with his other hand, and yanked roughly. The knot broke. Her breasts sprung out, and for a moment he imagined himself as a skillful potter who had shaped her breasts from finely kneaded clay.

Her breasts were firm and fresh like a potter's newly turned vessels. A shade darker than tan, they were completely unblemished and imbued with a strange radiance: just beneath the skin there seemed to be a layer of faint light giving off a spectral glow like a pond radiates light from beneath its turgid surface.

It was a monsoon day just like today. Outside the window, the peepal tree's leaves were fluttering. The girl slept entwined with Randhir, and her rain-soaked clothes lay in a messy heap on the floor. The heat spreading from the girl's dirty naked body felt the same to Randhir as what he had experienced when bathing in the grimy, hot public baths during the dead of winter.

All night the two clung to each other as though they had become one. They must not have said more than a couple of words, as what they had to communicate was accomplished by their breath, lips, and hands. All night Randhir caressed her breasts, arousing her small nipples and the nerves around her dark aureoles, and throughout the night tremors rippled up and down her body that were so strong that from time to time Randhir, too, quivered with delight.

Randhir knew all about such sensual pleasures. He had slept holding the breasts of countless girls. He had slept with girls so untrained that after cuddling up to him, they would go on to talk about all the household things you shouldn't mention to a stranger. He had also slept with girls who did all the work so that he could just lie there. But this girl, this girl who had been trembling beneath the tamarind tree and whom he had called up to his room, was very different.

All night her body emitted a strange smell at once alluring and repellent. With every breath Randhir took in this ambivalent odour that came from everywhere—her hair, her armpits, her breasts, and her stomach. All night he told himself that he wouldn't have felt that close to her if her naked body hadn't smelled that way, if that smell hadn't entered into his every fibre and invaded his every thought.

For one night this odour united Randhir and the girl. They became one, descending into an animal place where they existed only in pure pleasure, a place that despite being temporary was also eternal and that while being a sort of transcendent elation was also a quieted calm. They had become one, like a bird flying so high in the sky that it appears motionless.

This scent emanated from every pore of the girl's body. He recognized it but he couldn't describe it: it was like the pleasing aroma that dirt gives off after you sprinkle it with water. No, it wasn't like that at all. It was something different. It was without any of the artificiality of perfume, but pure and real. It was as real and old as the story of men and women itself.

Randhir hated the smell of sweat. After bathing, he would normally sprinkle aromatic baby powder under his armpits and elsewhere or use some other substance to cover up the smell. So it was amazing that he kissed the girl's hairy armpits over and over and was not at all disgusted, but rather found this surprisingly pleasurable. Her delicate armpit hairs were damp from her sweat that gave off this scent at once evocative and yet indefinable. Randhir felt like he knew this scent—it was familiar, he knew it in his bones, but he lacked the words to explain it to anyone.

It was a monsoon day just like today, exactly like today. When he looked through the window, he saw the leaves of the peepal tree trembling in the rain, rustling and fluttering in the breeze. It was dark and yet the night gave off a faint glow, as though the raindrops had stolen some of the stars' radiance. It was a monsoon day just like today back when Randhir had had only one teak bed in his room, though now there was another one along with a dressing table consigned to a corner. It was a monsoon day just like today, the weather was just the same, with the same twinkling rain, and yet the sharp aroma of henna hung in the air.

The second bed was empty. Randhir lay on his stomach,

his head turned to look out of the window at the leaves of the peepal tree quivering in the rain, and next to him a fair-skinned girl had fallen asleep after struggling unsuccessfully to cover herself with her naked limbs. Her red silk pants lay on the other bed, from which hung one knotted end of her pant's deep red drawstring. Her other clothes were strewn over the bed as well: her flowery kameez, her bra, underpants, and veil—and everything was red, bright red. And the clothes all smelled strongly of the pungent aroma of henna.

Her black hair was flecked with glitter, and her face was covered with rouge and a sparkly make-up that dissolved together to produce a sick greyish hue. The poor girl! Her bra's badly dyed fabric had run and stained her pale breasts red in places.

Her breasts were the colour of milk, white with a faint bluish tinge, and her armpits were badly shaven, leaving a greyish stubble. Over and over, when Randhir looked at the girl, he felt as though he had just exhumed her from some box, as though she were a book or a porcelain vessel: just as ink spots may mar the cover of a book sent from the printer's, or as scratches appear on porcelain treated roughly, he found the very same marks on her body.

Earlier, Randhir had untied the string fastening her bra, which had left deep lines on the tender flesh of her back and beneath her breasts. Her waist also bore the mark of her tight drawstring. Her necklace's heavy and sharp-edged jewels had left scratches across her chest that made it look as though she had torn at her skin with her nails.

It was a monsoon day just like today, the sound of the rain on the peepal tree's tender leaves was exactly the same, and

Randhir listened to it throughout the night. The weather was wonderful, and the breeze was pleasantly cool, but the overpowering aroma of henna lay thick in the air.

Randhir continued to caress the girl's milky white breasts. His fingers felt ripples of pleasure run up and down her tender body and faint tremors coming from its deepest recesses. When Randhir pressed his chest against hers, he felt every nerve in his body vibrate in response to her passion. But something was missing: the attraction he had felt to the ghatin girl's scent, the pull more urgent than a baby crying for his mother's milk, that instinctive call surpassing all words.

Randhir looked through the iron bars on the window. Nearby, the leaves of the peepal tree were fluttering, and yet he was looking beyond this at the distant overcast sky where the clouds cast an eerie glow that reminded him of the light of the ghatin girl's breasts.

A girl lay next to Randhir. Her body was as soft as dough made with milk and butter. The aromatic scent of henna rising from her sleeping body seemed to be fading little by little. Randhir could barely stand this poisonous, gut-wrenching odour: it smelled acidic, the strange type of acidity he associated with acid reflux—a sad scent, without colour, without exhilaration.

Randhir looked at the girl lying by his side. Feminine charm touched her only in places, just as drops of spoilt milk fleck water. In truth, Randhir still longed for the ghatin girl's natural scent, so much lighter and yet so much more penetrating than the scent of henna, the scent that was so welcome, that had excited Randhir so naturally. Trying for the last time, Randhir ran his hand over the girl's milky skin, but he felt nothing. Even though she was a respected judge's daughter, had graduated from college, and had hundreds of her male college classmates crazy about her, Randhir's new wife couldn't excite him. In the dying scent of henna, he tried to find the scent of the ghatin girl's dirty naked body that he had enjoyed when outside the window, the leaves of the peepal tree had glistened in the rain, exactly like today.

BABU GOPI NATH

I MET Babu Gopi Nath in 1940. In those days I was the editor of a weekly newspaper in Bombay. One day I was writing an article when Abdur Rahim Saindo entered the office along with a diminutive man. Saindo yelled out his greetings in his peculiar way and then introduced his companion, 'Manto Sahib, meet Babu Gopi Nath.'

I got up and shook his hand. As was his habit, Saindo began to heap praises on me, 'Babu Gopi Nath, you're shaking hands with India's number one writer. When you read what he writes, *ding-dong-dang* ... *vah*! He writes with such *topsy turvulence* that it clears your mind. What witticism was it that you wrote recently, Manto Sahib? 'Miss Khursheed bought a new car: God is a great car salesman!' What about that, Babu Gopi Nath? *Chingy ching*, right?'

Abdur Rahim Saindo had a completely unique way of putting things—'ding-dong-dang', 'topsy turvulence', 'chingy ching'—words he invented and then slipped spontaneously into conversations. After introducing me, he turned to Babu Gopi Nath, who was standing there in awe.

'Let me introduce you to Babu Gopi Nath, a great good-for-nothing. After sitting around doing nothing in Lahore, he decided to grace Bombay with his presence, and he brought a Kashmiri dove with him.'

Babu Gopi Nath smiled.

Abdur Rahim Saindo felt he hadn't said enough and so went on, 'If there's an award for the world's biggest fool, you're looking at the winner. People fill his ears with lies and take his money. Just for talking to him, I get two packets of Polson butter every day. Manto Sahib, I can say only this—he's an *anti-flow-Justian* kind of guy. Please come by his apartment this evening.'

God only knows what Babu Gopi Nath had been thinking when something startled him back to reality. 'Yes, yes, you must come by, Manto Sahib,' he said. Then he asked Saindo, 'Hey, Saindo, does he partake of you-know-what?'

Abdur Rahim Saindo erupted in laughter. 'Yes, he participates in all sorts of amusements. So, Manto Sahib, don't forget to come by this evening. I've also started drinking—after all, the booze is free.'

Saindo wrote down the apartment's address, and I showed up at about six in the evening as promised. It was a sparkling three-bedroom apartment with brand-new furniture. Saindo and Babu Gopi Nath were in the living room and with them were two men and two women. Saindo introduced me to them.

One was Ghaffar Sayyan, a pure Punjabi holy man wearing a cummerbund and a rosary with big beads. Saindo said, 'This gentleman is Babu Gopi Nath's legal advisor, get what I mean? Each and every Punjabi man with a snotty nose and drool dribbling from his mouth becomes a saint, and this gentleman, too, has either attained or is about to attain this revered status. He came with Babu Gopi Nath from Lahore because he had no hope of meeting any other such idiot there. At Babu Sahib's expense he smokes Craven A cigarettes, drinks Scotch, and prays for a happy end.'

Ghaffar Sayyan smiled as he listened to this.

The second man's name was Ghulam Ali. He was a tall and well-built young man with smallpox scars on his face. Saindo said, 'This is my disciple who is trying to follow in my footsteps. In Lahore, a famous courtesan's young daughter fell in love with him and in order to trap him, a lot of topsy turvulence was done. But he said, "It doesn't matter what you do or say, I'm not getting married." He met Babu Gopi Nath at a holy shrine drinking and bullshitting and has been clinging to him ever since. Every day he gets food and drink and a pack of Craven A.'

Ghulam Ali smiled throughout this introduction.

There was also a round-faced woman with a ruddy complexion. As soon as I entered the room, I understood that she was the Kashmiri dove Saindo had mentioned at my office. She was very clean and tidy. She had short hair that looked like she had cut it when in truth she hadn't. Her eyes were clear and sparkling. She looked inexperienced and innocent. Saindo introduced her, 'Zinat Begam. Babu Gopi Nath's pet name for her was Zinu. A very crafty madam plucked this apple from Kashmir and brought her to Lahore. From his CID people Babu Gopi Nath found out about her and then one night managed to take off with her. The madam filed a suit against him. The trial lasted two months and the police enjoyed themselves to their heart's content, but in the end Babu Sahib won the case and brought her here—ding-dong-dang!'

Now only one person remained, the woman with the

dark complexion sitting silently and smoking. She had a depraved expression that was concentrated in her bloodshot eyes. Babu Gopi Nath made a sign in her direction and said to Saindo, 'Tell us something about her too.'

Saindo slapped this woman's thigh and said, 'Sir, this is Tinputi Falfuti, Mrs Abdur Rahim Saindo, alias Sardar Begam. She was also born and bred in Lahore. We fell in love in '36. Within two years, she did a ding-dong-dang on me. Then I fled. Babu Gopi Nath called her here so I could feel at home. She also gets a pack of Craven A, and every evening she gets a two and a half rupee injection of morphine. Though she's dark-skinned, in fact, she's a tit-for-tat-type woman.'

Sardar gave him a coquettish glance that said, 'Don't talk nonsense.' It was exactly the type of glance used by prostitutes.

After introducing everyone, Saindo set out in his usual manner to sing my praises, but I interrupted him, 'Come on, stop, Saindo. Let's talk about something else.'

Saindo yelled to the servant, 'Hey, boy—whisky and soda!' Then he turned to Babu Gopi Nath.

'Babu Gopi Nath, we need some cash.'

Babu Gopi Nath reached into his pocket, pulled out a money clip full of hundred-rupee notes, sheared one from the stack and handed it to Saindo. Saindo took the note and rustled it in his fingers. Then he said, 'Oh, God! Oh, Lord of All Worlds! When will I be able to throw money around like this? Ghulam Ali, go get two bottles of Johnny Walker Still Going Strong!'

The liquor arrived and everyone started drinking. We kept it up for two or three hours, and as usual Abdur

Rahim Saindo talked the most. He downed the first glass in one swig.

'Ding-dong-dang, Manto Sahib, that's what I call whisky! From my throat to my stomach, it washed down crying out, "Long live the revolution!"' He turned to Babu Gopi Nath, 'God bless you, Babu Gopi Nath, God bless you!'

Throughout the proceedings Babu Gopi Nath, the poor soul, didn't say anything other than to chime in with an occasional 'yes' to whatever Saindo was saying. I thought, 'This guy doesn't have any opinion of his own. Whatever anyone says, he agrees to it.' The proof of his gullibility was Ghaffar Sayyan. Saindo had said he was Babu Gopi Nath's legal advisor although he actually meant that Babu Gopi Nath revered him. Regardless, I learned in the course of our conversation that back in Lahore, Babu Gopi Nath often spent time with fakirs and dervishes. I noticed that Babu Sahib looked lost in thought, so I decided to ask him a question.

'Babu Gopi Nath, what are you thinking about?'

My question startled him. 'Oh . . . I . . . I . . . nothing,' he said. Then he smiled and cast a loving look in Zinat's direction. 'I was thinking about beautiful women like her. What else is there for a man like me to think about?'

'He's a great good-for-nothing, Manto Sahib,' Saindo interjected. 'Yes, a great good-for-nothing. There wasn't a courtesan in Lahore that Babu Sahib didn't topsy turvulence.'

'Manto Sahib, now I have no stamina like that,' Babu Gopi Nath admitted with an awkward humility.

Then the conversation turned racy and to counting all the brothels of Lahore. Who was good, who was bad.

Which girl was working under which madam. Which virgins had Babu Gopi Nath slept with and at what price. And so on and so on. Sardar, Saindo, Ghaffar Sayyan, and Ghulam Ali carried on in the rarefied dialect of Lahore whorehouses, and although I didn't catch some expressions, I understood enough.

Zinat remained sitting silently. From time to time she would smile at something, and yet I sensed that the conversation didn't interest her. She drank from a glass of diluted whisky but without evincing any pleasure. She smoked without relish, and yet the irony was that she smoked more than anyone else. Was she really in love with Babu Gopi Nath? It didn't seem so. It was clear, however, that he took great care of her and provided her with every comfort. Nonetheless, I sensed a strange tension between them. I mean, instead of being close they seemed to hold each other at a distance.

Sardar went to Dr Majid for her morphine injection at about eight o'clock. Ghaffar Sayyan drank three shots of whisky, picked up his rosary, and lay down to sleep on the carpet. Ghulam Ali was sent to a restaurant to pick up some food. After Saindo had stopped his nonsense for a while, Babu Gopi Nath, now drunk, turned to Zinat. Looking at her with a loving expression, he asked me, 'Manto Sahib, what do you think about my Zinat?'

I didn't know what to say. I looked at Zinat, and she blushed. 'I think she's good,' I said casually.

Babu Gopi Nath liked my answer. 'Yes, Manto Sahib, she really is good. I swear to God, Zinat isn't into jewellery or anything else. So many times I've said, "My dear, shall I build you a house?" And guess what she says? "What would I do with a house? I'm all alone."' Then he asked, 'Manto Sahib, how much does a car cost?'

'I don't know.'

Babu Gopi Nath was surprised. 'What're you saying, Manto Sahib! *You* don't know how much cars cost? Impossible! Tomorrow come with me, and we'll buy Zinu a car. I've realized you have to have a car in Bombay.'

Zinat's face remained expressionless.

Then Babu Gopi Nath got very drunk. With his emotions running high, he said, 'Manto Sahib, you're a very decent man, but I'm a total ass. Tell me, how can I be of service to you? Yesterday when I was talking to Saindo, he brought up your name. I immediately hailed a taxi and said to him, "Take me to Manto Sahib." Forgive me if I've said anything rude. I've committed many sins.' Then he asked, 'Should I call for some more whisky?'

'No, no,' I said. 'I've already had plenty.'

He became even more emotional. 'Drink some more, Manto Sahib!' Then he got out his wad of hundred-rupee notes and started to separate one. Before he could finish, I grabbed the clip and stuffed it back into his pocket. 'What happened to the hundred rupees you gave Ghulam Ali?'

In truth, I had begun to feel some sympathy for Babu Gopi Nath. How many people had latched like leeches onto this poor soul! Really, he was such a fool, and yet he understood what I was asking. Smiling, he said, 'Manto Sahib, whatever change Ghulam Ali gets is sure to fall from his pocket or . . .'

Babu Gopi Nath hadn't finished the sentence when Ghulam Ali walked into the room and informed us in a tone of great distress that some bastard at the restaurant had pick-pocketed every last rupee. Babu Gopi Nath turned to me and smiled. Then he took out a new note. He gave it to Ghulam Ali and said, 'Hurry and bring us some food.'

After we met five or six times, I came to understand Babu Gopi Nath's true character. Well, I admit that you cannot know someone completely but I learned many extremely interesting things about him.

First, I want to say again that my initial opinion proved wrong: he wasn't an idiot at all. He knew very well that Saindo, Ghulam Ali, Sardar, and the others hung around only to use him. He bore with their scolding and insults and never got angry. He confessed, 'Manto Sahib, I've never asked anyone for advice. Whenever anyone gives me advice, I say, "Wonderful!" They think I'm stupid, but I think they're smart—at least they're smart enough to see how they can take advantage of me. The truth is that I've lived with dervishes and gypsies since I was a child. I love them and can't live without them. I've decided that I'm going to stay at a saint's shrine as soon as my money runs out. Whorehouses and shrines—I feel at peace nowhere else. I'll quit going to whorehouses soon enough because my money's about to run out. But India has thousands of saints. I'll go find one when my time comes.'

'Why do you like whorehouses and shrines?' I asked.

He thought for a moment and then answered, 'Because there, from top to bottom, it's all about deception. What better place could there be for a person who wants to deceive himself?'

'If you like listening to courtesans' singing, you must know a lot about music.'

'Not at all,' he replied. 'And this is good because hearing the singing of even the worst courtesan I can nod my head in appreciation. Manto Sahib, I've absolutely no interest in singing, but I get a lot of pleasure from taking a ten- or hundred-rupee note and showing it to a woman. I get out the note and show it to her. She stands up with a sexy flourish to come take it, but when she comes close I jam it in my pocket. She bends down and takes the note from my pocket and this makes me very happy. We playboys enjoy a lot of small things like that. Anyway, everyone knows that parents force their daughters into whorehouses to earn money, and people use God in the same way.'

I didn't know anything about Babu Gopi Nath's family, but I did find out that he was the son of a very stingy moneylender. When his father died, Babu Gopi Nath had inherited assets worth a million rupees that he liquidated and spent however he chose. He brought 50,000 rupees to Bombay. Back then everything was cheap, and yet he managed to spend one hundred or 125 rupees a day.

He bought a Fiat for Zinu. I don't remember exactly, but I think it cost about 3,000 rupees. He hired a driver, another worthless character. Babu Gopi Nath liked people like that.

We began to get together more frequently. I was interested in him, but he began to revere me as if I were a saint. He had faith in me and respected me more than he did the others.

One evening when I went to the apartment, I was surprised to see Shafiq there. You'll probably recognize the name, Muhammad Shafiq Tusi. He was very famous, both on account of his inventive singing and his wit and charm, and yet there was a part of his life that most people didn't know about. Very few people knew he had made three sisters his lovers—one after the other after the other—keeping each for three or four years before moving on, and how before that he had been their mother's lover too. Most people knew he didn't like his first wife (who died soon after they got married) because she didn't flirt with him like a courtesan. But everyone knew that he had slept with hundreds of women by the time he reached forty. He wore fancy clothes, ate excellent food, and owned the most luxurious cars. But he never spent even a single rupee on any prostitute.

His entertainer's personality was very attractive to women, especially prostitutes, and he could seduce them with hardly any effort.

When I saw him getting on so well with Zinat, I wasn't surprised. I only wondered how he got there: Saindo knew him, but they hadn't been talking to each other for a long time. It was only afterwards that I learned that no one other than Saindo had brought him and that the two had made up.

Babu Gopi Nath was sitting on one side of the room and smoking a hookah. (Perhaps I didn't mention earlier that he didn't smoke cigarettes.) Muhammad Shafiq Tusi was telling jokes about entertainers, jokes that pleased Sardar more than Zinat. When Shafiq saw me, he said, 'Oh, bismillah, bismillah! So you, too, come here?'

'Please come in, Angel of Death,' Saindo said to me. 'Here everything's ding-dong-dang.' I understood what he meant.

The gossiping continued for a while. I noticed Zinat and Muhammad Shafiq Tusi exchange suggestive glances. Zinat was completely untrained in this art of flirting, but Shafiq's mastery made up for her rawness. Sardar was looking at them as a wrestling coach sitting outside the wrestling ring watches two pupils feint and dodge.

Over the course of time, I gradually grew friendly with Zinat. She took to calling me 'bhai', and I quite liked this. She was sociable but didn't talk much; she was guileless and sincere.

But I didn't like her flirting with Shafiq. First of all, she did it awkwardly. The fact that she called me 'bhai' also had something to do with it. When Shafiq and Saindo got up and went outside, I asked her about this flirting but perhaps I did so too severely because suddenly tears welled in her eyes and she left crying for another room. Babu Gopi Nath, sitting in a corner and drawing on his hookah, quickly got up and followed her. Sardar said something to him through a series of glances, but I couldn't tell what. A little while later Babu Gopi Nath reappeared and called to me, 'Manto Sahib, please come with me.' I followed him.

Zinat was sitting on a small bed. When I came in, she covered her face with both hands and lay down. Babu Gopi Nath and I sat down in chairs next to the bed. In a very serious manner, Babu Gopi Nath said, 'Manto Sahib! I love this woman very much. She has been with me for two years. I swear by the saint Hazrat Ghaus-e-Azam Jilani that I've never had reason to complain. Her sisters, I mean other prostitutes, robbed me with both hands, but she's never taken more than a reasonable amount. If I went off and stayed for weeks at some courtesan's house, this poor soul would pawn her jewellery in order to get by. Like I said, I'll be leaving these worldly things soon enough. My money's going to last for just a few more days. I don't want her to have a bad life. In Lahore I tried to get her to understand her situation. "Try to pick up on what the other girls are doing. Today I'm rich but tomorrow I'll be poor. It's not enough for a courtesan to know just one rich man. If you don't seduce someone else before I'm gone, you'll be in a world of hurt." But, Manto Sahib, she didn't listen to anything I said. She stayed at home all day as though waiting for someone to arrange her marriage. I asked Ghaffar Sayyan for advice. He told me to take her to Bombay because he knew two prostitutes who'd become actresses there. I thought Bombay would be okay. Now it's been two months since I brought her here. I called Sardar from Lahore so that she could teach Zinat all the necessary skills. She can learn a lot from Ghaffar Sayyan too. No one knows me here. Zinat was worried that she would disgrace me. I said, "Stop worrying about that. Bombay's a huge city. There're hundreds of thousands of rich men. I bought you a car. Go find a man who's good for you." Manto Sahib, I swear to God that my heartfelt wish is to see her get on her own two feet and be wise to the world. I'm ready right now to put 10,000 rupees in the bank in her name. But I know that in fewer than ten days she'll be sitting outside and Sardar will have taken her every last rupee. You too tell her it's important to be a little savvy. Since I bought the car, Sardar's been taking her every evening to Apollo Bunder but so far nothing has happened. Today Saindo had a very difficult time getting Muhammad Shafiq to come. What do you think about him?'

I didn't think it was the right time to say what I thought. But Babu Gopi Nath began again, 'He looks like someone who lives well, and he's handsome too. Zinu dear, do you like him?'

Zinat didn't say anything.

Babu Gopi Nath's talk about bringing Zinat to Bombay confused me. I couldn't believe it was possible, and yet what I saw afterwards proved everything to be true—it was Babu Gopi Nath's heartfelt wish that Zinat become a rich man's mistress, or that she learn how to work men for their money. I say this because if Babu Gopi Nath wanted merely to get rid of her, that wouldn't have been so hard. He could arrange that in a single day. But since his intentions were honourable, he tried everything to secure Zinat's future. In trying to get her into acting, he invited over numerous men who, it turned out, were only pretending to be directors. Then he got a telephone installed in the apartment. But nothing came from any of this.

Muhammad Shafiq Tusi kept coming by for about a month and a half. He even spent several nights with Zinat, and yet he wasn't the type of man who can support a woman. One day, in a sorrowful and offended tone, Babu Gopi Nath said, 'Shafiq Sahib turned out to be a gentleman only in name. He carries himself as though he has a lot of pride but look—he tricked Zinat into giving him four sheets, six pillowcases, and 200 rupees. Now I hear he's dating a girl named Almas.'

This was true. Almas was the youngest daughter of Nazir Jan of Patiala, and Shafiq had already dated her three sisters. Shafiq spent Zinat's 200 rupees on seducing Almas, and their story ended when she tried to kill herself by swallowing poison after fighting over him with her sisters.

Zinat called me several times after Muhammad Shafiq Tusi stopped visiting her and asked me to find him and bring him back. I looked for him, but no one knew where he lived. Then I ran into him one day at the radio station. He seemed very worried. When I told him Zinat wanted to see him, he said, 'I already know. It's too bad, but I really don't have any time to spare these days. Zinat's a good woman, but she's too virtuous—I don't have any interest in women who act like wives.'

Zinat lost hope in Shafiq and started going again with Sardar to Apollo Bunder. Over the course of fifteen days and countless gallons of petrol, Sardar was able to entrap two men. Zinat got 400 rupees off them. Babu Gopi Nath thought things were improving because one of them (an owner of a factory that made silk clothes) told Zinat he wanted to marry her. But then this man didn't come by again, and soon one month had passed.

One day I was going down Hornby Road on some business when I saw Zinat's car near the pavement. Muhammad Yasin, the owner of the Naginah Hotel, was sitting in the back seat. 'Where did you get this car?' I asked.

Yasin smiled. 'Do you know the girl who owns it?'

'Yes, I know her.'

'Then you can understand how I got it,' Yasin said, winking. 'She's a good girl, isn't she?'

I smiled back.

Four days later Babu Gopi Nath came to my office in a taxi. He told me how Zinat had met Muhammad Yasin. One evening Zinat and Sardar had picked up a man at Apollo Bunder and taken him to the Naginah Hotel. This man fought with them over something and left, but Zinat struck up a friendship with the hotel's owner.

Babu Gopi Nath was satisfied because Yasin had given Zinat six top-of-the-line saris during the two weeks or so they had been seeing each other. Babu Gopi Nath thought that once their relationship got even stronger then he'd head back to Lahore. But things didn't work out that way.

A Christian woman was renting a room in the Naginah Hotel. Yasin began flirting with her young daughter, Muriel. Every morning and evening Yasin would take Zinat's car and drive Muriel around town while poor Zinat stayed in her room. When Babu Gopi Nath learned about this, he got very sad. He said to me, 'Manto Sahib! What kind of people are these? If you're tired of something, just say so! But Zinat's strange too. She knows well enough what's going on, but she doesn't even say, "If you want to go out with this Christian girl, then get your own car. Why're you using mine?" What should I do, Manto Sahib? She's a real good girl, but I don't know what to do. She has to learn to be less naïve.'

Zinat wasn't shocked when the affair with Yasin fell through.

After that nothing new happened for many days. Then I called one day and learned that Babu Gopi Nath along with Ghulam Ali and Ghaffar Sayyan had gone to Lahore to get some more money as he had already spent the 50,000, and that Babu Gopi Nath had told Zinat it would take some time because he had to sell some property there.

Sardar needed her morphine injections, and Saindo needed Polson butter. So they worked together to pick up two or three guys every day. They told Zinat that Babu

Gopi Nath wasn't going to return, and so she would have to look after herself. She earned 125 a day, out of which she kept half and Saindo and Sardar shared the rest.

'Why are you doing this?' I asked Zinat one day.

'I don't know anything, bhai jan,' she replied very innocently. 'I do whatever Saindo and Sardar say.'

I wanted to sit down next to her and explain to her at length that what she was doing wasn't right and that Saindo and Sardar were using her. But I didn't say anything. Zinat was annoyingly passive—she was dumb, lazy, and listless. The poor girl didn't know the value of her life. She was a prostitute, but she didn't have a prostitute's wiles. Oh, how annoyed I got just by looking at her! She didn't take an interest in anything—not in cigarettes, not in alcohol, not in houses, not in eating, not in telephones, not even in the sofa on which she spent so many hours stretched out.

Babu Gopi Nath came back after a month. When he went to Mahim, there was someone else living in his apartment. On Saindo and Sardar's advice, Zinat had rented the upper floor of a bungalow in Bandra. When Babu Gopi Nath came to see me, I told him the address. He asked about Zinat, and I told him what I knew, except the part about how Saindo and Sardar were being pimps for her.

Babu Gopi Nath had brought 10,000 rupees. He had had a hard time scraping it together and had left Ghulam Ali and Ghaffar Sayyan back in Lahore.

The taxi was waiting on the street, and Babu Gopi Nath insisted I go with him.

We reached Bandra after about an hour. The taxi was climbing Pali Hill when Saindo appeared on the narrow road in front of us. 'Saindo!' Babu Gopi Nath shouted.

'Ding-dong-dang!' Saindo said when he saw Babu Gopi Nath.

'Come on. Get in the taxi. Come with us,' Babu Gopi Nath called out. But Saindo said, 'Pull over. I need to talk to you alone.'

The taxi driver pulled over. Babu Gopi Nath got out, and Saindo took him ahead. They talked for quite a while. When they were done, Babu Gopi Nath returned to the taxi alone and instructed the driver, 'Take us back.'

Babu Gopi Nath was happy. When we got close to Dadar, he said, 'Manto Sahib, Zinu's getting married!'

'To whom?' I asked in surprise.

'A wealthy landlord from Hyderabad in Sindh. I pray to God they'll be happy together. It's good I got here in time. I'll use the money to buy things for her dowry.' Then he asked me, 'What do you think about all of this?'

I didn't have any opinion. I wondered who this Hyderabadi landlord was. I wondered if it was some trick staged by Saindo and Sardar. But later I learned it was true. There was, in fact, a wealthy Sindhi landlord who had met Zinat through a music teacher, himself from Hyderabad. This music teacher was trying without success to teach Zinat how to sing. One day he brought his patron, Ghulam Husain. (This was the Hyderabadi gentleman's name.) Zinat treated him very well. Upon Ghulam Husain's request, Zinat sang a couplet of Ghalib's, 'My beloved nitpicks. It's hard to tell her the sorrows of my heart.' Ghulam Husain fell intensely in love, and the music teacher told this to Zinat. Saindo and Sardar met them, and soon they had arranged the marriage.

Babu Gopi Nath was happy. He went to play the role

of Saindo's friend in the home of Zinat's fiancé and met Ghulam Husain. After meeting him, Babu Gopi Nath was twice as happy as before.

'Manto Sahib! He's a handsome and very decent young man. Before leaving Lahore, I stopped at Data Ganj Bakhsh's shrine and prayed, and my prayer was answered. I pray to God they'll be happy.'

Babu Gopi Nath spared no expense in making the arrangements for Zinat's wedding. He ordered 2,000 rupees worth of jewellery and the same amount of clothes. He also gave her 5,000 rupees in cash. Muhammad Shafiq Tusi, Muhammad Yasin, Saindo, the music teacher, Babu Gopi Nath, and I were all at the wedding. Saindo was the witness for the bride.

When the exchange of vows was over, Saindo whispered, 'Ding-dong-dang!'

Ghulam Husain was wearing a blue serge suit. Everyone congratulated him, and he gladly accepted our best wishes. He was very handsome, and Babu Gopi Nath looked like a quail in front of him.

Babu Gopi Nath had also arranged a banquet and when everyone had eaten, he washed their hands. When I went up to him to get my hands washed, he said to me in a child-like manner, 'Manto Sahib, please go inside for a moment and see how Zinu looks in her wedding clothes.'

I brushed aside the curtain and entered the room. Zinat was wearing a red shalwar kameez with gold brocade. Her red scarf also had a fancy border. She was wearing light make-up, and although I really dislike lipstick, it looked beautiful on her. She blushed and greeted me in a very endearing way. When I saw a bed in one corner covered with flowers, I couldn't help but smile.

'What kind of joke is this?' I asked.

Zinat looked at me with a dove's innocent expression. 'You're making fun of me, bhai jan!' she said, and then tears welled in her eyes.

I still hadn't understood my mistake when Babu Gopi Nath entered. He took out his handkerchief and with great affection wiped away Zinat's tears. Then he spoke to me in an offended tone, 'Manto Sahib, I took you to be a very understanding, decent man! You should've stopped to think before making fun of Zinat.'

Babu Gopi Nath's faith in me was broken. Before I could apologize, he began stroking Zinat's hair. With great affection he said, 'I pray to God that you'll be happy.'

He looked at me with eyes full of tears of sad reproach. Then he left.

JANAKI

It was the beginning of the racing season in Pune when Aziz wrote from Peshawar: 'I'm sending Janaki, an acquaintance of mine. Get her into a film company in Pune or Bombay. You know enough people. I hope it won't be too difficult.'

It wasn't a question of being difficult, but the problem was I had never done anything like that before. Usually the men who take girls to film companies are pimps or their like, men who plan to live off the girls if they can get a job. As you can imagine I worried a lot about this, but then I thought, 'Aziz is an old friend. Who knows why he trusts me so much, but I don't want to disappoint him.' I was also reassured by the thought that the film world is always looking for young women. So what was there to fret about? Even without my help, Janaki would be able to get a job in some film company or other.

Four days later Janaki arrived, and after a long journey—from Peshawar to Bombay, and then from Bombay to Pune. As the train pulled up, I started to walk along the platform because she would have to pick me out of the crowd. I didn't have to go far because a woman holding my photo descended from the second-class compartment. Her back was to me. Standing on tiptoes, she started looking through the crowd. I approached her.

'You're probably looking for me,' I said.

She turned around.

'Oh, you!' She looked down at my photo and then in a very friendly manner said, 'Saadat Sahib, the trip was so long! After getting off the Frontier Mail in Bombay, I had to wait for this train for so long, it nearly killed me.'

'Where are your things?'

'I'll get them,' she said and entered the compartment to bring out a suitcase and a bedroll. I called out for a coolie. As we were leaving the station she said to me, 'I'll stay in a hotel.'

I got her a room in a hotel just opposite the station. She needed time to wash up, change her clothes and rest, and so I gave her my address, told her to meet me at ten in the morning, then left.

At ten thirty the next morning she arrived in Parbhat Nagar where I was staying at a friend's small but newly built apartment. She had got lost trying to find the place, and I had been up late writing the night before and so had slept in. I bathed and changed into a T-shirt and pyjama. I had just sat down with a cup of tea when she showed up.

The previous day, though weary from her trip, she had been bursting with life both on the platform and at the hotel, but when she appeared that morning at Apartment #11 in Parbhat Nagar, she looked anxious and worn out: she looked as though she had just donated ten to fifteen ounces of blood or had an abortion.

As I already said, my friend's house was completely quiet. I was staying there to write a film script. There was no one else in the apartment except an idiotic servant, Majid, the type that makes a house only more desolate. I made a cup of tea and gave it to Janaki.

'You must have eaten breakfast at the hotel before coming,' I said. 'But, anyway, please have some tea.'

Biting her lips anxiously, she picked up the cup and began to drink. Her right leg was shaking violently, and her lips quivered. I could tell there was something she wanted to say, but she hesitated. I thought maybe during the night someone had harassed her. So I asked, 'You didn't have any problems at the hotel, did you?'

'What? Oh, no.'

I didn't press her to say any more. Then after we finished our tea, I thought I should say something. 'How's Aziz Sahib?'

She didn't answer. She set the cup down on a stool, got up, and hurriedly said, 'Manto Sahib, do you know any good doctors?'

'Not in Pune.'

'Aaggggh!' she screamed in frustration.

'Why? Are you sick?'

'Yes.'

She sat down in a chair.

'What's the problem?'

When she smiled, her sharp lips became thinner. She opened her mouth. Again she wanted to say something but couldn't find the courage. She got up, picked up my pack of cigarettes, took one out and lit it.

'Please forgive me, but I just can't quit.'

I learned later that she didn't just smoke but smoked with a vengeance. She held the cigarette in her fingers like a man and took a deep drag. In fact, she inhaled so deeply that her daily habit was the same as a normal person's smoking seventy-five cigarettes.

'Why don't you tell me what's wrong?'

Annoyed, she pounded her foot on the floor like a young girl.

'Hai, Allah! How can I tell you?' she asked. Then she smiled. Her teeth were extraordinarily clean and shiny. She sat down, and trying to avoid my gaze, she said, 'The problem is that I'm fifteen or twenty days late and I'm scared that . . .'

Until then I hadn't understood, but when she stopped so abruptly I thought I finally knew what was going on.

'This happens often,' I said.

She took another deep drag and blew out the smoke in a thick rush.

'No,' she said, 'I'm talking about something else. I'm afraid I'm pregnant.'

'Ah!' I exclaimed.

She took a final drag and then stubbed out the cigarette in the saucer. 'If I am, it'll be a big problem,' she went on. 'This happened once in Peshawar, but Aziz Sahib brought some medicine from a doctor friend, and then everything was okay.'

'You don't like kids?'

She smiled. 'Sure, I like them. But who wants to go through the trouble of raising them?'

'You know it's a crime to have an abortion.'

She became pensive. In a voice full of sadness, she said, 'Aziz Sahib said this too, but, Saadat Sahib, my question is, how is it a crime? It's a personal matter, and the people who make the laws know an abortion is very painful. Is it really a serious crime?'

I couldn't help laughing. 'You're a strange woman, Janaki.'

Janaki also laughed. 'Aziz Sahib says so too.'

As she laughed, tears came to her eyes. I have noticed that when sincere people laugh, they always cry. She opened her bag, took out a handkerchief, and wiped away her tears. Then in an innocent manner, she asked, 'Saadat Sahib, tell me, is what I'm saying interesting?'

'Very.'

'That's a lie.'

'Why?'

She lit another cigarette.

'Well, maybe it's interesting. I only know that I'm kind of silly. I eat too much. I talk too much. I laugh too much. You can see, can't you, how big my stomach's become from eating too much? Aziz Sahib always used to say, "Janaki, don't eat so much!" But I never listened. Saadat Sahib, the thing is whenever I eat less, it always feels like something's missing!'

Then she laughed again, and I did too. Her laughter was very strange. It sounded like the jingling of a dancer's ankle bells.

She was just about to say something more about abortions when my friend came in. I introduced him to Janaki and told him how she wanted to get into acting, and then my friend took her to his studio because he was almost sure that the director he was working with would give her some special role in his new film.

I did as much as I could to find work for Janaki at

the studios in Pune. At one place she had a voice test. At another, a screen test. One film company dressed her up in all different sorts of clothes, and yet nothing came from any of this. Janaki was already worried about her period being late, and she became even more stressed after suffering through these auditions for four or five days and with no result. In addition, the twenty green quinine pills she took each day to abort her baby made her listless. Then she was also worried about how Aziz Sahib was faring in Peshawar. She had sent him a telegram as soon as she had arrived in Pune and since then, every day without fail, had written a letter to him in which she urged him to take care of his health and to take his medicine on time.

I didn't know what was wrong with Aziz Sahib, and all Janaki told me was that he loved her so much that he would immediately do whatever she asked. Although he often quarrelled with his wife over his medicine, he never made a fuss with Janaki.

At first I thought Janaki was just putting on a show about worrying for Aziz Sahib, but her candid talk gradually convinced me she really cared about him. Moreover, there was proof because she would always cry after reading his letters.

Her efforts to get into film companies resulted in nothing, but one day Janaki's mood improved when she learned that her guess had been wrong—she was late, but she wasn't pregnant.

Janaki had been in Pune for twenty days. She was writing Aziz one letter after another, and he was writing her long love letters in return. Then Aziz wrote to me, saying that if Janaki couldn't get in anywhere in Pune, I should try the many studios in Bombay. This made sense, but it was difficult for me to get away because I was busy writing the script. I called a friend of mine, Sayeed, who was playing the hero in some film. As it happened, he wasn't in the studio just then, but Narayan was there. When he overheard I was calling from Pune, he took the phone and shouted in English, 'Hello, Manto! Narayan speaking from this end!' Then he slipped into Urdu, 'What do you want? Sayeed isn't here right now. He's at home separating his stuff from Razia's.'

'What do you mean?'

'They had a fight. Razia's started seeing another guy.'

'But what's there to sort out?'

'Man, Sayeed is really awful,' Narayan said. 'He's taking back all the clothes he ever bought for her. Anyway, enough of that. What's going on?'

'Actually, the thing is one of my good friends in Peshawar has sent a girl who wants to get into acting.'

Janaki was standing next to me. I realized I hadn't explained things quite right. I was about to correct myself when Narayan shouted, 'A woman? From Peshawar? Hey, send her quick! I'm a Qasuri Pathan too!'

'Don't be silly, Narayan. Listen, tomorrow I'm sending her on the Deccan Queen. Either you or Sayeed will have to go to the station to pick her up. Tomorrow, on the Deccan Queen. Don't forget.'

'But how will I recognize her?'

'She'll recognize you. But listen—try to get her into some studio or other.'

The conversation lasted only three minutes. I hung up and said to Janaki, 'You're going to Bombay tomorrow on the Deccan Queen. I'll show you photos of Sayeed and Narayan. They're tall and handsome young men, and so you'll have no problem spotting them.'

I showed Janaki a bunch of photos of Sayeed and Narayan, and she stared at them for a long time. I noticed that she looked at Sayeed's photos with greater attention.

She put the album aside, and trying to avoid my eyes, she asked, 'What kind of men are they?'

'What do you mean?'

'I mean what kind of men are they? I've heard that most men in films are bad.' There was a tone of serious inquiry in her voice.

'You're right. But why does the film industry need good men?'

'What do you mean?'

'There are two types of people in the world—those who understand pain from their own suffering and those who see the suffering of others and guess what pain is. What do you think—which one truly understands the essence of pain?'

She thought for a moment and then answered, 'Those that suffer themselves.'

'Exactly,' I said. 'Those who know from personal experience are good at acting. Only someone who has experienced heartbreak can portray this feeling well. A woman who spreads her prayer mat five times a day, or a woman who thinks she doesn't need love, when she tries to portray love in front of a camera, how can she be anything but a disaster?'

Janaki thought for a moment. 'You mean that before getting into films a woman should know everything?'

'That's not necessary. She can learn after she gets into acting.'

She didn't think seriously about my statement but returned to her original question. 'What kind of men are Sayeed Sahib and Narayan Sahib?'

'Do you want details?'

'What do you mean by details?'

'I mean which of them will be better for you?'

This upset Janaki. 'What are you saying?'

'Just what you want to hear.'

'Never mind,' she said and then smiled. 'I won't ask anything else.'

I smiled too. 'When you ask, I'll recommend Narayan.'

'Why?'

'Because he's a better person than Sayeed.'

I still think so. Sayeed is a poet, a very heartless poet. If he catches a chicken, he won't slaughter it but will wring its neck. Once he's done with that, he'll pluck out its feathers and make soup. Once he's drunk the soup and gnawed on the bones, he will retire to a corner to write a poem about the chicken's death, crying profusely as he writes.

He drinks, but he never gets drunk. This irritates me as it defeats the very purpose of drinking. He gets up slowly in the morning, and his servant brings him a cup of tea. If there's any rum left over from the night before, he pours it into the tea and drinks the mixture in slow gulps, as though he has no sense of taste.

When he gets a sore, he lets it fester until pus forms. There's the risk of developing a serious condition, but he will never look after it and will never go to a doctor. If you tell him to go, he responds, 'Sometimes disease becomes a part of your body. If it's not bothering me, why do I need to treat it?' Then he looks over his wound as if it were an impressive couplet.

He will never be able to act because he lacks sensitivity. I saw him in a film that was very popular because of the heroine's songs, and there was a scene in which he had to hold his beloved's hand and declare his love. I swear he took her hand as if he were grabbing a dog by the paw! I've told him on many occasions, 'Stop dreaming about being an actor. You're a good poet. Go home and write some poems.' But he's obsessed with acting.

I like Narayan a lot. He made up a list of principles for working in a studio, and I like them a lot too.

1) An actor should never marry during his acting career. If he marries, he should stop acting and open up a yoghurt business. If he's famous, he'll do well.
2) If an actress addresses you as 'bhayya' or 'bhai sahib', immediately ask her in a whisper, 'What's your bra size?'
3) If you fall in love with an actress, don't waste time dilly-dallying. Go meet her in private and recite the line, 'I, too, have a tongue in my mouth.' If she doesn't believe you, then stick the whole thing out.
4) If you fall in love with an actress, don't take so much as a single paisa from her. That money's meant for her husband or her brothers.
5) Remember, if you want to have a child with an actress, hold off until after independence!
6) Remember that an actor has an afterlife too. From time to time, instead of preening before a mirror, get a little dirty. I mean, do some charity work.

7) Out of all the people at the studio, give your highest respect to the Pathan guard. Greet him when you get to the studio in the morning. Something good will come of this, if not in this world then in the next, where there are no film studios.
8) Never get addicted to liquor and actresses. It's quite likely that Congress will suddenly outlaw them both.
9) A shopkeeper can be a Hindu shopkeeper or a Muslim one, but an actor can never be a Hindu actor or a Muslim one.
10) Don't lie.

These are 'Narayan's Ten Commandments' that he keeps in a notebook. They reveal his character. People say he doesn't obey them all. Maybe. But he abides by most of them. This is a fact.

Without Janaki's asking, I managed to get across what I thought about Sayeed and Narayan. In the end, I told her directly, 'If you go into acting, you'll need a man's help. I think Narayan will prove to be a good friend.'

She listened to my advice and then left for Bombay. The next day she came back very happy because Narayan had got her hired at his studio for a year on a salary of 500 rupees a month. How did she get this job? We talked about this for quite a while. When she finished, I asked her, 'You met both Sayeed and Narayan. Which one did you like more?'

Janaki smiled mischievously. She looked at me tentatively and said, 'Sayeed Sahib!' Then she became pensive. 'Saadat Sahib, why did you go to such lengths to praise Narayan?'

'Why?'

'He's so sleazy. In the evening, he sat down outside to drink with Sayeed Sahib. I called him 'bhayya', and then he leaned over and asked me my bra size! God knows how furious that made me! What a despicable man!' There was sweat on Janaki's forehead.

I laughed loudly.

'Why're you laughing?' she asked sharply.

'At his foolishness.' Then I stopped laughing.

After complaining for a while about Narayan, Janaki began going over her worries about Aziz. She hadn't received a letter from him for several days, and all sorts of fears tormented her. She hoped he hadn't got a cough again. He rode his bicycle so recklessly that she hoped he hadn't had an accident. She worried about whether he would come to Pune, as he had promised her when she left Peshawar, 'I'll show up when you're least expecting me.' After she had expressed all of her misgivings, she calmed down. Then she began to praise him, 'He cares a lot about his kids. Every morning he makes sure they exercise, then he bathes them and takes them to school. His wife is really lazy, and so he has to deal with the relatives. Once I got typhoid and for twenty days straight he took care of me just like a nurse would.' And so on and so on.

Then she thanked me in the nicest possible words and set off for Bombay, where the door to a new and glittering world had opened for her.

In Pune I finished my film script in about two months. I collected my pay and left for Bombay where I needed to sign another contract.

I arrived in Andheri at the bungalow that Sayeed and

Narayan were sharing, at about five in the morning. When I entered the verandah, I found the front door locked. I thought, 'They must be sleeping. I don't want to disturb them.' There was another door in the back usually left unlocked for the servant, and so I went around and entered there. Inside there were two beds. Sayeed was sharing one with a woman, her face hidden beneath their quilt.

I was very sleepy. Without taking off my clothes, I lay down on the second bed. There was a blanket at its foot that I spread over my legs, and I was just about to fall asleep when an arm adorned with bangles emerged from behind Sayeed and reached towards the chair next to the bed.

A white cotton shalwar was draped over the chair.

I shot up. Janaki was sleeping with Sayeed! I took the shalwar from the chair and threw it towards her.

I went to Narayan's room and woke him. When he told me his shooting had ended at two in the morning, I was sorry for waking the poor soul. Nevertheless he wanted to chat, and so we stayed up gossiping until nine in the morning, returning often to the subject of Janaki.

When I brought up the time he had asked Janaki about her bra size, Narayan laughed convulsively. Laughing away, he said, 'The best part about that was when I asked her, she blurted out, "Thirty-four!" Then she realized how rude my question was and cussed me out. She's just a child. Now whenever we run into each other, she covers her breasts with her dupatta. But, Manto, she's a very faithful woman!'

'How do you know?'

Narayan smiled. 'A woman that blurts out her bra size to strangers doesn't have it in her to cheat.'

It was strange reasoning, but in a very serious manner Narayan convinced me that Janaki was sincere. He said, 'Manto, you can't imagine how well she's looking after Sayeed. Taking care of such an absolutely careless person isn't easy, but Janaki does it very well. She's a dutiful and affectionate nurse. It takes half an hour to wake that bastard, but she actually has the patience to do it. She makes sure he brushes his teeth. She dresses him. She feeds him breakfast. And at night after he's had his rum, she closes all the doors and lies down with him. At the studio she talks only about Sayeed Sahib, "Sayeed Sahib's a great man. Sayeed Sahib sings really well. Sayeed Sahib's weight is up. Sayeed Sahib's pullover is ready. I ordered sandals from Peshawar for Sayeed Sahib. Today Sayeed Sahib has a light headache. I'm going to take him some Aspro. Today Sayeed Sahib wrote a couplet for me." And then when I run into her, she remembers the bra thing and scowls.'

I stayed at Sayeed and Narayan's for about ten days. During that time Sayeed didn't say anything to me about Janaki, maybe because it had already become old news. But Janaki and I talked a lot. She was happy with Sayeed, and yet she complained about his carelessness, 'Saadat Sahib, he never thinks about his health. He's completely absent-minded. I worry constantly about him because he never thinks about anything. You'll laugh, but every day I have to ask him if he's gone to the bathroom.'

Everything that Narayan said proved true. Janaki was always busy looking after Sayeed, and her selfless service impressed me very much. But I kept thinking about Aziz. Janaki used to worry a lot about him, and yet had she forgotten him after she started living with Sayeed? I would have asked her if I had stayed in Andheri any longer. But I got into an argument with the owner of the film company where I was about to sign a contract and left for Pune in order to escape the tension. It must have been only two days later when a telegram arrived from Aziz saying that he was coming. Then, after five or six hours, he was sitting next to me, and early the next morning Janaki was knocking on my door.

When Aziz and Janaki saw each other, they didn't show the usual excitement of reunited lovers. My relationship with Aziz had always been reserved, and so perhaps they felt embarrassed to show their love in front of me. Aziz wanted to stay in a hotel, but as my friend was doing an outdoor shoot in Kolhapur, I insisted they stay with me. There were three rooms. Janaki could sleep in one and Aziz in another. Although I should have let them share a room, I wasn't close enough to Aziz to ask him if that's what he wanted. Besides he had never made it clear what their relationship was.

That night they went to the movies, but I didn't go because I wanted to start a story for a film. I had given Aziz a key so that I wouldn't have to worry about opening the door. I stayed up until two o'clock that night. Regardless of how late I work, I always get up between three thirty and four to get a glass of water, and I got up that night too. But as soon as I got up, I realized my water pitcher was in the room I had given to Aziz.

If I hadn't been dying of thirst, I wouldn't have bothered him, but because I had drunk too much whisky my throat was completely dry. I had to knock on the door. After several moments Janaki opened the door while rubbing her eyes. 'Sayeed Sahib!' she said without looking up. Then when she saw it was me, she sighed, 'Oh!' Aziz was sleeping on the bed. I couldn't help but smile. Janaki smiled too, and then made a funny face, twisting her lips to the side. I took the pitcher and left.

When I woke in the morning, there was smoke in my room. I went into the kitchen where Janaki was burning paper to heat water for Aziz's bath. Tears were flowing from her eyes. When she saw me, she smiled and blew into the brazier. 'Aziz Sahib catches a cold if he bathes in cold water,' she explained. 'He was sick for a month in Peshawar without me to look after him. How did he expect to get better when he refused to take his medicine? Just look how skinny he's become.'

Aziz had a bath and left on some business, and then Janaki asked me to write a telegram to Sayeed. 'I should have sent him a telegram as soon as I arrived yesterday,' she said. 'What have I done? He must be so worried!' She dictated the telegram. She mentioned how she had arrived safely, but she was more interested in asking about his health and urged him to take his shots according to the doctor's orders.

Four days passed. Janaki sent Sayeed five telegrams, but he didn't reply even once. She was thinking about going to Bombay when one evening Aziz's health suddenly got worse. She dictated another telegram for Sayeed and then was busy taking care of Aziz all night. It was an ordinary fever, but Janaki was overcome with anxiety, which seemed strange until I realized that a part of it was due to her concern over Sayeed's silence. Over those four days, she said to me time and again, 'Saadat Sahib! I'm sure Sayeed Sahib is sick, otherwise he definitely would have written back.'

On the fifth evening we were all sitting around and Janaki was laughing about something when a telegram arrived from Sayeed. It read, 'I'm very sick. Come immediately.' As soon as Janaki read this, she fell silent. Aziz didn't like this at all, and when he addressed her, his tone was sharp. I left the room.

When I came back in the evening, Aziz and Janaki were sitting apart from one another as though they had been fighting. Janaki's cheeks were stained with tears. After we chatted for a while, Janaki picked up her purse and said to Aziz, 'I'm going, but I'll be back very soon.' Then she addressed me, 'Saadat Sahib, please look after him. He still has a slight fever.'

I went with her to the station. I bought a ticket on the black market, saw her to her seat and left. Then I returned to the apartment, and Aziz and I stayed up late talking but we never mentioned Janaki.

The third day, at about five thirty in the morning, I heard the door open and then Janaki impatiently asking Aziz about his health and whether he had taken his medicine in her absence. I couldn't hear how he replied, but half an hour later, with my eyes still heavy with sleep, I heard him speaking to her, and although I couldn't make out his exact words, he was clearly angry.

At ten in the morning Aziz had a cold bath, ignoring the water Janaki had heated for him. When I mentioned to her that he'd left the water untouched in the bathroom, her eyes welled with tears.

Aziz left after bathing, and Janaki flopped down on the bed. In the afternoon I went to check on her and discovered she had a high fever. When I went out to get a doctor,

I found Aziz putting his things into a horse-drawn carriage. 'Where are you going?' I asked. He shook my hand and said, 'Bombay. God willing, we'll meet again.' Then he sat down in the carriage and left. I didn't even have a chance to tell him Janaki had a severe fever.

The doctor examined Janaki and told me she had bronchitis. If she wasn't careful, it might turn into pneumonia. The doctor wrote a prescription and left, and then Janaki asked about Aziz. At first I thought I shouldn't tell her, but then I realized nothing would be gained from concealing the truth, and so I told her he had left. She was devastated. She buried her face in her pillow and cried.

The next day around eleven when Janaki's fever dropped one degree and her health seemed a little better, a telegram arrived from Sayeed. He wrote in a harsh tone, 'Remember, you didn't keep your promise.' Then in spite of her fever and my attempts to stop her, she left for Bombay on the Pune Express.

After five or six days a telegram arrived from Narayan, 'Urgent. Come to Bombay ASAP.' I thought he meant he had talked to some producer about my contract, but when I arrived in Bombay, I learned that Janaki's health was very poor. Her bronchitis had in fact turned into pneumonia. Moreover, after getting to Bombay, she had fallen and scraped both her thighs very badly while trying to board a local train to Andheri.

Narayan told me that Janaki had suffered through this with great courage. But after she had reached Andheri, Sayeed had pointed at her packed bags and had said, 'Please leave.' Narayan said, 'When she heard Sayeed's icy words, she turned completely to stone. The thought must have crossed her mind, "Why didn't I die underneath the train?" Saadat, say what you will, but no man should treat women like Sayeed does! The poor soul had a fever and then had fallen trying to board a train and only because she was rushing to see this bastard. But Sayeed didn't stop to think about this. He just repeated, "Please leave." Manto, he said this so coldly, it was as if he was reading from a newspaper.'

This made me very sad, and I got up and left. When I came back in the evening, Janaki wasn't there but Sayeed was, sitting on his bed, a glass of rum in front of him, and he was busy writing a poem. I didn't say anything but went straight to my room.

The next day at the studio, Narayan told me Janaki was at the house of one of the studio's extra girls and that her health was precarious. He said, 'I talked to the owner of the studio and then sent Janaki to the hospital. She's been there since yesterday. Tell me, what should I do? I can't go to see her since she hates me. You go and check on her.'

I got to the hospital, and she immediately asked about Aziz and Sayeed. After all they had done to her, it was impressive that she asked about them with affection.

Her health was very poor. The doctor told me that both of her lungs were inflamed and her life was in danger, and yet I was surprised by how Janaki bore all her difficulties with such manly courage.

When I returned from the hospital and looked for Narayan in the studio, I learned he had been missing since the morning. When he returned to the house in the evening, he showed me three small glass vials.

'Do you know what these are?' he asked.

'No. It looks like medicine.'

Narayan smiled. 'Exactly. Penicillin.'

I was very surprised because penicillin was in short supply. Despite the quantities produced in America and England, very little got to India and that was reserved for the military hospitals. I asked Narayan, 'Penicillin's so scarce. How did you get it?'

He smiled and said, 'When I was a boy, I was very good at stealing money from our safe at home. Today I went to the Military Hospital and stole these three vials. Come on, let's hurry. We've got to move Janaki from the hospital to a hotel.'

I took a taxi to the hospital and then took Janaki to a hotel where Narayan had already booked two rooms. Over and over again Janaki weakly asked me why I had brought her there, and each time I told her, 'You'll soon find out.'

And when she found out—meaning, when Narayan came into the room holding a syringe—she scowled and turned away. She said to me, 'Saadat Sahib, tell him to go away!'

Narayan smiled. 'My dear, spit out all your anger. This is going to save your life.'

Janaki got mad. In spite of her weak condition, she raised herself from the bed, 'Saadat Sahib, either kick this bastard out, or I'm going.'

Narayan shoved her back down and said, smiling, 'Nothing's going to stop this bastard from giving you this injection. If you muck this up, it's your loss!'

He grabbed Janaki's arm. He gave the syringe to me and then wet a cotton ball with alcohol. He cleaned her upper arm and then gave me the cotton ball and stuck the needle in her arm. She screamed out, but the penicillin had already entered her arm.

Narayan released his grip, and Janaki began to cry. But Narayan didn't care. He swabbed the injection site with the cotton ball and left for the next room.

This was at nine o'clock at night. The next injection had to be given three hours later, as Narayan told me that the penicillin would have no effect if more than three hours elapsed between injections. So he stayed up. At about eleven o'clock, he lit the stove, sterilized the syringe and filled it with medicine.

Janaki's breathing was raspy and her eyes were shut. Narayan cleaned her other arm and again stuck the needle in her arm. Janaki emitted a feeble cry. Narayan took out the needle, cleaned Janaki's arm, and said to me, 'The third's at three o'clock.'

I don't know when he gave the third and fourth injections, but when I awoke I heard the sound of the stove and Narayan's asking one of the hotel boys for ice since he had to keep the penicillin cold.

At nine o'clock, when we went into the room to give Janaki her injection, she was lying with her eyes open. She glared with hatred at Narayan but said nothing. Narayan smiled. 'How are you feeling, my dear?' Janaki didn't respond.

Narayan went over and stood next to her. 'These injections aren't injections of love. They're to cure your pneumonia. I swiped this penicillin from the Military Hospital. Okay, turn on your side a little, and slide down your shalwar so I can get at your hips. Have you ever had an injection here?'

Before Janaki could protest, Narayan slid down Janaki's shalwar and said to me, 'Get the alcohol swab ready.'

Janaki began to thrash her legs.

'Janaki! Stop thrashing!' Narayan said. 'Nothing's going to stop me from giving you this shot!'

Narayan gave her the fifth injection. There were fifteen left, and Narayan gave them on a schedule of one every three hours. It was forty-five hours' work.

Even though Janaki's health hadn't noticeably improved after the first five injections, Narayan still had faith in the penicillin's miraculous powers. He fully believed that she would make it, and we talked on and on about this new drug. At about eleven o'clock a servant brought a telegram for me. A film company in Pune wanted me to come immediately, and I had to go.

After ten or fifteen days, I returned to Bombay in connection with work. After finishing my work, I went to Andheri where Sayeed told me that Narayan was still at the hotel, but because the hotel was in a distant suburb, I spent the night at Sayeed's.

I reached the hotel at eight the next morning and found the door to Narayan's room ajar. I entered but the room was empty, and when I opened the door to the next room, guess what I saw?

When Janaki saw me, she hid underneath a quilt. Narayan, who was lying next to her, saw me leaving.

'Hey, Manto, come in!' he called out. 'I always forget to shut the door. Come over here, buddy! Sit over there. But first hand over Janaki's shalwar, will you?'

PEERUN

THIS happened back when I was dirt poor. I was paying nine rupees a month for a room that didn't have water or electricity. The building was horrific. Gnats fell from the ceiling in thousands, and rats were everywhere, bigger than any I've ever seen, so big the cats were scared of them.

There was only one bathroom in the chawl and its door was broken. The women of the building—Jewish, Marathi, Gujarati, and Christian—would gather there in the early morning to fill their buckets with water. The women would get together first thing in the morning and go to the bathroom where they would form a wall in front of the door and then one by one, they would bathe.

One day I got up late. I went to the bathroom and started bathing when the door suddenly opened. It was the woman who lived in the room next to mine, and she had a water pitcher under her arm. I don't know why, but she stood there staring at me for a moment. Then she abruptly turned around, and the pitcher slipped to the ground and began to roll down the hall. She ran away as though a lion was chasing her. I laughed a lot and then rose, closed the door, and continued bathing.

But soon the door opened again. It was Brij Mohan. I had already finished bathing and was putting on my clothes.

He said, 'Hey, Manto. Today's Sunday.'

Then I remembered that Brij Mohan had to go to Bandra to meet his friend Peerun, whom he met every Sunday. She was a Parsi girl that Brij Mohan had been in love with for about three years.

Brij Mohan asked me for eight annas every Sunday for the train ride. Once he got to Peerun's house, the two of them would talk for half an hour, Brij Mohan would give her the answers for the *Illustrated Weekly*'s crossword, and then he would come back. It was pointless. All day he would labour to solve the crossword for Peerun, and though he had won some small prizes, they all went to her, each and every one.

Brij Mohan had countless photos of Peerun—Peerun in a shalwar kameez, in tight-fitting pyjamas, in a sari, in a sundress, in an outfit she wore to weddings, in an evening gown. He must have had over a hundred photos. Peerun wasn't pretty at all, and in my opinion she was just the opposite, and yet I never told Brij Mohan what I thought. I never asked about her—who she was, what she did, how he met her, how he fell in love, or whether he planned to marry her—and Brij Mohan never talked to me about her. But every Sunday after breakfast, he would ask me for eight annas, go to meet Peerun in Bandra, and then come back in the afternoon.

I went back to my room, and after I gave him the money he left. When he returned that afternoon, for once he had something to say, 'It's over.'

'What's over?'

'I broke up with Peerun today,' he said, as though relieved. 'I told her, "Since I met you, I haven't worked at all. You're bad luck." And she said, "Then stop seeing me, and we'll see if you get a job or not. I might be bad luck, but you're a real slacker—no one's lazier than you." So now it's over, and, God willing, I bet I'll get a job tomorrow. Tomorrow morning if you give me four annas, I'll go meet Seth Nanu Bhai and I'm sure he'll give me a job as his assistant.'

Seth Nanu Bhai was a film director, and he had already turned Brij Mohan away countless times since he thought Brij Mohan was lazy. But the next day when Brij Mohan returned, he shared with me the good news that Seth Nanu Bhai had very happily given him a job at 250 rupees a month. The contract was for a year, and it was all signed and sealed. He reached into his pocket and took out a hundred-rupee note and told me, 'This is an advance. I really want to take the contract and money to Bandra and say to Peerun, "Hey, look here! I got a job." But I'm scared that Nanu Bhai will fire me immediately. That's happened to me many times. I get a job, go see Peerun, and everything's wrecked. I get fired on one pretext or another. God knows why this girl is such bad luck. I've made up my mind not to see her for at least a year. I hardly have any clothes left. Over the next year I can get some made, and then I'll go see her.'

Six months passed. It seemed as though Brij Mohan's work was going well. He had got some new clothes made and had bought a dozen handkerchiefs, and now he had everything that a bachelor needed. One day after he had left for the studio, a letter came for him. I forgot to give it to him that night, and it was only the next morning over breakfast when I remembered it. As soon as he got his hands on it, he cried out, 'Ah, hell!'

'What's wrong?'

'It's Peerun—and just when everything was going well,' he said, opening the envelope with his spoon. 'It's her, all right. I'll never forget her handwriting.'

'What does she want?'

'Shit—she says that she wants to see me this Sunday, that she has something to tell me,' he said and then put the envelope in his pocket. 'Look here, Manto. Just wait and see if tomorrow I don't get fired.'

'Come off it—what're you talking about?'

'No, Manto, just you watch,' he said, sure of himself. 'Tomorrow's Sunday. Seth Nanu Bhai will come up with some excuse and fire me before you know it.'

'If you're so sure, then don't go.'

'Impossible. If she wants me, I have to go.'

'Why?'

'Well, anyway, I'm kind of fed up with working. It's been more than six months now.' Then he smiled and left.

The next morning after breakfast he left for Bandra. When he returned, he didn't say anything, and so I asked him, 'Did you meet your unlucky star?'

'Yeah, I told her I'm sure to get fired soon.' Then he got up from the cot. 'Anyway, let's go eat.'

We ate at the Haji Hotel and didn't talk at all about Peerun during the meal. Then that night before going to bed, he said, 'We'll just see what tomorrow brings.'

I thought that nothing was bound to happen, but the next day Brij Mohan came back early. He laughed loudly when we met. 'I'm jobless!'

'Stop it,' I said, thinking he was joking.

'What had to be stopped has been stopped! What's left for me to stop? Nanu Bhai's up to his neck in it. He sold the studio, and all because of me!' Then he laughed again.

'This is quite a turn of events.'

'Well, the obvious needs no explanation!' Brij Mohan lit a cigarette, picked up a camera, and went out for a walk.

Things turned bad for Brij Mohan. After he spent all the money he had saved, he began asking me again for eight annas for Sunday trips to Bandra. I still didn't know what they talked about for those thirty or forty minutes. He was a great conversationalist, and yet what could he find to talk about with that girl—that girl who he was convinced brought him only bad luck? One day I asked him, 'Brij, does Peerun love you?'

'No, she loves someone else.'

'Why does she want to see you?'

'Because I'm clever. I can take her ugly face and think of a way to make it beautiful. I solve the crosswords for her and sometimes win her prizes. Manto, you don't know girls like that, but I do. Whatever her lover lacks, I make up for it. That way she gets a complete man.' He smiled. 'It's high fraud!'

'So why do you see her?' I asked, confused.

Brij Mohan laughed and then wrinkled his brow. 'I like it.'

'What about it?'

'The way she's bad luck. I've been testing it—how she's bad luck—and now I know it's definitely true. Ever since I've known her, I've been fired from each and every job. Now I just want to find a way to beat this.'

'What do you mean?'

'I want to quit before I'm fired,' Brij Mohan said very seriously. 'I mean, I want to fire my boss. I'll say, "Sir, I know you're about to fire me, and so I'm not going to let you go to the trouble. I'll leave on my own. Anyway, it wasn't really you firing me but my friend Peerun, whose nose is so big it punctures cameras like an arrow!" Brij Mohan smiled. 'This is my little wish. We'll see if it comes true or not.'

'That's an unusual desire.'

'Everything about me is strange,' he said. 'Last Sunday I photographed Peerun's lover. Just watch him submit it to some competition and win!' He smiled again.

One Sunday, Brij returned from Bandra and said, 'Manto, it's over.'

'You mean you and Peerun?'

'Yeah. My clothes are running out, and so I thought I'd better stop going. God willing, I'll get a job in a couple days. I think I'll go see Seth Nayaz Ali. He's supposed to be making a film. I'll go tomorrow, but could you find out where his office is?'

I asked a friend what Ali's new telephone number was and relayed this information to Brij Mohan. The next day he went there, and when he returned in the evening, he was smiling contentedly. 'Hey, Manto,' he said, then reached into his pocket to pull out a piece of typed paper. 'A contract for one film—200 rupees a month. It's not much, but Seth Nayaz Ali said he'll give me a raise. Not bad, eh?'

'When will you see Peerun?'

Brij Mohan smiled. 'When? I was wondering that too—

when should I see her? But, Manto, remember how I told you that I have one little wish that I want to see through? I want to see that through. I think I shouldn't act too rashly but earn a little money first. I got fifty rupees as an advance. Here, you take twenty-five.'

I took the money and paid off an outstanding bill at a restaurant. Everything started going very well. I was making a hundred rupees a month, Brij Mohan was getting 200, and we were very comfortable. Then after five months, suddenly a letter arrived from Peerun.

'Look, Manto, the Angel of Death!'

In fact as soon as I saw the letter, I got scared. Brij Mohan was smiling while he opened the envelope, and he took out the letter and read it. It was very short.

'What?'

'She says she wants to see me on Sunday. There's some very important business.' Then Brij Mohan put the letter back in its envelope and shoved it into his pocket.

'You're going?'

'I've no choice.' Then he began to sing the film song, 'Don't forget, traveller, one day you'll have to go.'

But I told him, 'Don't go and see her. We've been living real well. You won't remember, but I recall how I used to lend you eight annas every Sunday.'

Brij Mohan smiled. 'I remember everything, so it's too bad that those days are coming back again.'

On Sunday Brij left to see Peerun in Bandra. When he came back, he said, 'I told her that this will be the twelfth time that I've been fired because of her. Have mercy upon me!'

'What did she say to that?'

'Her words were, "You're a silly idiot."'

'Are you?'

'One hundred per cent!' Then he laughed. 'I'm going to tender my resignation tomorrow as soon as I get to the office. I already wrote it at Peerun's.'

He showed me the paperwork. The next day he rushed through breakfast and left quickly for work, and when he came back that evening, he had a long face. He said nothing to me, and so I was forced to ask, 'What, Brij? What happened?'

He shook his head without emotion. 'Nothing, it's all over.'

'What?'

'I gave my resignation notice to Seth Nayaz Ali, but then he smiled and gave me an official letter stating that my salary had been increased from 200 to 300 rupees, effective from last month!'

Brij Mohan lost interest in Peerun, and one day he told me, 'As soon as her bad luck wore out, I got bored of her. My game evaporated! Now who's going to screw things up for me?'

RUDE

WHEN I left Delhi to return to Bombay, I was upset because it meant parting with good friends and a job my wife approved of—stable, easy work that netted us 250 rupees on the first of each month. Nevertheless I was suddenly overcome by a desire to leave, and not even my wife's crying and carrying on could dissuade me.

I know hundreds of people in Bombay and seeing my friends again after many years brought me real joy, and yet my greatest joy turned out to be meeting Izzat Jahan.

You must know Izzat Jahan—who hasn't heard her name? If you are a Communist and live in Bombay, you must already have met her many times and know how she has spent years working for the Communist cause, and you probably also know that she just married some unknown man.

This unknown man is a good friend of mine, as I know Nasir from our student days at Aligarh Muslim University when I used to call him Nasu. Illness and a lack of funds forced me to withdraw from school, but Nasir somehow managed to get a BA and land a factory job in Delhi. Years later while I was living in Bombay, Nasir came down for another factory job. During those days we got together often, but then I was forced to leave Bombay for various reasons, and that was when I got that job in Delhi, which turned out to be a regular disaster.

Anyway, I said goodbye to Delhi after two years and moved back to Bombay, the home of many dear friends and of Izzat Jahan. I'm a Communist and have written hundreds of essays on Communism. I have also read Izzat Jahan's essays in various newspapers, and they deeply impressed me. For God's sake, please don't think I was enamoured! I just wanted to meet her and talk to her—I had read about her activities, and as adolescent boys just fallen in love want to talk about their love affairs, I wanted to talk about my boundless love for Communism.

I wanted to talk about the development of Communist philosophy from Hegel to Karl Marx and to discuss the viewpoints of Lenin, Trotsky, and Stalin. I wanted to tell her my opinion of India's Communist Movement and to hear hers too. I wanted to tell her stories of young men carrying Karl Marx's books tucked beneath their arms with only one idea in mind—to impress others. I wanted to tell her about a friend who possessed every English-language book ever published about Communism but still didn't know even its rudiments, a guy who dropped Karl Marx's name just as frequently as people with a celebrity in the family find a way of mentioning them. I wanted to tell Izzat Jahan how my friend, despite his shenanigans, was so sincere that he couldn't stand to hear one word said against the Communist cause.

Then I would tell her about the young men and women who become Communist as a way to meet the opposite sex. I would tell her how half the boys who join the Movement are, simply put, horny, and how they stare at the girl initiates with eyes filled with centuries of unrequited desire. I would tell her how most of the girls are rebellious daughters of fat-cat industrialists who read some introductory books then become active members just in order to stave off boredom. And I would tell her how some of these girls become mired in debauchery when they lose all respect for social and moral norms and become the sex toys of our national 'leaders'.

To make a long story short, I thought it would be a great pleasure to discuss in detail India's Communist Movement and its future implications. From reading her articles, I knew her incisive opinions and bold style, and I was sure we would agree on a lot.

When I got to Bombay I had to stay at a friend's apartment for a while while I looked for a place and furnished it. My wife was still in Delhi, and I told her I would call as soon as things were arranged.

My friends are all bachelor film directors and have interesting opinions about women. They don't want to get mixed up in a relationship with a girl on the set, and so when they feel the need, they contact any number of pimps who can supply them with what they want. My friends keep these girls for the night and send them on their way in the morning. They don't get married because they think they could never make their wives happy. They say, 'I'm a film director, you know. If the shooting's during the day, I have to stay on the set all day. If the shooting's at night, I have to stay out all night. If I work during the day, then I need to relax at night, and if I work at night, then I need to relax during the day. My wife would ask me to do things for her, but how could I when I'm all tired out? Every day a new girl is good. If I feel sleepy, I can tell her, "Get some sleep." If I get tired of her, I can call a taxi, pay the fare, and send her on her way. As soon as a woman becomes your wife, she becomes a big burden. I'm very dutiful, so I don't want that pressure. I don't want to get married.'

One day I accompanied my friend in his taxi while he was looking for a girl. A pimp friend of his brought out not one but two Dravidian girls. I was confused but my friend immediately said, 'Don't worry. What's the difference between one or two?'

The taxi turned back toward the apartment. After getting back, my film director friend, the two girls wearing kashta saris and I climbed the stairs to the third floor. I opened his apartment's door and what did I see inside but Nasir sitting in front of my Urdu typewriter, inspecting it. Sitting right next to him was a woman wearing glasses, and when she turned to look in our direction, I recognized her. It was Izzat Jahan.

My film director friend was nervous, but since the two girls had already entered the room it was useless to pretend.

I introduced my friend to Nasir, Nasir introduced us to his wife, and then I sat down next to them. I wanted to say something more about Izzat Jahan to my friend and when I looked at him, I found him lighting a cigarette. 'This is one of India's greatest Communist women,' I said. 'You must have read her essays.'

But my friend had no interest in Communism, and afterwards I learned he didn't even know what the word meant. He gestured to the young women that they should go into the other room and then said, 'Please excuse me. I'll be back in a minute.'

Izzat Jahan was staring at my friend's two companions and inspecting their clothes, their comportment, in short everything about them. The girls went into the other room, and my friend brazenly excused himself and closed the door behind him.

Izzat Jahan turned to me and said, 'I'm very happy to meet you. Every day Nasir used to say, "Let's go meet Manto, let's go meet Manto." But I was very busy then. And . . . ' Then something broke her train of thought and she started a new line of conversation. 'You're going to be living here, right? This house isn't bad at all!' She looked around the room and nodded.

'Yes, it's nice. There's a breeze.'

'It's breezy and clean.'

'If you open the middle door, you get a good breeze.'

'Oh, yes, there was a little earlier.'

We had been chatting for about half an hour about this and that, but I sensed that Izzat Jahan was distracted. She was probably trying to figure out why my friend hadn't returned as he had promised. Then suddenly she requested a glass of water.

The apartment had two hallways, one in the front and one in the back. I didn't think it was a good idea to disturb my friend, so I brought the water back by the long way. When I got back to the room, I saw that Nasir and Izzat Jahan were whispering to each other.

Izzat Jahan took the glass. 'You went to a lot of trouble.'

'No, it was no trouble at all.'

She drank the water, contracted her eyebrows behind

her thick glasses, and in order to make conversation, she noted how the apartment had two hallways.

We chatted again for a while, and when the conversation turned to Communism, both Izzat Jahan and I got excited. I set out to make my views on Communism known.

'Communism says that all human institutions—religion, history, politics and so on—are rooted in economic conditions. In the present system, with the division between the rich and the poor, the instruments of production are all in the hands of the elite who then use these instruments for their benefit alone. When this order is overturned, according to you, the Communist Age will begin and the tools of production, which determine our economic conditions, will be in the hands of the common people.'

'Yes,' Izzat Jahan confirmed.

'And then there will be a special executive body to represent the people's power.'

'Yes.'

'But it's worth considering how even under Communism, power will be restricted to a select group. This group, in accordance with the Communist doctrine, will act for the good of all the people and will have nothing to do with personal interests and profiteering. But who can say beyond the shadow of a doubt that this group, which is supposed to be for the people, won't turn into something capitalistic and seek to oppress others? Won't they abuse their power? After ruling for a while, won't these people begin to act out of personal motives?'

Izzat Jahan smiled. 'You sound like you're Bakunin's brother.'

'I admit that Bakunin always fought with Marx and

couldn't come to accept certain points, and that despite his sincerity he couldn't develop a logical and organized philosophy of his own. But he said this, and it wasn't a lie, that even democracy is a euphemism for a government in which a larger group oppresses a smaller one. I'm all for any political system that frees society from all rules and oppression.'

Izzat smiled again. 'So you want anarchism, which is impractical? Your Bakunin and Kropotkin can't make it work.'

I interrupted her, 'Communism was impractical, and people thought it was a crazy dream. But Marx presented it in the form of a practical social system. It's possible that anarchism, too, will get its Marx.'

Izzat Jahan looked at the closed door, and then as if she hadn't heard what I had just said, she asked, 'Why hasn't your friend returned?'

I decided to tell her the truth. 'Earlier he was just being polite. He didn't plan on coming back.'

'Why?' Izzat Jahan asked innocently.

I looked at Nasir and smiled. He was beginning to find our conversation interesting.

'He has two girls with him. Why would he leave them for our boring company?'

'Are they actresses?'

'No.'

'Friends?'

'He just met them today.'

Little by little I told her everything, including my friend's views on sex. She listened carefully and then pronounced her verdict, 'This is the worst kind of anarchism. If everyone thought like your friend, then the world would be depressing. Men and women would see each other only as sexual partners, right? I don't care who your friend is, what does he think women are? Sliced bread, cake, or biscuits? A warm cup of coffee or tea, so he can drink as much as he likes and toss the rest? Damn those women who put up with this disgraceful behaviour! I can't understand why some people think sex is so important, or why your friend can't live without women. Why does he need to sleep with a woman every night?'

I said what I thought, 'Men have a special need for women. Some feel it more, and some feel it less. My friend is the type that wants to sleep with a woman every night. If food, drink, and sleep are important to him, then a woman is just as important. Maybe he's wrong to think like this, but at least he doesn't pretend.'

Izzat Jahan's tone became even more bitter. 'Just because he doesn't hide it, doesn't make it right. If prostitutes consent to selling their bodies, it doesn't mean it's natural. It's because our way of doing things is wrong and it's unnatural that there are prostitutes. Your friend's nervous system isn't sound. That's why he can't tell the difference between women and food. You can't live without food, but surely you can live without sex!'

'Sure, you can live,' I said. 'But when did it become a matter of life and death? You know, not every man can get a woman, but all those who can, do.'

Nasir wasn't at all interested in our conversation. 'Okay, enough of this. It's late, and we have nineteen miles to go. Let's go, Izzat, shall we?'

Izzat didn't listen to Nasir, but said to me, 'Whatever

you say, but, really, your friend is very rude. I can't believe the three of us were sitting here chatting and in the next room he—lahaul wala quwat!'

Nasir was sleepy. 'All right, for God's sake, stop talking about it! Let's go!'

Izzat got mad. 'Look . . . look . . . now you're finally starting to act like a real husband.'

I couldn't help but laugh, and Nasir laughed too. When Izzat Jahan saw us laughing, a smile stole across her lips.

'How else can I put it?' she asked. 'This is exactly what husbands are like—I mean he's trying to bully me.'

Nasir and Izzat stayed for a bit and then left. Our first meeting was very interesting. Although I wasn't able to talk to her in any detail about the Communist Movement, she still impressed me, and I imagined that future meetings would provide a lot of food for thought.

Then I found an apartment, and my wife joined me. One day Izzat came by, and the two of them took to each other immediately. From then on Izzat Jahan would often come by our apartment in the evening on her way home. I wanted to discuss with her every aspect of Communism from Hegel, Marx and Engels to Bakunin, Kropotkin and Trotsky, but she and my wife would go off to the other room and lie down on the bed and talk about who knows what. If I happened to mention the effects of Stalin's current war policy on Communist theory, she would ask my wife the price of white wool. If I said anything about the hypocrisy of M.N. Roy, she would praise some song from the movie *Family*. And if I got her to sit down next to me and was able to begin a conversation, she would get up after several minutes to go into the kitchen to peel onions for my wife.

Izzat Jahan worked all day at the Party office. She lived twenty or twenty-five miles from there, and her commute was an hour by train each way, so she would return home tired every evening. Nasir worked in a factory, and every month he had to work fifteen nights as an overseer. But Izzat was happy. She repeated to my wife, 'The meaning of marriage is not just a bed, and the meaning of a husband is not just someone to sleep with at night. People were not made just for this.'

My wife liked these words very much.

Izzat Jahan put a lot of herself into her work, and so I didn't mind that she was too tired to talk to me. Nor did I mind that she spent more time with my wife, as it was clear she enjoyed her company more than mine. Nonetheless I was curious to see if Izzat would change my wife's thinking—which was an average middle-class capitalist perspective—into her own.

One day I came back from work early, probably around two. I knocked on the door, but instead of my wife opening it, it was Nasir. Straightaway I went to put my bag on my desk as I usually did. Nasir lay down on my bed, pulling a blanket over him. Izzat Jahan was lying on the sofa on the other side of the room.

'I think I'm coming down with a fever,' Nasir said.

I looked in Izzat Jahan's direction and asked, 'And you?'

'No, I'm just lying down.'

'Where's Ruqaiya?' I asked.

'She's sleeping in the other room,' Izzat said.

'What's this? Everyone's sleeping?' Then I called out for my wife, 'Ruqaiya! Ruqaiya!'

'Yes!' her sleepy voice answered.

'Come here. How long are you going to sleep?'

Ruqaiya came into the room, rubbing her eyes, and sat down next to Izzat. Nasir was still lying with the blanket pulled over him. I sat in a chair next to my wife, and we talked for a while about deep sleep because Ruqaiya always slept like a baby. Then Izzat and my wife began talking about needlework. In the meantime tea was made. Nasir drank a cup in bed, and I gave him two aspirins for his fever.

Izzat Jahan and Nasir stayed for a little less than two hours and then left.

When I lay down on my bed that night, I folded the top pillow in half as I always do, and what did I see but the bottom pillow did not have a pillowcase. Ruqaiya was standing next to me changing her clothes. 'Why isn't there a pillowcase on this pillow?' I asked.

Ruqaiya stared at the pillow, and in a tone of surprise said, 'Well, where *did* that pillowcase go? Oh, yes—it was your friend.'

Smiling, I asked, 'Nasir took it?'

'How should I know?' Ruqaiya said defensively. Then she relented. 'Oh, it's so embarrassing! I couldn't bring myself to tell you. I was sleeping in the other room and they were—your friend and his wife—damn them! They turned out to be very rude.'

The next day we found the pillowcase underneath the bed, and rats and cockroaches had soiled it. In addition to that, we also found the aspirin tablets I'd given to Nasir to relieve his fever.

HAMID'S BABY

WHEN Babu Har Gopal came from Lahore, Hamid found himself without anywhere to turn. As soon as Babu Har Gopal got there, he ordered Hamid, 'Hey, get a taxi, quick.'

'Why don't you take it easy for a while?' Hamid suggested. 'You must be tired after your long trip.'

But Babu Har Gopal was stubborn. 'No, no, I'm not tired at all. I came here to have fun, not lie around. It was hard for me to get these ten days off. You're all mine—you have to do whatever I say. This time I'm going to do everything I want. Now get me some soda water.'

'Look, Babu Har Gopal, don't start drinking so early in the morning.'

But his guest didn't listen. He opened a cupboard, took out a bottle of Johnny Walker and unscrewed the cap. 'If you're not going to get any soda, then at least get some water,' Babu Har Gopal said. 'Or don't I get any water, either?'

At forty, Babu Har Gopal was ten years older than Hamid. Hamid obeyed his guest because he was a friend of his deceased father. Hamid immediately ordered some soda water, and then implored, 'Look, please don't force me to drink. You know my wife is very strict.' But nothing he said had any effect on Babu Har Gopal, so Hamid had to drink too. As expected, after Babu Har Gopal downed four shots, he said, 'Okay, then, let's go see what we can see. But look, let's get a nice taxi, a private one, I like those a lot. I hate the meter ones.'

Hamid arranged for a private taxi. It was a new Ford, and the driver was also very good. Babu Har Gopal was very happy. He sat down in the taxi, took out his big wallet, and looked to see how much he had. He had a bunch of hundred-rupee notes. He sighed in relief and muttered to himself, 'That's enough.' Then he turned to the driver. 'Okay, then. Driver, let's go.'

The driver turned his hat on sideways and asked, 'Where to, sir?' Babu Har Gopal motioned to Hamid. 'You tell him.'

Hamid thought for a moment and then mentioned a destination, and the taxi headed in that direction. Minutes later, Bombay's most famous pimp was sitting next to them. They went around to a number of places to see the girls, but Hamid didn't like any of them. He liked things neat and tidy; he loved cleanliness. Hamid thought the girls looked dirty and vulgar in their make-up and wore the expression that all prostitutes share. This disgusted him. He wanted all women, even prostitutes, to maintain their dignity, and he didn't want whores to lose their feminine modesty just because of their job. On the other hand, Babu Har Gopal had dirty habits. He was very rich, and if he'd wanted, he could have ordered all of Bombay washed clean with soap and water. But he didn't care about personal cleanliness. When he took a bath, he used hardly any water, and he wouldn't shave for days on end. He would pour expensive whisky even into a dirty glass. And he didn't care whom he held deep in his nightly clasps. He would sleep with even a dirty beggar woman and then the next morning exclaim, 'That was great! She was wonderful!'

Hamid couldn't get over his surprise about the kind of person Babu Har Gopal was. He wore an extremely expensive shervani and yet his undershirt made Hamid want to vomit. He carried a hanky but used the hem of his kurta to wipe mucus from his runny nose. He ate off dirty plates and was unfazed. His pillowcase was soiled and stank, but he never thought of changing it. Hamid thought long and hard, but he couldn't understand him. He often asked, 'Babuji, why aren't you revolted by dirtiness?'

Babu Har Gopal would smile. 'I am revolted. But when you're obsessed by it, you see it everywhere. How can you cure yourself of that?'

Hamid had no answer, but his disgust didn't abate.

They drove through the streets for hours. When the pimp realized how picky Hamid was, he said to the driver, 'Go to Shivaji Park.' Then he thought to himself, 'If he doesn't like her, I swear to God I'll quit being a pimp.'

The taxi stopped near a bungalow by Shivaji Park. The pimp went upstairs. He came back after a little while to take up Babu Har Gopal and Hamid.

The room upstairs was spick and span, and the floor's tiles were sparkling. There wasn't even so much as a single mote of dust on any of the furniture. On one wall there was a picture of Swami Vivekanand. On the wall in front of them there was a picture of Gandhiji, as well as one of Subhas Chandra Bose. Marathi books lay on the table.

The pimp asked them to sit down, and they sat on the

sofa. Hamid was impressed by the house's cleanliness. There were few possessions but everything was in order. The atmosphere was very chaste and bore no traces of a prostitute's shameless love for the gaudy.

Hamid waited impatiently for the girl to appear. A man came out from the next room, whispered something to the pimp, looked in Babu Har Gopal and Hamid's direction and then said, 'She's coming. She was washing up. Now she's putting on some clothes.' Then he left.

Hamid began inspecting the room. In the corner by the table there was a pretty, brightly coloured floor mat. On the table, ten or fifteen magazines lay next to the Marathi books. Beneath the table there was a pair of finely made sandals, and it looked as though the wearer had just taken them off her feet. Rows of books looked out from the glass-fronted bookcase opposite them. When Babu Har Gopal used his sandals to squash his cigarette on the floor, Hamid got upset. He was just about to pick up the cigarette butt and throw it outside when he heard a sound like that of rustling silk coming from the next room. He turned to look and saw a fair-skinned girl coming in barefoot and wearing a new kashta sari, the edge of which slid from her head. Her hair was parted in the centre. She came up to them and pressed her hands together in a gesture of welcome. Hamid saw a white leaf pinned to her bun, thick and neatly put together, which nicely accentuated her beauty. Hamid got up and greeted her, and blushing, the girl sat in the chair near them.

Hamid guessed she was no older than seventeen. She was of average height and so fair-skinned that her complexion seemed to have a light pink hue. She looked as new and fresh as her sari. After she sat down in the chair, she lowered her big black eyes, and Hamid was captivated. The girl was clean and full of light.

Babu Har Gopal said something to Hamid, but Hamid didn't hear him. It was as though someone had just shaken him awake. 'What did you say?' he asked.

Babu Har Gopal repeated his question, 'Say something, will you?' Then he lowered his voice. 'I don't like her that much.'

Hamid got angry. He looked at her again. Youth itself was sitting before him in its purest form—fresh, stainless youth wrapped in silk—and he could have her, not just for one night but for many, as once he paid for her, she would be his. And yet this thought saddened him. He didn't know why such things happened—this girl should never be sold like merchandise. But then he realized if that were true then he could never have her.

'So what about her?' Babu Har Gopal asked crassly.

'What do I think?' Hamid was again startled. 'You don't like her, but I . . .' He couldn't make himself say what he wanted to.

Babu Har Gopal took good care of his friends. He got up and in a business-like voice asked the pimp, 'So how much for her?'

'Look at the girl,' the pimp began. 'She's just started working.'

'Okay, okay,' Babu Har Gopal interrupted him. 'Just answer my question.'

The pimp lit a bidi. 'A hundred rupees for a day or a night. Nothing less.'

'So what do you think?' Babu Har Gopal addressed Hamid.

The transaction offended Hamid. He felt as though the girl was being disgraced—one hundred rupees for this alluring, radiant youth? It upset him to think this rare beauty was only one hundred rupees, but at the same time he was grateful she was available. She was the type of girl to give up everything for.

'So what do you want to do?' Babu Har Gopal asked him again.

Hamid didn't want to admit what he felt. Babu Har Gopal smiled, took his wallet from his pocket, and gave the pimp a hundred-rupee note. 'Not any less, not any more.' Then he turned to Hamid. 'Okay, let's go. Everything's settled.'

They went down and sat in the taxi while the pimp brought the girl down. Still blushing, she sat next to them. Then they drove to a hotel, booked a room, and Babu Har Gopal went out to look for a girl of his own.

The girl was sitting on the bed with downcast eyes. Hamid's heart raced. Babu Har Gopal had left a half full bottle of whisky, and Hamid called for some soda water and then downed a large shot. The liquor gave him some courage. He sat down next to the girl and asked, 'What's your name?'

The girl raised her eyes. 'Lata Mangalaonkar.'

She had a sweet voice. Hamid drained another big shot, and then pulling the end of the sari from her head, he stroked her shiny hair. Lata bashfully batted her eyes. Hamid unwrapped the sari from her shoulders and saw how Lata's plump breasts were trembling beneath her tight bra. Hamid's entire body quivered. He wanted to be the bra fastened against Lata's body, and he wanted to feel her soft warmth and fall asleep!

Lata didn't know Hindi. She had come from Mangaon two months before, and she spoke only Marathi, which though a choppy language became tender in her mouth. She tried to answer Hamid in broken Hindi, but he told her, 'No, Lata, speak Marathi. It's really good, really changli.'

When Lata heard him say 'changli', she burst out laughing and corrected his pronunciation, but Hamid couldn't make the sound between 's' and 'ch', and so they laughed again. Hamid didn't understand her Marathi but enjoyed listening, and from time to time he would kiss her lips and say, 'These sweet, sweet words you're saying, drop them into my mouth—I want to drink them.'

She didn't understand any of this and would laugh. Hamid would hug her. Lata's arms were svelte and fair, and her bra's tiny sleeves hugged her arms, which Hamid kissed over and over. He loved everything about her body.

When Hamid dropped Lata off at her house at nine that night, he felt hollow. The touch of her soft body was sheared from him like bark from a tree, and he spent the entire night tossing and turning. In the morning Babu Har Gopal came back, and when they were alone, he asked Hamid, 'So how was it?'

'Fine.'

'You want to go back then?'

'No, I have something to do.'

'Don't talk crap. I told you, you're mine for these ten days.'

Hamid assured Babu Har Gopal that he really did have some important work to attend to in Pune where there was a man he had to meet. At last Babu Har Gopal relented and left to continue his carousing alone.

Hamid took a taxi to the bank where he withdrew some money. Then he went straight to Lata's house. She was bathing, and the same man who had been there the day before was sitting in the front room. Hamid spoke to him for a while and then gave him a hundred-rupee note. Then Lata came. She looked even fresher than before. She pressed her hands together in her traditional greeting, and Hamid got up and told the man, 'I'm going. Bring her down. I'll get her back on time.'

He went down to the taxi. Lata came and sat next to him. When she touched him, Hamid felt all his tension flush from his body. He wanted to hold her, but Lata raised her hand, forbidding him to.

He dropped her off at seven thirty that evening and immediately lost all peace of mind. He was restless all night. Hamid was married and had two small children, and he knew he was being truly foolish. If his wife found out, there would be a scene. If he had seen Lata just once, that would have been one thing but it looked as though the affair wasn't going to end anytime soon. He resolved never again to go to Shivaji Park, but by ten the next morning he was sleeping with Lata at a hotel.

Hamid went to Lata's for fifteen straight days and in the process spent 2,000 rupees. On top of this, his absence had put his business in trouble. Hamid knew what was happening but Lata had taken possession of his heart and soul. Finally Hamid drew up his courage: he forced himself to go back to his business, stay busy, and forget Lata.

In the meantime Babu Har Gopal finished his research into filth and debauchery and went back to Lahore.

Four months passed, and Hamid kept his promises. But one day he happened to be going by Shivaji Park, and he spontaneously told the driver, 'Stop here.' The taxi stopped. Hamid thought, 'No, this isn't right. I should tell the driver to drive on.' But he opened the door, exited the taxi and went up.

When Lata came out, Hamid saw she had put on weight. Her breasts were fuller, and her face had become chubby. Hamid handed over the hundred rupees and took her to a hotel. Once they were there she told him she was pregnant, and he lost all presence of mind. Stunned, he asked, 'Who—who is the father?'

Lata didn't understand what he was asking, and once he finally got through to her, she shook her head and said, 'I don't know.'

'You don't have any idea?'

'No.'

Hamid cleared his throat. 'So—it's not mine?'

'I don't know.'

When Hamid questioned her in detail he found out that Lata's keepers had tried to get her to abort the baby, but nothing had worked. No drug had any effect, other than the one that made her so sick that she had to spend a month in bed. Hamid thought things over, but only one thing made any sense, and that was that he needed to get a good doctor's advice as soon as possible because they were planning to send her to her village.

Hamid dropped her off at her house and went to see a doctor friend who told him, 'Look here, this is very dangerous, a matter of life and death.'

Hamid was at his wit's end, 'It's a matter of life and death for me too! It's got to be mine. I've calculated it carefully, and I've asked her too. For the love of God, think about what this means for me. What if it's a girl? The thought makes me tremble. If you don't help me, I'm going to go crazy thinking about this.'

The doctor gave him some medicine, and Hamid gave it to Lata. He was almost rabid in his expectation of good news, but the medicine did nothing. He managed to get a hold of another drug but that one didn't work either. Now Lata's pregnancy was showing. They wanted to send her to her village, but Hamid told them, 'No, wait a little longer. I'm going to try something else.'

But he didn't do anything. Hamid became paralysed from thinking too much. What should he do, what shouldn't he do? He couldn't figure anything out. He cursed Babu Har Gopal over and over, and he cursed himself too. If Lata had a girl, she too, would become a prostitute. He couldn't bear this thought—it was reason enough to drown himself.

He began to hate Lata. Her beauty no longer stirred the emotions it once had, and if he happened to touch her, he felt as though he had thrust his hand into burning embers. He wanted her to die before giving birth to his baby. She had been sleeping with other guys—why the hell did she have to get pregnant with his kid?

Hamid wanted to stab her swollen stomach, or do something else to kill the child, and Lata too, was beside herself with worry. She had never wanted to have a baby. Moreover it was physically painful. In the beginning she was weak from throwing up, and now she had abdominal cramps. But Hamid imagined she didn't care—if she didn't care about her own situation, then at least she should look at what he was going through, feel some pity, and do away with the baby!

After the drugs failed, Hamid tried charms and quack remedies. But the baby was stubborn. Admitting defeat, Hamid gave permission to Lata to go back to her village, but he also went in secret to see where her house was. According to his reckoning, the baby was due in the first week of October. Hamid decided to get someone to kill the baby and so started hanging out with Dada Karim, the gangster. He wined and dined him, wasting a lot of money in order to prime him for his request.

Then Hamid told Dada Karim everything, and the price was set at 1,000 rupees. Hamid immediately handed over the money, and then Dada Karim said, 'I don't have it in me to kill such a young baby. I'll bring it to you, and you can do whatever you like with it. Your secret will die with me—you don't have to worry about that.'

Hamid agreed. He planned to put the child on the railroad tracks so a passing train would crush it—that or something else. He took Dada Karim to Lata's village. Dada Karim learned that the child had been born fifteen days earlier, and suddenly Hamid felt the same joy rising in him that he had felt when his first boy had been born. But he immediately repressed this and said to Karim, 'Look, let's get it over with tonight.'

At midnight Hamid was waiting in an abandoned field; a strange storm was raging in his mind. With great difficulty, he had resolved to commit the murder at hand. The stone on the ground before him was large enough to kill the baby, and several times he had picked it up to measure its weight.

At twelve thirty, Hamid heard footsteps. His heart began to beat so strongly that he thought it would burst from his chest. Dada Karim appeared from out of the darkness, and he was carrying a small bundle wrapped in cloth. He came up to Hamid, put the bundle in his trembling arms, and said, 'My part's done. I'm out of here.' Then he left.

Hamid was shaking badly. The baby was squirming in the bundle. Hamid put it on the ground and tried to get his trembling under control. When he calmed down a little, he picked up the heavy stone. He felt over the bundle for the baby's head and was about to bring the stone down when he thought he should look at least once at the baby. He put the stone aside and with his tremulous hands got out his box of matches and lit one. It burnt out in his fingers, as he couldn't bring himself look at the baby. He thought for a moment. He gathered his courage, lit another match, and pulled back the cloth. After a quick glance, he looked back at the baby. The match fizzled out. Wait—who did the baby look like? He had seen this face somewhere, but when and where?

Hamid quickly lit another match and examined the baby's face. Suddenly the face of a man came into focus, the man who lived with Lata at Shivaji Park. Hamid swore, 'Well, fuck this! It's his spitting image. Just like him!'

And bursting with laughter, he walked off into the night.

MUMMY

HER name was Mrs. Stella Jackson, but everyone called her Mummy. She was middle-aged and of average height. Her husband had been killed in the First World War, and she had been getting his pension for about ten years.

I don't know how she got to Pune or for how long she had been living there. In fact I never tried to figure out where she came from. She was so immediately interesting that you never thought to ask about her past, and you never worried whether she had any relatives because she was connected with everything that happened in Pune. It's possible I'm exaggerating a little, but it seems like each and every one of my memories of Pune include her.

I met her nowhere else but in Pune. Let me tell you how it happened.

I am extremely lazy. There are a lot of things I would really like to see, but I never get past talking about them. I might go on about how I'm going to climb Kanchenjunga or some other impressive peak in the Himalayas, and while that's theoretically possible, it's also likely that if by some miracle I manage to get to the top, I'd be too lazy to come back down.

You can see how lazy I am by the fact that I had been living in Bombay for God knows how many years (wait—

why don't I count? I moved to Bombay with my wife and then our boy died four years ago—why don't we say I was in Bombay for eight years) and yet I never once saw Victoria Gardens or went to any museum. I wouldn't have thought of going even to Pune if I hadn't got into an argument with the owner of the film company I was working for. Then I thought it would be good to get away for a while, and Pune was the best choice as it was close and I had friends there.

I had to get to Parbhat Nagar where one of my old film buddies lived. Outside the station we had already hired a tonga when I learned it was rather far away. Slow-moving things usually irritate me, but I had gone to Pune to unwind and so decided not to let the prospect of a long ride bother me. Unfortunately the tonga was just absurd—even more so than a horse-cart in Aligarh—and we were in constant danger of falling off. The horse was in front, the passengers in the back, and after we had rambled through one or two dust-covered bazaars, I felt sick. I asked my wife what we should do, considering the circumstances. She mentioned the heat, and how the other tongas she had seen were no different, and how it would clearly be more difficult if we got off and walked. I agreed; the sun was really hot.

We must have gone about an eighth of a mile when another broken-down tonga passed. I glanced at it, and then suddenly someone yelled out, 'Hey, Manto, you ass!'

I was startled. It was Chaddah and a haggard white woman sitting thigh to thigh. My first reaction was one of great disappointment. What was Chaddah thinking? Why was he sitting next to such a trashy old hag? I couldn't guess her exact age, but her gaudy layers of powder and rouge couldn't cover up her wrinkles. All in all, it was a depressing sight.

I hadn't seen Chaddah in a while. He was a close friend. I usually would have shouted some insult in return, but seeing that woman made me hesitate.

I stopped the tonga, and Chaddah also told his driver to stop. Then he turned to the woman and said in English, 'Mummy, just a minute.' He jumped from the tonga and with his hand raised in my direction yelled, 'You—how did you get here?' Then he abruptly grabbed the hand of my shy wife and said, 'Bhabhi jan, great job! You finally plucked this precious rose and brought him here!'

'So where are you off to?' I asked.

'I'm going somewhere on work,' he said pretentiously. 'Why don't you go straight . . . .' Then he turned to my driver and said, 'Look here, take this gentleman to my house. Don't charge him anything.' He turned again to me and in his bossy manner said, 'Go on now. There'll be a servant there. The rest you'll have to manage on your own.'

He turned and jumped back into his tonga where he addressed the old woman beside him as 'Mummy'. Hearing him call her that comforted me a little, and my earlier heavy-heartedness lightened considerably.

His tonga set off down the road. I didn't say anything to my driver, but he started up and then after about a half mile, stopped near a building that looked like an old government resthouse. He got down. 'Let's go, Sahib.'

'Where?'

'This is Chaddah Sahib's house.'

'Oh', I said and then looked questioningly at my wife. Her disapproving glance told me what she thought about his house, and in truth, she didn't want to be anywhere in Pune—she was sure that under the excuse of needing to relax I would drink myself into oblivion with my drinking buddies. I got down from the tonga, picked up my small briefcase and instructed my wife to follow. She caught on that I was in no mood to be contradicted and so silently obeyed.

It was an ordinary house. It seemed that some military people had quickly built the small bungalow, used it for a little while and then left it for good. The plasterwork was poor and crumbling in places. Inside it looked like a bachelor lived there, perhaps a film star working for a company that paid him every third month and then only in instalments.

I knew my wife was sure to feel uncomfortable in that drab setting, but I imagined that once Chaddah came, we would all go to Parbhat Nagar to my old film buddy's, and then my wife, poor thing, could spend two or three days there with his wife and children.

Chaddah's servant didn't make it any better. He was useless. When we got there, all the doors were open and he wasn't anywhere to be seen. When he showed up, he didn't pay any attention to us but treated us as though we had been sitting there for years and were content to sit there until eternity. He walked right by. At first I wondered whether he might be some aspiring actor living with Chaddah, but when I asked him about the servant, I found out that this fine gentleman was none other than the man in question.

Both my wife and I were thirsty, and when I asked for some water he set off in search of glasses. Quite a while later he came back to pull a broken mug from underneath the wardrobe and then mumbled, 'Last night Sahib ordered a dozen glasses, but who knows where they are now.'

I pointed at the broken mug he was holding and asked, 'So are you going to get some oil or not?'

'To get some oil' is a special Bombay idiom, and even though my wife didn't understand it she laughed anyway. The servant was puzzled. He said, 'No, Sahib. I . . . I . . . was thinking where a glass might be.'

My wife told him to forget the water, and he put the broken mug beneath the wardrobe as if that were its rightful place, and were he to put it anywhere else, the order of the whole house would be overturned. Then he turned up his nose and left.

I was sitting on a bed, probably Chaddah's. On the other side of the room were two easy chairs, and my wife was sitting in one and fidgeting. We sat in silence. Then Chaddah arrived, but he didn't behave as though he had guests. As soon as he came into the room, he said to me, 'Wait is wait . . . it couldn't be helped.' Then with his sorry apology over, he continued, 'So you've come, old boy. Let's go to the studio for a bit. If I take you, it'll be easy for me to get an advance. This evening . . .' His glance fell on my wife and he stopped. Then he laughed, 'Bhabhi jan, I hope you haven't turned him into a maulvi yet!' He laughed even louder. 'Let all the maulvis go to hell! Let's go, Manto! Let's let bhabi jan sit for a while. We'll be right back.'

My wife had been angry, but now she was seething. I went out with Chaddah, as I knew that she would fall asleep after fuming for a while.

The studio was nearby and once there, Chaddah

badgered his boss into giving him 200 rupees. We returned in just under an hour to find my wife asleep in the easy chair, and since we didn't want to bother her, we went into another room that functioned like a storage room—things broken to the point of uselessness were lying about in heaps, and everything was covered in dust, a virtue insomuch as it gave the room a bohemian feel.

Chaddah left abruptly to look for his servant. When he found him, he gave him a hundred-rupee note and said, 'Prince of China! Get two bottles of the cheapest rum—I mean XXX rum—and a half dozen glasses.' (Later I learned Chaddah called his servant not only the 'Prince of China' but also the prince of whatever country came to mind.) The Prince of China took the money, and snapping the note in his fingers he disappeared.

Chaddah sat down on a bed with broken springs and smacked his lips thinking about the upcoming XXX rum. Then he said, 'Wait is wait . . . so you've finally found your way over here.' Suddenly he became pensive, 'But what should we do about your wife? She's going to get pissed.'

Chaddah was unmarried but was always considerate of others' wives. In fact he respected them so much that he decided never to marry. He always said, 'My inferiority complex has denied me this reward. When the question of marriage comes up, I always feel like I'm ready for it, but afterwards I think I'm not worthy of a wife and so I gather up all my marriage plans and deep-six them.'

The rum came quickly and the glasses too. Chaddah had asked for six, but the Prince of China had brought only three because the other three had broken on the way. Chaddah didn't seem to care about the broken glasses but thanked God that the alcohol was safe. Without wasting any time, he opened one bottle, poured the rum into the brand-new glasses and then said, 'Welcome to Pune!'

We downed our drinks in one shot.

Chaddah poured another round and then got up and went to the other room. When he came back he said that my wife was still sleeping and he seemed concerned about this. He said, 'I make so much noise that I bet I'll wake her up. So let's . . . no, wait . . . first I'll order some tea.' Then he took a sip of rum and called his servant, 'Oh, Prince of Jamaica!'

The Prince of Jamaica came at once and Chaddah told him, 'Look here, tell Mummy to make some first-class tea and send it over ASAP!'

The servant left. Chaddah finished his glass and poured himself a smaller shot. 'I'm not going to drink a lot,' he said. 'The first four shots make me very emotional, and I have to help you take bhabi to Parbhat Nagar.'

Half an hour later, the tea arrived. The dishes were clean and arranged nicely on the tray. Chaddah took off the tea cosy, smelled the tea and exclaimed, 'Mummy is a jewel!' Then he suddenly started to curse at the Prince of Ethiopia, and he was yelling so loud that my ears began to throb. Then he picked up the tray and said to me, 'Come on.'

My wife was now waking up. Chaddah gently placed the tray down on a rickety stool and respectfully intoned, 'Your tea, Begam Sahib.' My wife didn't like Chaddah's obsequious joke, but the tea service looked so good that she couldn't refuse it. Her mood improved after she drank two cups, and in an insinuating tone she said, 'You two already had your tea?'

I said nothing, but Chaddah bowed and then confessed,

'Yes, it was wrong of us, but we knew you'd forgive us.'

My wife smiled, and Chaddah laughed loudly. 'We two are very high-class pigs—nothing is forbidden to us!' he said. 'Let's go, we'll take you to the mosque.'

My wife didn't like this joke either, and in fact, she hated everything about Chaddah. While she basically hated all my friends, she reserved a special hatred for him because he mocked social conventions. But I don't think he ever thought about etiquette, or if he did he felt that such nonsense was a waste of time, on par with a game of Snakes and Ladders. His eyes gleamed as he looked at my angry wife, and then he called out, 'Prince of the Country of Kebabs! Go get a tonga, a Rolls Royce one!'

The Prince of the Country of Kebabs left with Chaddah for another room. My wife and I found ourselves alone, and I tried to convince her that she shouldn't be angry. I explained that sometimes you find yourself in circumstances you never could have imagined, but that the best way to get through them is to let things go. But as usual she didn't listen to my Confucian advice and continued to grumble to herself. Then the Prince of the Country of Kebabs came in to announce the Rolls Royce tonga outside, and we set off for Parbhat Nagar.

It was fortunate that only my film buddy's wife was there. Chaddah asked her to entertain my wife for a while and in doing so said, 'Wives prefer their own company. When we come back, we'll see how you two ladies got along.' Then he turned to me, 'Manto, let's get your friend from the studio.'

Chaddah went about things in such a whirlwind that he never gave anyone time to contradict him. He grabbed my arm and led me outside before my wife could stop us. Once we were in the tonga, Chaddah relaxed, 'Okay, that's over with. Now what are we going to do?' Then he burst out laughing. 'Mummy! Great Mummy!'

I was about to ask him who exactly Mummy was when Chaddah started talking about something and I couldn't get a word in.

The tonga returned to Chaddah's house. It was called Sayeedah Cottage, but Chaddah called it Kabidah Cottage because he said everyone living there was depressed. And yet later I found out that this wasn't true.

The cottage looked uninhabited from the outside, but in fact many people lived there. Everyone worked for the same film company, which paid monthly salaries every three months and then not even in full. When I was introduced one by one to everyone who lived there, I learned they were all assistant directors: some were chief assistant directors, and some were aides to these assistants and some aides to these aides. Every other person was an assistant to someone and was trying to raise cash in order to set up his own film company, though if you judged them by the way they carried themselves, you would have thought they were all film stars. Back then it was the era of wartime rationing and yet no one had a ration card, so they bought on the black market even those things you could get cheap with just a little effort. They went to the tracks in the racing season; otherwise, they gambled with predictable results. They lost money every day.

There were so many people living in the house that the garage was also used as a living space for the family of a woman named Shirin and her husband who, maybe just to break the monotony of their pursuits, wasn't an assistant director but worked for the film company as a driver, although I never saw him there and had no idea when he came and went. Shirin was very pretty and had a little boy who was the centre of attention whenever anyone had free time, and yet she herself spent most of her time in the garage.

The best part of the house went to Chaddah and his two buddies—two actors who got roles but weren't yet stars. One was Sayeed, whose stage name was Ranjit Kumar. Chaddah would say, 'Sayeedah Cottage got its name from this bastard, otherwise it would be Kabidah Cottage.' Sayeed was handsome but didn't talk much, and sometimes Chaddah would call him 'Tortoise' because he did everything so slowly.

I never found out the real name of the other actor but everyone called him Gharib Nawaz. He was from a rich Hyderabadi family and had come to Pune to get into acting. His salary was 250 rupees a month, yet he had been working for a year and had received that much just once, and that time he had given it to Chaddah who was being pressured by some bloodthirsty Pathan to pay back a loan. He wrote romances for the film company, and sometimes he tried his hand at poetry. Everyone who lived in the Cottage had an outstanding debt with him.

There were also the brothers, Shakil and Aqil. Both were assistants to some assistant director and always wrapped up in impossible schemes.

The three big ones—I mean, Chaddah, Sayeed, and Gharib Nawaz—treated Shirin extremely well, but they never went into the garage at the same time. There was no fixed visiting schedule, and if they found themselves together in the house's main room, one would go to the garage where he would stay for a while, sitting and talking to Shirin about household affairs, and the other two would busy themselves doing their own things. Those who were the assistant types did favours for Shirin: sometimes they brought things back from the market, sometimes they ran laundry errands, and sometimes they comforted her crying child.

But nobody was depressed—just the opposite. On those few occasions when they turned to talk about what was wrong with their lives, they did so cheerfully. They were really an interesting cast of characters.

We were just about to push open the cottage's gate when Gharib Nawaz came out. Seeing him gave Chaddah an idea, and he took some money out of his pocket. Without counting it, he gave some to Gharib Nawaz and told him, 'We need four bottles of Scotch. If this isn't enough, you'll have to make up the difference. If there's change, give it back to me.'

Gharib Nawaz smiled mischievously. Chaddah laughed loudly, looked in my direction and then said to Gharib Nawaz, 'This is Mr One Two, but I can't let you talk to him because he's been drinking rum. If there's some Scotch tonight, you can talk to him then. But please go get the Scotch.'

Gharib Nawaz left and we went inside. Chaddah let out a loud yawn and picked up the half finished bottle of rum. He held the bottle up to the light, glanced to see how much was left and shouted, 'Oh, Prince of Kazakhstan!' When the servant didn't appear, Chaddah poured himself a large drink and said, 'The idiot must have passed out drunk!'

After finishing his drink, Chaddah became worried. 'Hey, you shouldn't have dragged Bhabhi here. I swear, it's a big responsibility!' But then he comforted himself. 'I don't think she'll get bored where we left her.'

'Yes,' I answered, 'she's okay over there. For the time being she'll forget about wanting to kill me.' Then I poured some rum into my glass even though the stuff tasted like rotten molasses.

The storage room had two iron-barred windows through which we could see an empty lot. From out there someone shouted out Chaddah's name. I was startled. I looked again and saw the music director, Vankatre. I couldn't figure out what race he was—Mongolian, African, Aryan, or God knows what else. You would be about to decide on one when you would see something that contradicted your first impression and force you to revise your thoughts again. Actually, he was Maratha, and yet, instead of having an aquiline nose like Shivaji he had this surprising apparatus, broad and pressed down, which he said was necessary for producing good nasal sounds. When he saw me, he shouted, 'Manto! Sir Manto Seth!'

Chaddah shouted back in an even louder voice, 'To hell with all this sir-seth business! Come on, get in here!' Vankatre immediately came in. Laughing, he pulled a bottle of rum out of his pocket and set it on the footstool and said, 'Hell, I went over to Mummy's. She said my friend had come, and I wondered who the hell it could be—hell, I had no idea it was fucking Manto!'

Chaddah thumped Vankatre on his pumpkin-shaped

head and said, 'Stop fucking talking about him, would you? At least you brought some rum.' Vankatre rubbed his head. Then he picked up my empty glass and poured himself a drink. 'Manto, when we met today,' he said, indicating Chaddah, 'the first words out of this bastard's mouth were how he felt like drinking, but I didn't have any money and so didn't know what to do.'

Chaddah pounded him on the head again, 'Sit down, will you? You make it sound like you really cared.'

'Hey, if I didn't care, who the hell brought this big bottle? Your dad give it to me?' Then Vankatre slugged down his rum. Chaddah didn't pay any attention to Vankatre's chatter but asked, 'So what did Mummy say? Anything? When will Mozelle come? Oh, yes—the platinum blonde!'

Vankatre wanted to say something but Chaddah grabbed my arm and began talking. 'Manto, I swear to God, she's so great. I'd heard of platinum blondes but yesterday I saw my first. Her hair is like delicate silver threads! It's great! I swear to God, Manto! Long live Mummy!' Then he looked fiercely at Vankatre and snapped, 'You idiot, Vankatre! Repeat with me—"Long live Mummy!"'

Chaddah and Vankatre shouted together, 'Long live Mummy!' After several rounds of shouting, Vankatre tried again to answer Chaddah's question, but Chaddah stopped him, 'Okay, enough of that. I'm all emotional now.' Then he went on, 'You know how the beloved's hair is usually black, like black clouds? This is something else.' He turned to me again. 'Manto, it's very confusing. Her hair is like beautiful silver threads! But I can't say it's silver, and I don't know what colour platinum is because I've never seen it. It's a strange colour, a mixture of steel and silver.'

Vankatre finished his second shot and suggested, 'And then add a little XXX rum to that.'

This made Chaddah furious and he shouted, 'Don't talk shit!' He turned again to me with a compassionate look and said, 'Man, I have really become emotional! Yes—that colour—I swear to God it's unprecedented. Have you seen it? You'll find it on a fish's stomach—no, no, not just their stomachs—on pomfret fish—what are those things on fish called? No, no—on snakes—on their delicate scales—yes, scales—just that colour—scales—I learned that word from a fisherman. It's such a beautiful thing and yet such an absurd word! In Punjabi we call it 'chane'—shining—yes, that—it's exactly how her hair is. Her hair is so beautiful, it could kill you!' Then he suddenly got up. 'Fuck all this! Man, I've got all emotional!'

Then Vankatre asked very innocently, 'What do you mean by "emotional"?'

'It means "sentimental",' Chaddah answered. 'But you won't understand, you, the son of Balaji Baji Rao and Nana Farnavis!'

Vankatre poured himself another shot and turned to me. 'This bastard Chaddah thinks I don't know any English,' he said. 'Hey I graduated from high school! Fuck, my father . . . he loved me so much . . . he . . . .'

Chaddah interrupted him, 'He made you into Tansen. He twisted your nose so you could make good nasal sounds. He taught you how to sing dhrupads when you were still a child. When you cried for milk, it was in Mian ki Todi, and when you cried to go to the bathroom it was in Adana and the first words out of your mouth were in Patdeep. And your father . . . he was a great musical guru, better than even Baiju Bawara. And now you're better than your father, and that's why your name is One-Up Vankatre!' He turned to me. 'Manto, this bastard . . . whenever he drinks, he starts going on about how great his father was. Why should I care if his daddy loved him? And should I tear up my BA and throw it out the window just because this fool graduated from high school?'

Vankatre wanted to fend off this storm of insults, but Chaddah wouldn't let him. 'Be quiet! I already said I've become emotional—yes, the colour of pomfret fish—no, no—like a snake's fine scales—yes, that's just that colour—God only knows how Mummy charmed this girl out of hiding.'

Then Vankatre said, 'Ask for a peti. I'm going to play something.'

Chaddah laughed. 'Sit down, will you, you idiot savant!'

Vankatre poured the rest of the rum into his glass and then said, 'Manto, if he doesn't get this platinum girl, Mr Chaddah is going to go to some peak in the Himalayas and become a yogi.' And then he tossed down his drink.

Vankatre started to open the bottle he had brought and then said, 'But, Manto, this girl's really great.'

'We'll see,' I said.

'Actually tonight—tonight I'm going to give a party,' Chaddah said. 'Fortunately for me, you came and so Mr One-Hundred-Eighty Mehtaji gave me that advance, otherwise things would have been really tough. Tonight . . . tonight . . . ' Chaddah began to sing in a very coarse voice, 'Tonight, don't play any sad melodies . . .'

Poor Vankatre was about to protest against Chaddah's awful singing when Gharib Nawaz and Ranjit Kumar came in. Both had two bottles of Scotch, which they set down on the table. I knew Ranjit Kumar well enough, but we weren't close friends and so we exchanged only a couple words, 'When did you come?'

'I came just today.' Then we toasted each other and began to drink.

Chaddah really had become quite emotional, and whatever the conversation he brought up the platinum blonde. Ranjit Kumar finished off a fourth of a bottle, Gharib Nawaz drank three shots of Scotch and everyone got drunk, except me (I was saved because I was used to drinking a lot). I guessed from their conversation that the four of them were badly infatuated with the new girl Mummy had brought in from God knows where. Her name was Phyllis. She worked in a hairdressing salon somewhere in Pune and usually went around with a boy who looked like a eunuch. Gharib Nawaz wanted her so badly that he was ready to sell his Hyderabadi inheritance to get her. Chaddah had only one thing going for him, his looks. Vankatre was sure his singing would be enough to win her. And Ranjit Kumar thought that coming on strong would be the best approach. But in the end everyone knew that Mummy herself would decide the lucky one, the one who would get Phyllis, the platinum blonde.

As they went on about Phyllis, suddenly Chaddah looked at his watch and said to me, 'To hell with this girl! Let's go, your wife's probably getting upset over there. The only problem is I might get sentimental there too. Well, look after me, will you?' He shook the last few drops into his mouth and shouted out, 'Oh, Prince of the Country of Mummies! Oh, Prince of Egypt!'

The Prince of Egypt appeared rubbing his eyes as though after centuries of rest he had just been excavated from some tomb. Chaddah flicked some rum on his face and said, 'Get us two tongas, two Egyptian chariots!'

The tongas arrived, and we got in and headed for Parbhat Nagar.

Harish, my old film buddy, was at home. The inconveniences of entertaining there were great because of his apartment's far-flung locale, and yet he hadn't overlooked the smallest detail in making sure my wife felt comfortable. Chaddah let him know with a glance where everything stood, and this proved quite useful. My wife didn't seem upset in the least, and in fact, it looked like she had had a good time, which was likely because Harish knew how to please women with his interesting banter. He asked my wife if she would like to see that day's shooting.

'Are you filming any songs?' she asked.

Harish answered, 'No, that's tomorrow. I think you should go then.'

Harish's wife was tired of going to shootings, as she had ferried countless people to her husband's sets. She quickly said to my wife, 'Yes, tomorrow will be good.' Then she turned to her husband and said, 'She's still tired from travelling.'

We all breathed a sigh of relief. Harish entertained everyone for a while with his witty conversation and then said to me, 'Come on then. Let's go.' He looked at my friends. 'Let them stay. Our producer wants to hear your story.'

I looked at my wife and then told Harish, 'Ask for her permission.'

My naïve wife was caught in the trap, and she said to Harish, 'When we were leaving Bombay I told him to take his briefcase, but he said it wasn't necessary. Now what will he show him?'

'He can recite something from memory,' Harish suggested. Then he looked at me, asking for my confirmation.

'Yes,' I said nonchalantly, 'that's possible.'

Chaddah put the finishing touch on the little drama.

'Okay, then. We're going,' he said. The four of them got up, said their goodbyes and left. A little while later Harish and I left too. Chaddah and the others were waiting with tongas at the edge of Parbhat Nagar. When he saw us, he cried out, 'Long live King Harish Chandar!'

We all went to Mummy's, except for Harish who had to meet one of his girlfriends. Mummy's house was a bungalow, and from the street it looked like Sayeedah Cottage although inside it was clean and orderly, which reflected Mummy's good taste. The furniture was ordinary, and yet everything was so well arranged that the house looked as if a designer had put it together. When we left Parbhat Nagar I had expected a brothel, but the house didn't look anything like that. It was as respectable as a middle-class Christian house and somehow seemed much younger than Mummy, as it didn't have any false touches like her make-up's obvious attempts at deception. When Mummy entered the living room, I suddenly realized that while everything around her was actually very old, Mummy alone continued to age. God knows why, but while looking at her garish make-up, I suddenly wanted to see her young again.

Chaddah introduced me, and then he introduced Mummy, 'This is Mummy, the great Mummy!'

Hearing Chaddah's words, she smiled at me and then turned back to Chaddah and spoke in English, 'You ordered tea in your usual panic—you didn't even tell me if he liked it or not.' Then she said to me, 'Mr Manto, I'm very ashamed. In fact all this mischief is due to your friend Chaddah, my incorrigible son.'

I complimented her on the tea and expressed my thanks, but Mummy told me not to offer empty praise. She said to Chaddah, 'Dinner's ready. I made it because I knew that if I didn't, you'd come at the last minute and make my life hell.'

Chaddah hugged Mummy. 'You're a jewel, Mummy! Let's eat!'

'What? No, you won't!' Mummy said, startled.

'But we left Mrs Manto in Parbhat Nagar,' Chaddah explained.

'May God strike you down!' Mummy yelled. 'Why the hell did you do that?'

'Because of the party!' Chaddah laughed.

'But I cancelled it when I saw Mrs Manto in the tonga,' Mummy said.

Chaddah was crestfallen. 'No, how could you! We made all these plans just for the party!' He sat down dejectedly in a chair and addressed everyone, 'Well, all our dreams are shattered! The platinum blonde whose hair is the colour of a snake's belly's delicate scales . . .' He got up and grabbed Mummy's arms. 'You cancelled it! You cancelled it in your heart. Here, I'm going to reverse it—I'm going to write "swad" on your heart.' Then he made the Urdu letter 'swad' on Mummy's heart and shouted, 'Hurray!'

Mummy had just said the party was cancelled, but I could tell she didn't want to disappoint Chaddah. She patted his cheek affectionately and said over her shoulder, 'Okay, General Vankatre, go bring the cannons in from headquarters.'

Vankatre saluted and left to carry out his orders. Sayeedah Cottage was very close, and in under ten minutes he returned with not just the liquor bottles but also Chaddah's servant. Chaddah welcomed him, 'Come here—come here—Prince of the Caucusus—that—that girl whose hair is the colour of snake's scales is coming. You, too, should try your luck!'

Ranjit Kumar and Gharib Nawaz did not like the way Chaddah was opening up the competition for the platinum blonde, and they both told me how Chaddah often got out of line in this way. As usual, Chaddah kept bragging about himself while the two of them sat quietly in the corner, sipping their rum and enumerating their sorrows.

I kept thinking about Mummy. Gharib Nawaz, Ranjit Kumar, and Chaddah were sitting in the living room like small children waiting for their mother to come back with toys. Chaddah was confident he would get the best toy because he was the oldest and also his mother's favourite, and Ranjit Kumar and Gharib Nawaz sympathized with each other because their problems were the same. Liquor was like milk in that setting, and the image of the platinum blonde was like a little doll. If every place and time has its own melody, then the melody that night was rather flat—Mummy was the mother, the others were the boys, and that was that.

My aesthetic taste had suffered a shocking blow earlier when I had seen Mummy with Chaddah in the tonga. I was sorry I had had such bad thoughts about them, but it troubled me over and over why she used so much ugly make-up. It demeaned her—it ridiculed her maternal feelings for Chaddah, Gharib Nawaz, and Vankatre and God knows who else.

I asked Chaddah, 'Hey, why does your Mummy use so much flashy make-up?'

Chaddah answered, 'Because people like bright things. It's very rare to find simpletons like us, people who like soft music and muted colours, people who don't want to be young again and who don't try to trick old age by acting young. People who call themselves artists are fools. I'll tell you an interesting anecdote. It was during the Baisakhi fair in your Amritsar, in Ram Bagh where the prostitutes live. Some farmers were passing by. A strong young man raised on pure milk and butter and whose new shoes were dangling on his staff looked up at a whorehouse and saw a dark-skinned whore. She was wearing wild-coloured make-up and her oil-soaked hair was grotesquely pasted onto her forehead. Elbowing the ribcage of his friend, he said, "Hey, Lehna Sayyan, look up on the fifth floor—there's—"' God knows why Chaddah didn't go ahead and finish his sentence because he usually didn't have any reservation about swearing. He laughed, filled my glass with rum, and said, 'For this farmer, this witch was a fairy from Mount Caucasus, and the beautiful girls of his village were like clumsy buffaloes. We're all fools—mediocre fools—mediocre fools because nothing in this world is high class—it's second or third class—but—but—Phyllis is very special—like a snake's scales—'

Vankatre raised his glass, poured rum on Chaddah's head and said, 'Scales, grails—you're out of your mind.'

Chaddah licked the rum dripping off his forehead and said to Vankatre, 'Now tell me, bastard, how much did your daddy love you? You've cooled me off, so tell me how much!'

Vankatre turned serious and said to me, 'By God, he loved me a lot. I was fifteen when he arranged my marriage.'

Chaddah laughed loudly, 'He made you into a cartoon, that bastard! May God give him a kaserail ki peti in heaven so that he can woo a beautiful bride for you!'

Vankatre became even more serious. 'Manto, I don't lie—my wife is truly beautiful. In our family . . .'

'Your family be damned. Talk about Phyllis,' Chaddah said. 'No one can be more beautiful than her.' Chaddah looked toward the corner where Gharib Nawaz and Ranjit Kumar were sitting. He yelled at them, 'Founders of the Gunpowder Plot! Listen, no conspiracy on your part will work! Chaddah's going to win!' Then he turned to his servant. 'Hey, isn't that right, the Prince of Wales?'

The Prince of Wales was looking yearningly at the fast-emptying rum bottle. Chaddah erupted in laughter, poured half a glass and gave it to him. Gharib Nawaz and Ranjit Kumar were whispering to each other about Phyllis and secretly scheming against each other.

The lights were now on in the living room, as the light had faded outside. I was telling Chaddah the latest news from the Bombay film industry when we heard Mummy's shrill voice on the verandah. He shouted out in excitement and went outside, and Gharib Nawaz and Ranjit Kumar exchanged suggestive glances and looked toward the door. Mummy entered the room chatting with the five Anglo-Indian girls accompanying her, each one different from the others—Polly, Dolly, Kitty, Elma, and Thelma—and the boy Chaddah called Sissy because he looked like a eunuch. Phyllis came in last, accompanied by Chaddah who had his arm wrapped around the thin waist of the platinum blonde—a conquering display that Gharib Nawaz and Ranjit Kumar didn't like.

With the arrival of the girls, the party broke into full swing. All of a sudden everyone was talking English so quickly that Vankatre couldn't keep up, and yet he did the best he could. When none of the girls paid any attention to him, he sat down on a sofa next to Elma's older sister, Thelma, and asked her how many more Indian dance steps she had learnt. He started explaining Dhani, and as he kept time out loud—'one, two, three!'—he choreographed some steps. On the other side of the room, the other girls were gathered around Chaddah as he recited dirty English limericks from his trove of thousands. Mummy was ordering some soda and snacks, Ranjit Kumar smoked and stared intently at Phyllis, and Gharib Nawaz kept saying to Mummy that if she needed any money, she should just ask.

The Scotch was opened and the first round of drinking began. When Phyllis was called in, she gave her platinum blonde hair a light shake and then said that she didn't drink whisky. Everyone insisted, but she didn't listen. Chaddah pouted, and so Mummy poured Phyllis a small drink and raised it to her lips saying sweetly, 'Be a brave girl and drink it up.'

Phyllis couldn't refuse. This made Chaddah happy, and in his good mood he raced through another few dozen risque limericks.

Everyone was having a good time. Suddenly it occurred to me that people must have started wearing clothes all those millennia ago when they got sick of their nakedness, and similarly, people run to nakedness nowadays when they get sick of their clothes. Modesty and debauchery reach a balance, and debauchery has at least one virtue in that it momentarily frees people from the boredom of routine. I looked toward Mummy sitting arm in arm with the young girls and laughing at Chaddah's limericks. She was wearing the same trashy make-up beneath which you could still see her wrinkles, and yet she was happy. I wondered why people consider escapism so bad, even the escapism on display right then. At first it might appear unseemly, but in the end its lack of pretension gives it its own sort of beauty.

Polly was standing in a corner talking with Ranjit Kumar about her new dress, telling him how it was due to her cleverness alone that she had got herself something so nice for so cheap, as she had transformed two worthless pieces of cloth into a beautiful dress. And Ranjit Kumar replied in earnest, promising to have two new dresses made for her despite the fact that he worked for a film company and so could never hope to receive the needed money in one single payment. Dolly was trying to get Gharib Nawaz to lend her some money, promising him that once she got her salary from the office she would repay him, and while Gharib Nawaz knew that this wouldn't happen just as it hadn't in the past, he nonetheless accepted her promises. Thelma was trying to learn the very difficult steps of Tandau dancing, and while Vankatre knew she would never succeed, he kept instructing her. Thelma, too, knew she was wasting their time, and yet she was memorizing the lesson with passionate concentration. Elma and Kitty were quickly getting drunk and talking about some Ivy who last time at the racecourse had placed a bad bet on their behalf in order to take revenge for God knows what. Chaddah was putting Phyllis's blonde hair in the golden Scotch and drinking the liquor. Sissy kept digging a comb out of his pocket to tend to his hair. Mummy went around the room, talking here and there, ordering a soda bottle to be opened or broken glasses picked up from the floor, and she was watching over everyone like a dozing cat that keeps track of her five kittens through half-opened eyes, always knowing where they are and what mischief they are up to.

What part—what colour or what line—was wrong with this picturesque scene? Even Mummy's make-up seemed like a necessary part of the whole. Ghalib says, 'The prison of life and the chains of grief are one. / How can people escape grief before death?' If the prison of life and the chains of grief are truly one, what law prevents people from trying to escape a little suffering? Who wants to wait around for the Angel of Death? Why shouldn't we be allowed to play the interesting game of self-deception?

Mummy was praising everybody profusely, and she had a motherly affection for everyone. It occurred to me that perhaps she wore so much make-up so people won't know the truth about her—that she couldn't be a mother to everyone and so had chosen just a handful of people to lavish her affection on while leaving the rest to fend for themselves.

Mummy went into the kitchen to fry some potato chips and so wasn't around to see Chaddah give Phyllis a strong shot of liquor right in front of everyone. Phyllis became drunk, stumbling drunk.

Midnight passed. Vankatre moved on from teaching Thelma how to dance to telling her how much his father loved him—while he was still a child, his father had arranged his marriage, his wife was very beautiful and so on. Gharib Nawaz had already forgotten about the money he'd just loaned to Dolly, and Ranjit Kumar had taken Polly somewhere outside. Having exhausted their topics of gossip, Elma and Kitty were tired and wanted to lie down. Mummy, Phyllis and Sissy were sitting near a stool, and next to them sat a subdued Chaddah. It was the first time Phyllis had ever been drunk and Chaddah was eyeing her as though he wanted to eat her up, and yet Mummy didn't notice.

A little while later, Sissy got up and stretched out on the sofa where after combing his hair for a minute, he fell asleep. Gharib Nawaz and Dolly got up and went off together. Elma and Kitty were talking about some Margaret when they said goodbye to Mummy and left. For the last time Vankatre mentioned his wife's beauty, cast an amourous glance first at Phyllis and then at Thelma, who was sitting next to him. Without further ado, he grabbed Thelma's arm and took her out to the lawn to show her the moon.

God knows why, but suddenly Mummy and Chaddah were yelling at each other. Chaddah's speech was slurred, and like a rebellious son, he started to curse her. Phyllis tried gently to calm them down but Chaddah was too worked up to listen. He wanted to take Phyllis with him to Sayeedah Cottage but Mummy was against this. She tried to get him to understand why he shouldn't do this but he wouldn't listen. He said over and over, 'You're crazy! You old bitch—Phyllis is mine—ask her!'

Mummy withstood his curses and then explained what was what, 'Chaddah, my son, why don't you understand? She's young. She's very young.' Her voice quavered with both entreaty and rebuke. It was a frightening scene but Chaddah just didn't understand. He was thinking only about Phyllis and how to get his hands on her. I looked at Phyllis and for the first time realized how young she was—not more than fifteen. Now she seemed upset, and her fair face trembled.

Chaddah grabbed her arm and pulled her toward him. He clutched her to his chest like a film star, and Mummy screamed in protest, 'Chaddah, let go of her! For God's sake, let her go!'

When Chaddah didn't release Phyllis, Mummy slapped him on the face. 'Get out! Get out!' she yelled.

Chaddah was stunned. He pushed Phyllis away, stared furiously at Mummy and then left. I got up, said my goodbyes and followed Chaddah.

When I got to Sayeedah Cottage, Chaddah was lying face down on his bed with all of his clothes on. I didn't say anything but went into another room and fell asleep on a big desk.

I woke up at ten o'clock. Chaddah had gotten up early and gone out though no one knew where. Coming out of the bathroom, I heard his voice coming from the garage. I stopped. He was saying to someone, 'She's beyond compare. I swear to God, she's beyond compare. Pray that when you reach her age, you'll be that great.'

His tone was strangely bitter, but I couldn't tell whether his bitterness was directed at himself or the person to whom he was talking. I didn't think it was right to linger and so I went inside. I waited for about half an hour and when he didn't come inside, I set off for Parbhat Nagar.

My wife was in a good mood. Harish was not at home, and when his wife asked about him, I said he was still sleeping at Chaddah's. We had had a good time in Pune, and so I told Harish's wife that I was ready to go back to Bombay. She made a show of trying to stop us, but in coming from Sayeedah Cottage I'd already decided that the night's events had been more than enough for me.

We left and on the way to the station, we talked about Mummy. I told my wife exactly what had happened, and she suspected that Mummy had fought with Chaddah because Phyllis was either her relative or else she wanted to give her to a good customer. I didn't say anything as I didn't really know.

Several days later Chaddah sent a letter in which he mentioned the events of that night, and he had this to say for himself, 'I turned into an animal that night—what an ass!'

Three months later, I had to go to Pune on some important business, and after getting there I went straight to Sayeedah Cottage. Chaddah wasn't there, but I met Gharib Nawaz when he came out of the garage, playing with Shirin's young boy as would an affectionate uncle. He greeted me very warmly and we went inside. A little while later Ranjit Kumar came walking in as slow as a turtle and sat down without saying a word. When I tried to make conversation, he barely responded, but I learned that Chaddah had not gone back to Mummy's house and that Mummy had not come by Sayeedah Cottage. The day after the party, Mummy had sent Phyllis back to her parents. Ranjit Kumar was upset because he had been confident that if Phyllis had remained in Pune for a few more days, he would have won her over. Gharib Nawaz didn't have any similar regret and was only sad that she had left.

Then I learned that Chaddah's health had been poor for several days. He had a fever but hadn't gone to the doctor and instead wandered pointlessly around town all day. When Gharib Nawaz began to tell me this, Ranjit Kumar got up and went outside and through the iron-barred windows I saw him head toward the garage.

I was just about to ask Gharib Nawaz about Shirin when Vankatre entered in an extremely agitated state. He told us Chaddah had just lost consciousness in the tonga as the two were coming back to Sayeedah Cottage. We all ran outside to see the tonga driver propping him up. We lifted him out, carried him inside and laid him down. I put my hand to his forehead—his fever must have been at least 106 degrees.

I told Gharib Nawaz that we should immediately call a doctor. He discussed this with Vankatre and then took off, saying he'd be right back. Then he came back with Mummy who was huffing and puffing and trying to catch her breath. As soon as she entered, she looked at Chaddah and screamed, 'What's happened to my son?'

When Vankatre told her that Chaddah had been sick for several days, Mummy yelled, 'What kind of people are you? Why didn't you tell me?' Then she gave us our orders: one had to rub Chaddah's feet, another had to get some ice, and the third had to fan him. When Mummy saw how weak Chaddah was, she was beside herself with worry. But then she gathered her strength and went to get a doctor.

I don't know how Ranjit Kumar found out in the garage, but he came back as soon as Mummy had left and asked what was going on. Vankatre recounted how Chaddah had fallen unconscious on the ride over and how Mummy had just left to get a doctor. Hearing this last bit of news, he visibly relaxed. In fact the three of them looked relieved, as though Mummy's involvement had absolved them of their responsibility for Chaddah's ill health.

They rubbed Chaddah's feet and put ice packs on his forehead in accordance with Mummy's instructions, and by the time she returned with the doctor, Chaddah had regained some degree of consciousness. The doctor took his time examining the patient, and his grave expression made it seem as though Chaddah's life was in danger. Once he was done, the doctor motioned to Mummy and the two left the room. I turned to look out through the iron-barred windows and saw the garage's sackcloth curtains swaying in the breeze.

A little while later, Mummy returned. One by one she told Gharib Nawaz, Vankatre, and Ranjit Kumar not to worry. Chaddah was listening with opened eyes, and when he saw Mummy, he didn't react with surprise and yet he did seem confused. But when he realized why Mummy was there, he took her hand, squeezed it and said, 'Mummy, you are great!'

Mummy sat next to him on the bed. She truly embodied

affection—she rubbed her hand over Chaddah's hot forehead and said, 'My boy, my poor boy.'

Chaddah's eyes welled with tears but he tried to hold them back. 'No', he said. 'Your boy is a first-class scoundrel. Get your dead husband's pistol and shoot him in the chest!'

Mummy lightly slapped Chaddah's cheek. 'Don't talk nonsense,' she said. Then like an attentive nurse she got up and said, 'Boys, Chaddah's sick and I have to take him to a hospital, okay?'

Everyone understood. Gharib Nawaz went and got a taxi, and we lifted Chaddah and put him in. He kept protesting that this fever wasn't bad enough to warrant taking him to the hospital, but Mummy said that in any event, the hospital would be more comfortable.

Chaddah was admitted to the hospital, and Mummy drew me aside and said that he was very sick with the plague. When I heard this, I nearly fainted. Mummy herself was very worried, but she hoped that this setback would pass and Chaddah would soon get healthy.

Treatment continued for some time. It was a private hospital, and the doctors gave Chaddah a lot of attention. But even then many complications arose: his skin began to crack in places and his fever mounted, and finally the doctors suggested we take him to Bombay. But Mummy didn't agree and she took Chaddah back to her house.

I couldn't stay in Pune. I returned to Bombay and called from time to time to ask about his health. I thought he would die, but I learned that his health was slowly improving. Then I had to go to Lahore in connection with a trial, and when I returned fifteen days later, my wife handed me a letter from Chaddah in which he wrote, 'The great Mummy saved her wayward son from the jaws of death!'

There was an ocean of emotions in those few words. Unusually for me, I got very sentimental while recounting to my wife how Mummy had cared for Chaddah. My wife was moved too, 'Women like that are usually very caring.'

I wrote to Chaddah two or three times but received no answer. Afterwards I learned that Mummy had sent him to one of her girlfriends' house in Lonavala, thinking that a change of scenery would do him some good. Chaddah spent a month there but got bored and came back.

I happened to be in Pune on the day of his return. He was weak from fighting off the plague, but otherwise he was his usual rowdy self and he talked about his sickness just as someone would mention a minor bicycle accident—now that it was over, he thought it pointless to talk about it in detail.

Small changes had come about at Sayeedah Cottage. The brothers, Aqil and Shakil, had left when they decided that Sayeedah Cottage's atmosphere was not conducive for establishing their own film company. In their place came Sen, a Bengali music director, along with a runaway from Lahore named Ram Singh who had got just before Chaddah went to Lonavala and had won permission to stay. Everyone in Sayeedah Cottage ended up using the boy for their work, since he was very courteous and obliging. The boy set his stuff up in Sen's room where there was extra space.

Then Ranjit Kumar was cast as the hero in a new film and the film company promised that if the film did well, he would be given the chance to direct. Chaddah somehow secured 1,500 rupees of his two years' unpaid salary and all of that in one lump sum. He told Ranjit Kumar, 'You know, if you want to get some money, pray for the plague. It's better than being an actor or director!'

Gharib Nawaz had recently come back from Hyderabad, and so Sayeedah Cottage was enjoying some good times. I noticed expensive shirts and pants drying on the clothesline outside the garage and how Shirin's little boy had new toys.

I had to stay in Pune for fifteen days. Harish was busy trying to win the love of the heroine of a film he was shooting, but he was scared because the heroine was Punjabi and her husband sported a big moustache and bulging muscles. Chaddah encouraged him, 'Don't worry about that bastard. Macho Punjabi guys are horrible lovers. Listen, for just a hundred rupees a word, I'll teach you ten or twenty hardcore Punjabi swear words that'll come in handy.'

At Chaddah's rate (basically a bottle of liquor for each swear word), Harish memorized six Punjabi insults, complete with a Punjabi accent, but he hadn't yet had an opportunity to test their effectiveness.

Mummy was throwing her usual parties with Polly, Dolly, Kitty, Elma, Thelma and everyone else. Vankatre instructed Thelma in Kathakali, Tandau, and Dhani, shouting 'one, two, three . . .' to count out the measures, and Thelma was trying her best to learn. Gharib Nawaz was lending money right and left, and Ranjit Kumar (a film star at last) continued to escort girls outside to enjoy the breeze. And just like old times, Chaddah's raunchy limericks made everyone erupt in laughter. Only one person was absent—Phyllis, the one for whose hair colour Chaddah had spent so much time trying to find the proper simile. But Chaddah didn't look for her. Nevertheless when Chaddah's and Mummy's glances met, sometimes he would lower his gaze, and it seemed that he still felt bad about that one night's craziness. After his fourth shot, he would shout at himself, 'Chaddah, you're such a pig!' Then Mummy would give a sweet little smile that seemed to say, 'Don't be silly.'

And as usual, Vankatre and Chaddah would quarrel. Vankatre would get drunk and start to praise his father and beautiful wife, but Chaddah would cut him off as if with an enormous battle axe. Vankatre, the poor soul, would stop talking and fold his high school diploma and put it in his pocket.

Mummy was still everyone's 'Mummy' and she put together the parties with her usual affection. Her make-up remained the same ugly fare and her clothes were still tasteless and flashy; her wrinkles still showed from beneath layers of powder and rouge but now it all looked sacred: her shadow had protected Chaddah, and the plague's insects hadn't dared touch her. When Vankatre's beautiful wife had a miscarriage, Mummy intervened to save her life. When Thelma, because of her interest in learning Indian dance, fell into the clutches of a Marwari Kathak dancer who passed on to her a sexually transmitted disease, Mummy scolded her ferociously and was ready to abandon her for good. But seeing her tears, Mummy's heart melted. She told her boys what had happened and asked them to get Thelma treated. When Kitty got 500 rupees for solving a crossword, Mummy forced her to give half of it to poor Gharib Nawaz because suddenly he didn't have any money. She told Kitty, 'Give it to him now, you'll be able to get it back later if you want.' During my fifteen days in Pune, she often asked me about my wife, expressing concern that we hadn't had another child after our first son's death. She didn't talk to Ranjit Kumar with much interest, and it seemed as though she didn't like his love for showing off. (In fact, she had said as much to me on several occasions.) She hated the music director, Sen, and always complained when Chaddah brought him along, 'Don't bring that awful man here.' When Chaddah asked why, she would reply, 'He seems insincere. I don't like him.' Then Chaddah would laugh.

I always had a good time at Mummy's parties. Everyone drank, got drunk, and flirted. Things were full of sensual possibility and yet they never got out of hand because everybody knew where things stood.

I returned to Bombay. On my second day back, I read in the paper that Sen had been killed at Sayeedah Cottage. The murderer was reported to be a fourteen- or fifteen-year-old boy named Ram Singh. I immediately called Pune but couldn't reach anyone.

A week later, a letter arrived from Chaddah in which he recounted all of the murder's details. It was at night, while everyone was sleeping. Suddenly someone fell onto his bed, and he woke with a start. When he turned on the light, he saw that it was Sen, dripping with blood. Chaddah was trying to process this when Ram Singh appeared in the doorway with a dagger in hand. Immediately, Gharib Nawaz and Ranjit Kumar appeared too and soon everyone woke up. Gharib Nawaz and Ranjit Kumar grabbed Ram Singh and pried the dagger from his hand, while Chaddah laid Sen on his bed. He was about to ask Sen about his wounds when the music director took his last breath and died. Gharib Nawaz and Ranjit Kumar were holding Ram Singh and both were trembling. Then Ram Singh asked Chaddah, 'Bhapaji—did he die?'

Chaddah nodded his head, and then Ram Singh said to the two men holding him, 'Let me go. I won't run away.'

Chaddah didn't know what to do and so immediately sent his servant to fetch Mummy. Everyone relaxed when Mummy came as they were confident that she would resolve the situation. She told Gharib Nawaz and Ranjit Kumar to let go of Ram Singh and then she took him to the police station where his formal statement was entered into the books. For days afterwards, Chaddah and his friends were harried first by the police investigation and then the trial, and Mummy was frantically running here and there, trying to help Ram Singh's cause.

Chaddah was confident the boy would be acquitted, and in fact his innocent manner impressed the judge so much that the lower court did so. Before the trial Mummy told him, 'Son, don't worry, just tell the truth.' Then Ram Singh gave an exact account of what had transpired, the same that he had given at the police station. Ram Singh loved music and Sen was a very good singer—eventually Sen convinced him to try to become a playback singer. Swayed by the man's promises, Ram Singh submitted to his sexual advances. But he hated Sen terribly, and time and again he cursed himself. Finally, he grew so sick of the situation that he told Sen that if he forced himself upon him once more, he would kill him. And that was just what happened.

Ram Singh offered this testimony to the court. Mummy was there providing her support, and her glances reminded him of what she had earlier said, 'Don't worry, just tell the truth because the truth always wins. You killed him, but what he was doing was sordid. It was depraved, a crime of unnatural passion.'

In his letter Chaddah wrote, 'In this age of lies, there was a surprising victory for the truth, and all the credit goes to my old Mummy.'

Chaddah invited me to the party that Sayeedah Cottage was throwing to celebrate the acquittal, but I was too busy to go. The 'brothers, Shakil and Aqil L had moved back, as they hadn't been able to find a more suitable place to get their film company up and running. They were again assistants to some assistant in their old film company and had only a couple hundred rupees of their original capital. Chaddah asked them to chip in for the party, and they gave all of their remaining money to make the party a success. Chaddah said, 'I'll drink four shots and pray your film company gets on its feet.'

Chaddah told me that at the party Vankatre, quite out of character, praised neither his asshole father nor his beautiful wife. Kitty told Gharib Nawaz she needed some money, and so he lent her 200 rupees. Gharib Nawaz said to Ranjit Kumar, 'Don't play with the poor girls. Your intentions might be good, but as far as accepting money goes, the girls aren't going to pay it back. Anyway, if you want, give them something, just don't expect anything in return.'

At the party Mummy coddled Ram Singh and advised

everyone to encourage him to go home. Suddenly it was decided, and the next day Gharib Nawaz bought his ticket. The day of his departure, Shirin made him some food for the trip, and everyone went to the station to see him off. As the train pulled out, everyone stood waving until it disappeared.

I learned all this about the party ten days afterwards when I had to go to Pune on some important business. Nothing had changed at Sayeedah Cottage, which seemed like a caravanserai that stays the same even after thousands of travellers have stopped there, the type of place that never grew old. When I arrived, sweets were being distributed because Shirin had given birth to another boy. Vankatre had bought a Glaxo baby carriage for her new son. Finding it had been difficult but he had managed to procure two, one of which he kept for his own family. Chaddah stuffed the last two sweets into his mouth and said, 'So you got this Glaxo carriage—that's great. Just don't mention your damn father and beautiful wife.'

'You idiot, I don't drink any more,' Vankatre said, before adding, 'My wife speaks Urdu, you know—yes, by God—she's very pretty!'

Chaddah erupted in such obnoxious laughter that Vankatre couldn't say anything else. Then Chaddah, Gharib Nawaz, and Vankatre turned to me and we started to talk about the story I was writing for a film company there in Pune. Then we brainstormed for quite a while for a name for Shirin's baby. We thought of hundreds, but Chaddah didn't like any of them. At last I pointed out that the boy's birth was auspicious because he was born at Sayeedah Cottage and so suggested that his name should be Masud. Chaddah didn't like this either but for the time being accepted it.

It seemed that Chaddah, Gharib Nawaz, and Ranjit Kumar were out of sorts. I reasoned that it might be due to the change in weather or because of Shirin's new baby, but neither of those could explain it all. Or maybe it was the traumatic memory of Sen's murder. I didn't know why but everyone seemed sad—they were laughing and carrying on but inside they were upset.

I was busy writing at Harish's for a week. I often wondered why Chaddah didn't come by; neither did Vankatre. As for Ranjit Kumar, I wasn't close enough to him to expect him to travel out of his way to see me, and then I thought Gharib Nawaz might have gone to Hyderabad. Harish was around but he was probably over at his Punjabi heartthrob's house trying to build up the resolve to flirt with her in the presence of her hulk of a husband.

I was writing the story's most interesting part when Chaddah appeared from out of nowhere. As soon as he entered the room, he asked, 'Do you get anything for this nonsense?'

He was referring to my story. Two days earlier I had received my second payment, so I said, 'Yeah, I got the second instalment of 1,000 rupee two days ago.'

'Where is it?' Chaddah looked at my coat.

'In my pocket.'

Chaddah thrust his hand into my pocket, took out four hundred-rupee notes and said, 'Come to Mummy's tonight, there's a party.'

I was about to ask him the details but he left. He still seemed dejected and as though something was bothering him. I wondered what it might be, but my mind was absorbed in the scene I was writing and I soon forgot about his problems.

I updated Harish's wife on my wife's activities and left at about five. I arrived at Sayeedah Cottage at seven. Wet baby clothes hung on the clothesline, and Aqil and Shakil were playing with Shirin's older boy near the hand-pump. The garage's canvas curtain was pulled open and Shirin was talking to Aqil and Shakil, probably about Mummy. They stopped talking when they saw me. I asked after Chaddah, and Aqil said he was at Mummy's.

When I arrived at Mummy's, it was very loud and everyone was dancing—Gharib Nawaz with Polly, Ranjit Kumar with Kitty and Elma, and Vankatre with Thelma. Vankatre was instructing Thelma in the hand gestures of Kathakali. Chaddah was carrying Mummy in his arms and jumping around the room. Everyone was drunk and it was as if a storm had broken. Chaddah was the first to shout out his greetings to me and then there was a cannon-like burst of Indian and English voices, the echo reverberating in my ears. Mummy greeted me with genuine warmth. She took my hand and said, 'Kiss me, dear!'

But instead she kissed me on the cheek and then dragged me into the centre of the dancers. Chaddah cried out, 'Stop—it's time for drinking!' Then he shouted, 'Oh, Prince of Scotland! Bring a new bottle of whiskey.' The Prince of Scotland brought a new bottle. He was dead drunk. When he started to open the bottle, it fell and broke into pieces. Mummy wanted to scold him but Chaddah stopped her. 'It was only a bottle, Mummy,' he said. 'Forget it—there are people here with broken hearts.'

The party hit a lull, but then Chaddah got things going with his raucous laughter. Another bottle arrived, and everyone drank a strong shot. Chaddah began to deliver an incoherent speech, 'Ladies and gentlemen, you all may go to hell! Manto is here. He thinks he's a famous writer, an expert in human psychology. How should I put it, "He penetrates the deepest recesses of human psychology." But it's all nonsense! People like him are just the idiots who would lower themselves into a well—it's like lowering yourself into a well.' He looked around the room and then began again, 'It's too bad that there aren't any fishermen here. There's a Hyderabadi who says "khaf" when he should say "qaf" and who acts like he met you two days ago even though it was really ten years. To hell with his Nizam of Hyderabad and his tons of gold and tens of millions of jewels! But no, Mummy—yes—it's like lowering yourself into a well. What did I say but that it's all nonsense. In Punjabi we say that fools understand human psychology better than people like Manto. And that's what I'm talking about.'

Everyone shouted, 'Hurray!'

Chaddah continued, 'It's all a conspiracy! Manto's conspiracy! Like Herr Hitler, I signalled you all to shout, "Death! Death to you all!" But first, me—me—' He was extremely worked up. 'I—who that night got mad at Mummy over the girl with the platinum blonde hair—God knows what kind of Don Juan I took myself for. But, no, getting her wasn't hard at all. I swear by my youth that in a single kiss I could have sucked all the blessed purity straight out of her! But this was wrong. She was too young, so young, so weak, so characterless . . . so . . .' He looked at me with a questioning glance. 'Tell me, what would you call her in high-class Urdu, or Farsi, or Arabic? Characterless. Ladies and gentlemen, she was so young, so weak, and so characterless that if she had committed a sin that night, she would either have regretted it for as long as she lived or have forgotten it completely. Regardless, she would never have remembered it as pleasurable. This makes me sad. It was good that Mummy put an end to it right there. Now I'm just about done with this nonsense. I actually intended to deliver a longer speech, but I can't speak any more. I need another shot.'

He drank another shot. Everyone had been quiet during his speech, and they remained so afterwards. God knows what Mummy was thinking. She looked old and lost in thought. Chaddah seemed suddenly hollow. He wandered here and there, as if looking for some corner of his mind where he could safeguard something. I asked him, 'What's wrong, Chaddah?'

He broke out laughing and answered, 'Nothing—the thing is that today the whiskey isn't kicking in.' But his laughter was spiritless.

Vankatre pushed Thelma aside and made me sit down next to him. Soon enough, he began praising his father who he said had been a very accomplished man who had held audiences spellbound with his harmonium playing. Then he mentioned his wife's beauty and how his father had selected this girl for him to marry when he was still a child. When the Bengali music director, Sen's, name came up, he said, 'Mr Manto, he was a very bad man. He said he was a student of Khan Sahib Abdul Karim Khan, but that was a lie, an utter lie. Actually, he was some Bengali pimp's student.'

It was two in the morning, and Chaddah was sullen. He carelessly pushed aside Kitty, stepped forward, slapped Vankatre's pumpkin-shaped head and said, 'Stop talking nonsense. Get up and sing something. But watch out if you sing a classical raag . . .'

Vankatre began to sing rightaway, but his voice wasn't good and the notes weren't crisp. But whatever he sang, he sang very sincerely. In Malkos he sang two or three film songs that made everyone sad. Mummy and Chaddah looked at each other and then turned away. Gharib Nawaz was so touched that tears sprang from his eyes, and Chaddah laughed loudly and said, 'People from Hyderabad have weak tear ducts—they start leaking from time to time!'

Gharib Nawaz wiped away his tears and began to dance with Elma. Vankatre put a record on the gramophone's turntable and set the needle down. The song was an oldie. Chaddah picked up Mummy again and cavorted around the room, and his voice became hoarse, like those singing women who ruin their voices by wailing away at weddings.

This tumult lasted for two more hours, and Mummy had fallen silent. But then she turned to Chaddah and said, 'Okay, that's enough!'

Chaddah raised a bottle to his lips. He drained it, threw it to the side and said to me, 'Let's go, Manto, let's go.'

I got up. I wanted to say goodbye to Mummy, but Chaddah pulled me away, 'Today no one will say goodbye.'

We were leaving when I heard Vankatre begin to cry. I said to Chaddah, 'Wait, what's going on?' But he pushed me ahead and said, 'That bastard's tear ducts are defective too.'

On the way home Chaddah didn't say anything. I wanted to ask him about the strange party, but he said, 'I'm dead tired.' Once we got back to Sayeedah Cottage, he lay down on his bed and immediately fell asleep.

I woke the next morning and went to the bathroom. When I came out, I saw Gharib Nawaz next to the garage's canvas curtain. He was crying, and when he saw me, he wiped away his tears and started to walk away. But I went up to him and asked why he was crying. He said, 'Mummy left.'

'Where has she gone?'

'I don't know.' Then he turned toward the street.

Chaddah was lying on his bed. It looked as though he had not slept at all. When I asked him about Mummy, he smiled and said, 'She's gone. She had to leave Pune on the morning train.'

'Why?'

Chaddah was bitter. 'The government didn't like her being around. They didn't like the way she looked. They were against her parties. The police wanted to exploit her. They wanted to call her 'mum' and use her as a madam. There was an investigation into her activities, and finally, the police convinced the government and forced her to leave the city. They forced her out. If she was a prostitute, a madam, if her existence was a menace to society, then they should have killed her. Why did they tell her—the quote-unquote filth of Pune!—that she could go wherever she pleased as long as it wasn't here?' Chaddah laughed loudly but then fell silent. He began again in an emotional voice, 'I'm sorry, Manto. With this "filth" someone pure has left, the one who set me on the right path that night.

But I shouldn't be sorry. She's left Pune, and yet wherever she ends up, there'll be young men like me who have the same depraved passions. I entrust my Mummy to them. Long live Mummy! Long live . . .' He stopped abruptly. 'Let's go. We've got to find Gharib Nawaz. He must be weak from crying. These Hyderabadis have real weak tear ducts. They spring leaks from time to time.'

I noticed tears in Chaddah's eyes. They floated there like corpses on water.

SIRAJ

DHUNDHU was outside the Iranian restaurant across from the small park near the Nagpada Police Station, and he was leaning against the electricity pole that he manned from sunset until four in the morning. I don't know his real name but everyone called him Dhundhu, which was fitting because his job was to find girls that satisfied his customers' varied tastes. He had been a pimp for about ten years and in that time he had pimped thousands of girls of every religion, race, and temperament.

Since the beginning, he had been working from the same pole outside the Iranian restaurant across from the small park. It had become his symbol, so much so that the two were inseparable in my mind. Whenever I went by the pole and saw the white chuna lime and red kattha betel stains where people had wiped their fingers, I mistook it for Dhundhu chewing throat lozenges and betel paan.

Dhundhu was tall. The pole was too, and a mess of wires coiled at its top. One wire extended far across to another pole, where it merged with the entanglement of wires there. Another wire looped across to a building, and yet another went to a store. It seemed that this pole commanded a large area, and that its influence radiated out through other poles to encompass the entire city.

The Telephone Department had installed a box on the pole so that from time to time they could check to see if the wires were working. I often thought that Dhundhu was also a type of box, one there next to the pole to collect information about men's sexual desires. He knew all the rich men, both those in the surrounding neighbourhoods and in the far-flung ones, men who from time to time (or always) wanted to have sex, either to check if their plumbing still worked or to relieve stress.

He also knew all the girls in the trade. He knew everything about their bodies, as well as their temperaments—he knew very well which one was right for which customer at which time. There was only one, Siraj, whom he couldn't figure out.

Dhundhu had said to me many times, 'The bitch's crazy. Manto Sahib, I don't understand her. She's very moody. Sometimes she's all fire, and sometimes she's like ice. She cracks up laughing, and then suddenly she starts crying. The bitch can't get along with anyone. She fights with every trick. I've told her many times, "Look, straighten up, or go back to wherever you came from. Your clothes are rags. You have hardly any money for food. You know, fighting and cheating's not the way to get ahead." But she's a real live one. She doesn't listen to anyone.'

I had seen Siraj once or twice. She was really skinny but beautiful, and her prominent eyes overshadowed every other feature of her oval face. When I saw her for the first time on Clare Road, I was puzzled. I wanted to tell her eyes, 'Excuse me, please move aside a little so I can see Siraj.' Needless to say, it didn't happen.

She was small, and her body was like a carafe and her

spirit was like liquor so strong that someone had added water, although this adulteration strangely didn't make the liquid any less intoxicating but merely more abundant. Her body radiated allure.

Seeing her, I could guess she was upset. Her matted hair, sharp nose, clenched lips, and fingernails—which looked like the pointy tips of cartographers' pencils—advertised her irritable disposition. She seemed upset at Dhundhu, at the pole, at the customers he brought to her, but also at her big eyes and at her thin, long fingers, perhaps because she wanted to use them like cartographers employ their pencils to make something fine and yet she couldn't accomplish this. But this is the impression of a short story writer who in describing a tiny facial mole can make it seem as large as the sang-e-aswad in Mecca.

Listen to what Dhundhu had to say about her. One day he told me, 'Manto Sahib, Siraj, that bitch, got into a fight with a trick again today. I don't know what good deed God was rewarding me for, maybe it's just that I'm friends with the officers at the Nagpada Police Station. Anyway, thank God for small favours because otherwise I would certainly have been locked up. She made such a scene. I kept thinking, "Oh my God, oh my God, this is it."'

'What happened?'

'The same as always.' Then he continued, 'Afterwards I cursed my parents for having brought me into the world. Over and over I said to myself, "You bastard, you know what she's like—why bother? Is she your mother or sister?" I don't get her, Manto Sahib.'

We were sitting in the Iranian restaurant. Dhundhu poured his coffee-mixed tea into his saucer and slurped it down. Then he said, 'Actually, the thing is I've started to feel for her.'

'Why?'

'Who knows why. Hell, if I knew, wouldn't I try to stop?' He turned his cup upside down in his saucer and said, 'You've heard, right? She's still a virgin.'

I couldn't believe what he was saying. 'A virgin!'

'I swear.'

'No, no, Dhundhu,' I said, trying to get him to reconsider.

My disbelief upset him and he said, 'I'm not lying to you, Manto Sahib. She's really a virgin. Want to bet?'

'That's impossible.'

'Why?' Dhundhu asked full of confidence. 'Girls like Siraj can spend their entire lives as prostitutes and never get laid. The bitch doesn't let anyone touch her. I don't know that much about her, but I do know she's Punjabi. She was living with a madam on Lamington Road until she got kicked out for fighting with her tricks. She had managed to stay there for two or three months only because there were so many other girls. But, Manto Sahib, no one's going to feed you for free forever! The madam kicked her out with no more than what she was wearing, and she went to live with another madam on Faras Road. But she didn't listen to anyone there either, and she lost her shit in front of a trick. She stayed there for two or three months. But the bitch is still full of fire. Who's going to take the time to cool her off? God save her. Anyway, she went to live in a hotel in Khetwadi, but she made a scene there too. The manager got so fed up with her that he sent her packing. What should I say, Manto Sahib? The bitch doesn't think about food. Her clothes are full of lice, and she doesn't wash her hair for two months or more at a time. If she gets a joint or two from somewhere, she smokes them right up or goes to stand near some hotel so that she can listen to the film songs filtering out.'

These details are enough. I don't want to tell you what I thought because it's not relevant to the story. Just to string the conversation along, I asked, 'If she doesn't like what she's doing, then why don't you send her back? I'll even buy the ticket.'

'Manto Sahib, it's not about the fucking money!'

'So why don't you send her back?'

Dhundhu fell silent. He took a cigarette stub from behind his ear, lit it, and blew the smoke strongly through his nostrils. 'I don't want her to go.'

Then I understood. 'You love her?'

Dhundhu reacted immediately. 'How can you say things like that, Manto Sahib?' He pulled on his earlobes to show he was telling the truth. 'I swear on the Koran that I've never had any of those dirty thoughts. I only . . . ' He stopped. 'I only like her a little.'

'Why?'

Dhundhu gave the best answer possible. 'Because . . . because she's not like the others. All the other girls worship money—those are the bitches to watch out for. But this girl, she's really different. When I go get her, she never refuses. We agree on a price. We get into a taxi or the tram. But, Manto Sahib, tricks come for pleasure. They spend a little money and so they want to feel her up. Naturally they go for her breasts. Then she goes crazy. She starts hitting. If the guy's not the fighting sort, he leaves immediately. If he's drunk—or a bastard—then all hell breaks loose. I always have to go clean up her mess, give the guy his money back and grovel for forgiveness. I swear on the Koran I'd do this only for Siraj. And, Manto Sahib, I swear my business has been cut in half because of this bitch.'

I don't want to tell you what I thought about Siraj, and yet what Dhundhu said didn't square with my impression of her.

One day it occurred to me that I should meet Siraj on my own. She lived near Byculla Station in an extremely dirty neighbourhood dotted with garbage heaps that served as an open toilet. The city had built tin shacks there for the poor, and I won't mention the nearby high-rises because they have nothing to do with this story, only that in this world there will always be the rich and the poor.

Dhundhu had told me where her shack was, and I went to find it, feeling self-conscious about my nice clothes.

Anyway, I went. There was a goat tied up outside, and it began to bleat as soon as it saw me. An old woman came out, propping herself up with a cane, just like in the old stories when an old madam emerges from some hellhole. I was just about to turn away when I saw a pair of large eyes looking out from behind a sackcloth curtain full of holes. Her eyes looked sad, and I looked over her face and got angry. I don't know what she had been doing inside, but when she saw me she immediately came out, not even bothering to look at the old woman, and asked, 'How did you find me?'

'I wanted to meet you.'

'Come in.'

'No, come with me.'

When she heard this, the horrid old woman said coldly, 'It'll be ten rupees.'

I got out my wallet and gave the old woman the money. Then I said, 'Come on, Siraj.'

For a moment Siraj's large eyes relented. Her face opened up and again I saw how beautiful she was: it was a reserved beauty, a preserved beauty, like something protected for centuries in a grave, and I felt almost like I was in Egypt ready to excavate the old treasures there.

I don't want to get into the details, but Siraj was with me at a hotel. She was sitting in her filthy clothes right in front of me, and I couldn't stop looking at her eyes. They seemed to protect not just her face but her entire being—they cut her off from me and I had no idea what she was thinking. I had already given the old woman her money, but I gave Siraj forty rupees more. I wanted her to fight with me in the way I had heard she fought with others, and so I didn't say anything complimentary. And at the same time her eyes were frighteningly intense and penetrating, as though they could not only see right through me but through everyone.

She said nothing. In order to provoke her, I was going to have to force myself to do something nasty, and so I drank four shots of whisky. Then I came on to her in the offensive way that an ordinary trick would, but she didn't do anything to stop me. Then I did something very bad. I thought it would make her explode, but I was surprised to see it only calmed her. She got up and said, 'Get me a joint.'

'How about a drink?'

'No, I want a joint.'

I got her a joint, and she smoked it like a real addict. When she looked at me again, her eyes had lost their effect, and her face seemed like a ransacked empire, a ravaged country. There was a sense of desolation in everything about her, but what had brought it about? She seemed like a city attacked by invaders, a city so new that its walls, built up to only a yard in height, were left in incomplete ruins.

I was confused, so confused that it's best not to remember. I didn't want to know whether Siraj was a virgin or not, and yet I caught a glimpse of something in her sad and glassy eyes that was beyond description. I wanted to talk to her, but she wasn't interested at all. I wanted her to fight with me, but she disappointed me here too. I took her back to her house and went home.

Dhundhu was very angry when he found out about my secret mission. His feelings of friendship, as well as his sense of professionalism, were badly injured. He didn't give me a chance to explain but said, 'Manto Sahib, I didn't expect this from you.' Then he walked off.

When I didn't see him at his spot the next evening, I thought he might be sick, but he wasn't there the next day either.

A week passed. I thought of Dhundhu each morning and evening when I passed by the pole. I also went to look for Siraj in the filthy neighbourhood next to Byculla Station, but I found only the old madam. I asked about Siraj, and she tried instead to entice me in a sickening manner. Through her toothless grin she said, 'She's gone, but there are others. Do you want me to get one for you?'

I wondered why Dhundhu and Siraj were missing, and just after my secret meeting. I wasn't worried about whether I would see them again but only puzzled about their whereabouts. I didn't think they were in love. Dhundhu was above these things—he had a wife and three kids and loved them very much. But how was it that they disappeared at the same time?

I thought Dhundhu might have suddenly decided that Siraj should go home. Before he had been reluctant to consider this, but perhaps he had decided she should.

A month went by.

Then one evening I saw Dhundhu next to his pole, and I felt as though the electricity had come back after a long power outage, as though the pole had come alive and the telephone box too. Even the tangled wires seemed to be whispering in every direction. I walked up to him and he smiled.

We went to the Iranian restaurant. I didn't make him explain anything, and he ordered a coffee-tea mixture and a cup of tea for me. Then he positioned himself as though he were about to tell me something important, and yet instead he said, 'So what's new, Manto Sahib?'

'What's there to say, Dhundhu? Life goes on.'

Dhundhu smiled. 'Isn't that the truth—life goes on and will keep going on. But, hell, it's strange how life does that. To tell you the truth, everything about this world is strange.'

'I agree.'

The tea came and we started to drink. Dhundhu poured coffee-mixed tea into his saucer and said, 'Manto Sahib, Siraj told me everything. She said, "Your rich friend is crazy."'

I laughed. 'Why?'

Dhundhu answered, 'This is what she said, "He took me to a hotel and gave me some money. But he didn't act like a rich man."'

Her comments upon my clumsiness embarrassed me,

'I was actually there for another reason, Dhundhu.'

Dhundhu erupted in full-bellied laughter. 'I know! Please forgive me for getting angry with you that day.' Then he said in a friendly way, 'But all that's over with now.'

'All of what?'

'That bitch Siraj, who else?'

'What happened?'

Dhundhu told his story, all chopped up into pieces, 'The day she went with you, she came back and said, "I got forty rupees. Let's go, take me to Lahore." I said, "Bitch, what's come over you all of a sudden?" She said, "No, come with me, Dhundhu, you have to!" And, Manto Sahib, you know I couldn't refuse her. "Let's go," I said. So we got tickets and boarded the train. In Lahore we stayed at a hotel. She asked me to get her a burqa and so I did. She put it on and left immediately to wander around. Days passed. I said to myself, "Look at what's going on, Dhundhu. Siraj, that bitch, is just as crazy as before, and, hell, now you've gone crazy too, travelling to such a far-off place with her!"'

'Manto Sahib, one day we were riding in a tonga when she asked the driver to stop. She pointed to a man and said, "Dhundhu, bring that man to me. I'm going back to the hotel." I was at my wit's end. By the time I got out of the tonga, the man was walking away. I followed him. Thank God I can read people easily—we spoke for just a moment but I could tell he was a playboy. I said, "I have some special merchandise from Bombay." He said, "Let's go right now." I said, "No, show me your money." He showed me a lot of money, and I said to myself, "Okay, Dhundhu, why not do some business here?" But I couldn't understand why that bitch Siraj had chosen this man from out of all of those in Lahore. I said to myself, "It'll do." We got a tonga and went straight to the hotel. I told Siraj I had brought him. She said, "Wait a minute." So I waited. A little while later I took this good-looking man inside. That bastard reared like a colt when he saw Siraj, and Siraj grabbed him.'

Dhundhu poured his cold coffee-tea into his saucer, drank it in one gulp and then lit a bidi.

'Siraj grabbed him?'

Dhundhu raised his voice. 'Yes! She grabbed that bastard and said, "Where do you think you're going? Why did you force me to leave my home? I loved you, and you said you loved me. After we ran off from Amritsar, we came here and stayed in this very hotel, remember? And then you disappeared in the middle of the night and abandoned me. Why did you bring me here? Why did you convince me to run off with you? I was ready for anything, but you fled at the last moment. Come here. Now I've got you here again. I still love you. Come here." And, Manto Sahib, she threw herself on him. Tears started rolling down that bastard's cheeks. He begged for forgiveness, "It was wrong of me. I was scared. I'll never leave you again . . ." Who knows what he was blabbering. Then Siraj motioned for me to leave and I went out.

'In the morning I was sleeping on a cot when she woke me. "Let's go, Dhundhu," she said. "Where to?" "Back to Bombay." "What about that bastard?" "He's sleeping. I put my burqa over him."'

Dhundhu ordered another coffee-mixed tea, and then Siraj came in. Her face looked fresh and her large eyes were poised and calm.

MOZELLE

FOR the first time in four years, Trilochan found himself looking up at the night sky, and that was only because he had come out onto the terrace of the Advani Chambers to think things over in the open air.

The sky was completely clear but hung like an enormous ash-coloured tent over all of Bombay. For as far as he could see, lights burned through the night. It seemed to Trilochan as though countless stars had fallen from the heavens and had attached themselves to the buildings, which in the dark of the night loomed like enormous trees, around which the fallen stars glimmered like fireflies.

For Trilochan this was a completely new experience, a new plane of existence, to be out beneath the night sky. He realized that for four years he had lived caged in his apartment, oblivious to one of nature's greatest gifts. It was about three o'clock, and the wind was delightfully light. Trilochan had grown used to the electric fan's artificial breeze, which oppressed his very existence: every morning he got up feeling as though someone had been pummelling him all night long. But now he felt rejuvenated, as the morning's fresh breeze washed over his body. He had come up to the terrace feeling anxious, but after only half an hour, the tension had eased. He could now think clearly.

Kirpal Kaur lived with her family in a neighbourhood known for its fanatic Muslims. Many houses had already been burned, and several people had died. Trilochan felt it was no longer safe for them to live there, but a curfew was in effect and no one knew how long it would last, maybe forty-eight hours. He felt he could do nothing because he was surrounded by Muslims of the most violent sort. Then troubling news reports were coming one after another from the Punjab saying that Sikhs were terrorizing Muslims. At any moment, any Muslim could very easily seize delicate Kirpal Kaur's wrist and lead her to her death.

Her mother was blind. Her father was paralysed. And her brother was staying in Deolali to supervise his newly acquired construction contracts there.

Trilochan was very upset with Niranjan, Kirpal Kaur's brother. Trilochan read the paper every day and had told Niranjan a full week before about the intensity of the sectarian violence, advising him in clear words, 'Niranjan, drop this small-time contracting work. We're passing through a very delicate time. Whatever your obligations are here, you really have to leave. Come to my place. No doubt there's less space there, but we can find a way to get by.'

But Niranjan hadn't listened. He had let Trilochan finish his lecture, then smiled through his thick beard and said, 'Hey, you're worrying for no reason. I've seen a lot of this sort of thing here. This isn't Amritsar or Lahore. It's Bombay, Bombay! You've been here for, what, four years? I've been living here for twelve years, twelve years!'

Who knows what Niranjan took Bombay to be. He must have thought the city kept some charm so that when violence broke out, it would quell itself. Or he thought it was like a mythical fort, upon which no harm could be wreaked.

But in the cool morning breeze, Trilochan could clearly see that the neighbourhood was not safe at all. He was even preparing himself mentally to read in the morning papers that Kirpal Kaur and her parents had already been killed.

Trilochan actually didn't care about Kirpal Kaur's paralysed father and blind mother. If they died and Kirpal Kaur escaped, it would suit him just fine. And if Niranjan was killed in Deolali, it would be even better because then no obstacle would remain. At the moment Niranjan sat like a boulder in his path, and so whenever Trilochan got the chance to talk to Kirpal Kaur, instead of calling him Niranjan Singh he would call him 'Boulder' Singh.

The morning breeze blew slowly over Trilochan's close-cropped hair, pleasantly chilling it. But his worries wouldn't subside. Kirpal Kaur had just entered his life. Unlike her brother, she was very gentle and delicate. She had grown up in the countryside but hadn't absorbed that hardness, that wear and tear, that manliness, usually found in Sikh country girls who spend their lives moving from one strenuous labour to the next.

She had a slim figure, as if she still hadn't filled out. She had small breasts, which would have been more pleasant if plumper. In comparison to average Sikh country girls, her skin was fair, more like the colour of raw cotton, and her body was glossy like the texture of mercerized clothes. She was extremely shy.

They were from the same village, but Trilochan hadn't spent much time there. He had left for high school in the city, where he had begun to live permanently. After high school he had enrolled at college, and while during those years he had gone to his village countless times, he had never heard of Kirpal Kaur, probably because he was always in a hurry to get back to town as soon as possible.

Then his college days had become a distant memory. Ten years had passed since he had last seen his college hostel, and in that time many strange and interesting events had taken place in Trilochan's life: Burma—Singapore—Hong Kong—then Bombay, where he had been living for four years.

And in these four years, this was the first time he had seen the clear night's sky. A thousand lights glowed, and the breeze was pleasant and light.

While thinking about Kirpal Kaur, Trilochan thought of Mozelle, a Jewish girl who had lived in the Advani Chambers. Trilochan had fallen hopelessly in love with her, a kind of love he had never experienced in his thirty-five years.

He crossed paths with Mozelle the very day he got an apartment on the second floor of the Advani Chambers through the help of one of his Christian friends. At first she seemed frighteningly crazy. Her bobbed brown hair was in irremediable disarray, and her lipstick, cracked in spots, clung to her lips like clotted blood. She was wearing a loose white gown whose open collar revealed a generous view of her breasts, large and marked with blue veins. Her upper arms, which were bare, were covered with a dusting of extremely fine hairs as though she had just come from a beauty salon where during her haircut these hairs had fallen onto her arms to stick like crushed nuts on sweets.

But more than anything, her lips held his attention: they weren't that thick, but she had smeared burgundy lipstick across them in such a way that they seemed as fat and as red as chunks of buffalo meat.

Trilochan's apartment was directly opposite Mozelle's and only a narrow corridor separated their doors. Trilochan was walking towards his door when Mozelle came out from her apartment wearing wooden sandals. Trilochan heard their sound and stopped. Through her dishevelled hair, Mozelle looked at him and laughed, and this unnerved Trilochan. He took the key from his pocket and quickly started towards his door, but as they passed each other Mozelle slipped and fell on the slick cement.

Before Trilochan realized it, Mozelle was lying on top of him with her long gown at her waist and her naked, fleshy legs on either side of him. Trilochan tried to get up, but in his embarrassment he only entangled himself further with Mozelle, as if her body were coated with a soapy lather and he couldn't find a grip.

Panting, Trilochan apologized earnestly. Mozelle adjusted her gown and smiled, 'These sandals are completely worthless.' Then she recovered her lost sandal, fit it between her big toe and the toe next to it, got up, and went down the corridor.

Trilochan thought it might not be easy to get to know Mozelle, but she opened up to him very quickly. And yet she was very self-centred, and she gave no weight to what he said or did. He bought her food and drinks, treated her to movies, and stayed with her all day when she went swimming at Juhu Beach. But when he wandered beyond her arms or lips, she scolded him. He became so subservient that he waited on her hand and foot and catered to her every whim. Trilochan had never been in love. In Lahore, Burma, and Singapore, he had gone to prostitutes, but he had never imagined that as soon as he reached Bombay, he would fall deeply in love with a careless, self-centred Jewish girl. Whenever he asked her to the movies, she would immediately get ready. But after they reached their seats in the theatre, she would start glancing through the crowd and if she spotted any of her acquaintances, she would wave vigourously and without asking for Trilochan's permission go and sit by them.

On other occasions they would be at a restaurant, and Trilochan would order a huge spread just for her. But if she saw one of her close friends, she would leave in the middle of eating, and Trilochan could only watch and fume.

Mozelle would often infuriate him when she would callously leave him to go out with her close friends and then not come back for days, sometimes on the excuse of a headache, and sometimes an upset stomach, although Trilochan knew hers to be as strong as steel.

When she ran into him again, she would say, 'You're a Sikh. You can't understand these delicate matters.'

Trilochan would burn with anger. 'Which delicate matters? Your ex-lovers'?'

Putting her hands on her wide hips, Mozelle would spread her powerful legs and say, 'Why do you keep on bringing them up? Yes, they're my friends and I like them. If you're jealous, then be jealous.'

In a pleading manner, Trilochan would ask, 'How long will we last like this?'

Mozelle would laugh loudly. 'You really *are* a Sikh! Idiot!

Who told you we were together? If you're so concerned about having a lover, go back to wherever you're from and marry some Sikh girl. I don't care what you say, I'm not changing.'

Trilochan would yield. Mozelle had become his big weakness, and he always wanted to be with her. And yet she often humiliated him in front of worthless Christian boys. While the usual reaction to humiliation and insult is revenge, for Trilochan this wasn't the case. Many times he made himself forget what she said and forgive her for how she acted. It didn't matter because he loved her—not just loved her, but as he had told his friends over and over he was completely head over heels in love with her. There was nothing left to do but relinquish himself heart and soul to love's quagmire.

For two years he suffered like this. At last one day, when Mozelle was in a giddy mood, he threw his arms around her and asked, 'Mozelle, don't you love me?'

Mozelle shook herself free, sat down in a chair, and began looking at the hem of her gown. Then she raised her big Jewish eyes, batted her thick eyelashes and said, 'I can't love a Sikh.'

Trilochan felt as though someone had tucked a bunch of burning coals into his turban. He flew into a rage.

'Mozelle, you always make fun of me. But it's not me you're making fun of, it's my love!'

Mozelle got up and, in her alluring way, shook her well-trimmed brown hair. 'Shave your beard and let your hair down. If you do this, guys are going to wink at you—you're beautiful.'

This spurred Trilochan into action. He strode forward,

brusquely drew Mozelle to him, and pressed his lips against hers.

'Don't!' said Mozelle, as she pushed him away, disgusted. 'I already brushed my teeth this morning. Don't trouble yourself.'

'Mozelle!' Trilochan cried out.

Mozelle took out a small mirror from her purse and looked at her lips where she saw scratches on her thickly laid lipstick. 'I swear, you don't know how to put your beard to good use. It could really clean my navy blue skirt. I'd only have to apply a little detergent.'

Trilochan became so angry that he gave up. He sat down calmly on the sofa, and Mozelle came and sat beside him. She let down his beard, sticking the pins one by one between her teeth.

Trilochan was beautiful. Before his beard had started to grow, people always mistook him for a striking young girl. But now his beard hid his features beneath its bushy mass. He knew it obscured his beauty, but he was obedient and respected his religion. He didn't want to lose those things that showed his faith was complete.

After Mozelle finished letting out his beard, Trilochan asked her, 'What are you doing?'

With the pins between her teeth, she smiled. 'Your beard is very soft. I was wrong to say it could clean my navy blue skirt. Triloch, shave it off and give me the clippings and I'll weave them into a first-class coin purse.'

Trilochan could feel his face turning red with anger beneath his beard. In a deliberate voice, he said, 'I've never made fun of your religion, so why do you make fun of mine? Look, it's not nice to do that. I would never tolerate it except I'm helplessly in love with you. Don't you know this?'

Mozelle stopped playing with his heard. 'I know.'

'And so?'

Trilochan drew his beard together neatly and took the pins from between Mozelle's teeth. 'You know my love isn't nonsense. I want to marry you.'

'I know.' Giving her hair a light toss, she got up and began looking at a painting hung on the wall. 'And I've nearly decided to say yes.'

Trilochan jumped up. 'Really?'

Mozelle's red lips grew into a broad smile, and her white teeth sparkled for an instant. 'Yes.'

With his beard half folded, Trilochan squeezed her to his chest and said, 'So—so—when?'

Mozelle pushed herself away. 'When you cut your hair and shave.'

Trilochan was resigned to his fate. Without thinking, he said, 'I'll get it cut tomorrow.'

Mozelle began to do a tap dance. 'You're talking nonsense, Triloch. You're not that courageous.'

Suddenly religion was the last thing on his mind. 'You'll see.'

'I *will* see,' Mozelle repeated. Quickly she came up to Trilochan, kissed him on his beard, and left, grimacing.

It is impossible to describe how much Trilochan suffered that night as he thought about getting his hair cut. The next day in a Fort barbershop he got his hair cut and beard shaved. He kept his eyes clamped shut throughout the proceedings. When the business was finally over, he opened his eyes and stared for a long time in a mirror—now he would draw the attention of even the most beautiful girls in Bombay!

Trilochan felt the same strange coldness he had felt after leaving the barbershop. He began to pace back and forth on the terrace over to where there were a number of water pipes and tanks. He didn't want to remember the rest of the story, but he couldn't stop himself.

The first day after getting his hair cut, Trilochan didn't leave his apartment. The second day he sent a note to Mozelle through his servant saying he was sick and asking if she could come by for a moment. Mozelle came. Seeing Trilochan, she stopped short. 'My darling Triloch!' she cried out before throwing herself onto him and kissing him so much that his face turned red from her lipstick.

She stroked Trilochan's soft, clean cheeks, ran her fingers like a comb through his short English-style hair, and began babbling in Arabic. She was so emotional that her nose began to run. When she noticed this, she took up her skirt's hem and used it as a handkerchief. This embarrassed Trilochan, and he drew her skirt down and reproached her, 'You should really wear something down there.'

His words didn't have any effect on Mozelle. She smiled, her lips smeared with stale and spotty lipstick, and then she said, 'They make me uncomfortable. This way's better.'

The memory flashed through his mind of how that first day he had run into her and the strange mix-up that had followed. He smiled and drew her to his chest. 'Let's get married tomorrow.'

'Of course,' Mozelle said, rubbing the back of her hand over his soft chin.

It was decided that the wedding would be in Pune. Because it was a civil marriage, they had to give ten to fifteen days' notice. This was a legality. Pune was the best place for the marriage as it was close to Bombay and Trilochan had some friends there. They decided to leave for Pune the very next day.

Mozelle was a salesgirl in a store in the Fort. There was a taxi stand near her store where she asked him to wait. Trilochan arrived at the agreed upon hour and waited for an hour and a half, but Mozelle didn't show up. The next day he learned that she had left for Deolali with an old friend who had just bought a brand-new car and that she was going to stay there for a while.

What happened then to Trilochan? That is a very long story. The short version is that he drew up his courage and resolved to forget her. Soon after that, he met Kirpal Kaur and fell in love with her. Then he realized that Mozelle was nothing more than a wild girl with a cold heart who jumped from here to there like a bird. At least, he consoled himself, he hadn't made the mistake of marrying her.

Despite this he would think about Mozelle from time to time. These were bittersweet moments: she didn't care about anyone's feelings, but Trilochan still liked her, and so he couldn't help but wonder what she was doing in Deolali—whether she was still with the guy with the new car or if she had left him and was with someone else. Regardless, it was painful for Trilochan to think that she was living with someone other than him, but at the same time such behaviour was nothing but in character.

He had spent not just hundreds but thousands of rupees on her. But he had done so willingly, and furthermore

Mozelle's tastes weren't expensive. She liked cheap things. Once Trilochan took her to get some earrings he had picked out for her, but when they got to the store, Mozelle became fascinated with a pair of gaudy, cheap imitation ones, and rejecting Trilochan's favourites, begged him to buy the others instead.

Trilochan really couldn't understand Mozelle. They would spend hours kissing, and he would run his hands all over her body. But she never let him go further. To irritate him, she would say, 'You're a Sikh. I hate you.'

It was obvious that Mozelle didn't hate him. If she had, she would never have agreed to spend time with him. She didn't put up with things she didn't like, and so the thought of her spending two years hanging out with him and hating every minute of it was ridiculous. Mozelle made up her own mind about things. For example, she didn't like underwear because they felt tight. On many occasions Trilochan had stressed their absolute necessity and even tried to shame her into wearing them, but she never reformed her ways.

When Trilochan raised the subject, she would get irritated and say, 'This shame-blame stuff is nonsense. If you get offended, close your eyes. Tell me, you're naked underneath your clothes, and so where are the clothes to cover that up? Where are the clothes that can prevent you from imagining what's underneath? Don't give me that crap. You're a Sikh. I know you wear those silly baggy underpants. They're a part of your religion—just like your beard and your hair. You should be ashamed. You're an adult but still think your religion is hidden in your underpants.'

When they had first met and Mozelle said things like this, Trilochan would get angry, but as time passed he started to consider what she was saying, and sometimes his prejudices gave way. Then, after getting his hair cut, he was overcome by the feeling of how much time he had wasted carrying around his heavy mess of hair.

Trilochan stopped near the water tanks. He cursed Mozelle and forced himself to stop thinking about her. Kirpal Kaur, pure and innocent Kirpal Kaur, whom he loved, was in danger. She lived in a neighbourhood full of the most violent sort of Muslims and already two or three incidents had taken place. The problem was that there was a forty-eight-hour curfew in effect. And yet who really cared about that? Muslims living in her building could very easily kill her and her parents at any time.

Concentrating on this, Trilochan sat down on a large water pipe. His hair had grown out, and he was sure that in under a year it would look as though he had never cut it. His beard had grown fast as well. Nonetheless, he didn't keep it as long as he used to, and there was a barber in the Fort who trimmed it so neatly that it looked as though it was untouched.

He stroked his long, soft hair and sighed deeply. He was about to get up when he heard the hard slap of wooden sandals. He wondered who it might be, as there were many Jewish women in the building and they all wore the same wooden sandals when at home. The noise grew closer. Then he glimpsed Mozelle near the next water tank—she was wearing the special loose gown of Jewish women and, with both arms raised above her head, was stretching in such a sexy way that Trilochan felt as though the air itself would shatter.

Trilochan got up from the water pipe and asked himself, 'Where in the hell did she come from? What's she up to now?'

Mozelle stretched again, and Trilochan's bones throbbed with desire.

Mozelle's large breasts heaved beneath her loose gown, and suddenly the thought of their delicate veins flashed through Trilochan's mind. He coughed loudly. Mozelle turned and looked in his direction but didn't seem surprised at all. She approached him, and her sandals clapped against the ground. Once she reached him, she looked at his dwarfish beard and asked, 'You've become a Sikh again, Trilochan?'

His face began to burn.

Mozelle came forward and rubbed the back of her hand against his chin. Then she smiled. 'Now this brush could clean my navy blue skirt! But I left that in Deolali.'

Trilochan didn't respond.

Mozelle pinched his arm. 'Why don't you say something, Sardar Sahib?'

Trilochan didn't want to be made foolish again, but he couldn't help but look searchingly at her. No special change had taken place, other than how she looked a little weaker. 'Have you been sick?'

'No,' Mozelle said and gave her bobbed hair a light shake.

'You look weaker than before.'

'I'm on a diet.' Mozelle sat down on the water pipe and began to rap her sandals against the ground. 'So you're trying to be a Sikh again?'

'Yes,' Trilochan said nonchalantly.

'Congratulations!' Mozelle took off one of her sandals and beat it against the water pipe. 'Have you fallen in love with some other girl?'

'Yes,' Trilochan said flatly.

'Congratulations. Is it someone in this building?'

'No.'

'That's really wrong.' Fixing her sandal, Mozelle got up. 'You should always give first consideration to your neighbours.'

Trilochan remained silent. Mozelle got up and tickled his beard with all five fingers. 'Did she tell you to grow it out?'

'No.'

Trilochan felt uneasy, as though he were unsnarling his beard with a comb, and when he said 'no', there was a curt edge to it.

Mozelle's red lipstick made her lips look like old meat. When she smiled, Trilochan felt as though he had entered a village butcher shop where the butcher had just cut a thick-veined piece of meat in two.

Then she laughed. 'Now if you shave your beard, I swear I'll marry you.'

Trilochan wanted to tell Mozelle how much he loved Kirpal Kaur and how he was going to marry her, and how in comparison to her, Mozelle was wanton, ugly, faithless, and unkind. But he wasn't spiteful. 'Mozelle, I've already decided to get married to a simple girl from my village who upholds our religion. For her sake I've decided to grow out my hair.'

Mozelle usually didn't spend any time thinking about details, but she reflected for a moment and after pivoting on one of her sandals, she asked, 'If she obeys your religion, then how can she accept you? Doesn't she know you've already cut your hair?'

'She doesn't know yet,' Trilochan admitted. 'Right after you left for Deolali, I started to grow out my beard, just to spite you. Then I met Kirpal Kaur. I do up my turban in a way so that even one man in a hundred has a hard time telling I cut my hair. Anyway, it's going to grow back very soon.' Trilochan ran his fingers through his hair.

Mozelle lifted her long gown and scratched her pale voluptuous thigh. 'That's good. But look at this stupid mosquito! See how hard it bit me!'

Trilochan turned his gaze away from her. With her finger, Mozelle applied saliva to where the mosquito had bitten her and then let go of her gown and stood up. 'When's the wedding?'

'I don't know yet,' Trilochan said before suddenly becoming pensive.

For several seconds Mozelle didn't speak. Then noticing his worried demeanour, she asked in a very serious manner, 'Trilochan, what are you thinking about?'

At that moment Trilochan needed someone to talk to. Even Mozelle would do. He told her about the danger Kirpal Kaur was in, and then Mozelle laughed and said, 'You're a first-class idiot! Go get her! What's hard about that?'

'Hard? Mozelle! You would never understand the delicacy of this situation, the delicacy of any situation. You're so careless. That's why our relationship didn't work out, something I'll be sorry about forever.'

Mozelle banged her sandal against the water pipe. 'To hell with your regret! Stupid idiot. You should be thinking about how to get your what's-her-name out of there, but you sat down to cry about the old days. We would never have lasted. You're a silly coward and I need a fearless man. But enough of that. Come on, let's go rescue your girl.'

She grabbed Trilochan's arm. 'From where?' he asked in fear.

'From where she lives. I know that neighbourhood inch by inch. Come on.'

'But listen! There's a curfew.'

'Not for Mozelle. Come on.'

She grabbed Trilochan's arm and pulled him towards the door leading to the stairs. She was about to open the door and go down the stairs when she stopped and looked at Trilochan's beard.

'What?' Trilochan asked.

'Your beard. But it's okay. It's not that big. If you don't wear a turban, no one will take you for a Sikh.'

'Don't wear a turban?' Trilochan was taken aback. 'I won't go without a turban.'

'Why?' Mozelle asked, feigning ignorance.

Trilochan pushed back some stray hairs. 'You don't understand. I have to wear it there.'

'Why?'

'Why don't you understand? Up till now she hasn't seen me without my turban. She doesn't know I've cut my hair, and I don't want her to know.'

Mozelle rapped her sandal against the door's threshold. 'You really are an idiot. Stupid ass! It's a matter of life and death for your what's-her-face.'

Trilochan tried to explain, 'Mozelle, she's a very religious girl. If she sees me without a turban, she'll hate me.'

This irritated Mozelle. 'Ah, screw your love! I wonder if all Sikhs are so stupid. Her life's in danger and you're insisting on wearing a turban—and maybe your silly underwear too?'

'I always wear it.'

'Good for you! But we're going to a neighbourhood where it's Muslim after Muslim and they're not the type you want to mess with. If you wear a turban, you'll be slaughtered the moment you get there.'

Trilochan responded curtly, 'I don't care. If I go, I'm going to wear a turban. I'm not going to risk losing her love.'

This incensed Mozelle. She writhed in anger, and her breasts twitched and trembled. 'You ass, what will her love matter if you're dead? What's your slut's name? When she's dead—and her family's dead as well—then, well, you really are a Sikh. I swear to God, you're a Sikh and a real dumb one too!'

Trilochan was furious. 'Stop talking nonsense!'

Mozelle cackled. She put her arms around Trilochan's neck and swung lightly from side to side. 'Okay, darling, as you wish. Go and put on your turban. I'll be waiting for you outside.'

She began to walk downstairs. Trilochan called out, 'You're not going to put on any other clothes?'

Mozelle shook her head. 'No, I'm okay like this.'

She continued walking down, her sandals slapping against the stairs. Trilochan listened to her reach the last stair, then he smoothed back his long hair and descended towards his apartment. Inside he changed his clothes quickly. His turban was already made up. He fixed it carefully into place, locked the door, and went downstairs.

Outside on the pavement, Mozelle had her sturdy legs spread wide and was smoking just as a man would. When Trilochan approached, she mischievously blew a mouthful of smoke in his face. 'You're really awful,' Trilochan said angrily.

Mozelle smiled. 'That's not very original. I've heard that before.' Then she looked at Trilochan's turban. 'You've really tied it up well. It looks like you still have all your hair.'

The market was completely deserted. The wind blew so slowly that it seemed as though it, too, was afraid of the curfew. Lamps were lit but their light seemed sickly. Usually at that hour the streets would spring to life, as the trams started up and people began to come and go, but now it was so quiet it seemed as though no one had ever used this road and never would.

Mozelle was walking ahead. Her sandals clattered against the pavement and their noise echoed through the silence. Beneath his breath Trilochan was cursing her for not having taken two minutes to change out of her stupid sandals. He wanted to tell her to take them off and walk barefoot, but he knew she wouldn't listen.

Trilochan was so terrified that when a leaf stirred, his heart lurched, and yet Mozelle walked ahead fearlessly, puffing on her cigarette as though she were enjoying a thoughtless stroll.

They reached an intersection and a police officer's voice burst upon them, 'Hey, where're you going?'

Trilochan flinched. Mozelle approached the policeman, and once she reached him she gave her hair a light shake and said, 'Oh, you—don't you recognize me? It's Mozelle.' Then she pointed down an alley. 'There, over there. My sister lives there. She's not feeling well. I'm bringing a doctor.'

The officer was trying to remember Mozelle, when from God knows where she took out a pack of cigarettes and offered him one, 'Here, have a cigarette.'

The officer accepted. Mozelle took the cigarette from her mouth and extended it towards the officer. 'Let me give you a light.'

The officer took a drag. Mozelle winked at the officer with one eye and at Trilochan with the other, and rapping her sandals against the ground, she set off for the alley leading to Kirpal Kaur's neighbourhood.

It seemed to Trilochan that Mozelle got a strange pleasure from defying the curfew, and it was true that she liked to play dangerous games. When they used to go to Juhu Beach, she was a headache. She would dash against the ocean's enormous waves, swimming out so far that Trilochan feared she would drown. When she came back, her body always had bruises all over it, and yet she didn't care.

Mozelle forged ahead, and Trilochan followed, surveying from side to side skittishly, fearful that a knife-wielding assailant would spring upon him. Mozelle stopped, and when Trilochan caught up with her, she explained, 'Triloch, dear. Being scared like this doesn't help. If you're scared, something bad will certainly happen. Believe me, I'm talking from experience.'

Trilochan remained silent.

Leaving one alley, they made for one that led directly into Kirpal Kaur's neighbourhood. Mozelle stopped abruptly. A little way ahead, people were looting a Marwari's shop. She considered the scene and then said, 'It's nothing. Let's go.'

They set off. Suddenly a man carrying a large brass basin on his head ran into Trilochan, and the basin fell. The man looked Trilochan up and down and realized Trilochan was a Sikh. Quickly, he reached for something inside his waistband, but Mozelle stumbled forward as if in a drunken stupor and rammed into him. 'Hey, what're you doin'?' she asked in a drunken voice. 'You wanna hit your own brother? I'm gonna marry him.' Then she turned to Trilochan. 'Karim! Pick up the basin and put it on this man's head.'

The man withdrew his hand from his waistband and leered lasciviously at Mozelle; then he went up to her and nudged her breasts with his elbow. 'Enjoy yourself, lady. Enjoy yourself.' Then he picked up the basin and ran off down the road.

'How rude, the dirty bastard,' Trilochan muttered.

Mozelle rubbed her breasts. 'It wasn't that bad. Shit happens. Come on, let's go.'

She set off quickly and Trilochan hurried after her.

After passing through this alley, they found themselves in Kirpal Kaur's neighbourhood. 'Which alley is it?' Mozelle asked.

'Third alley—corner building.'

Mozelle started off in that direction. The road was completely empty. The buildings were crammed full of people, but not even the cry of a baby could be heard.

When they approached the alley, they saw something suspicious ahead: a man rushed from a building to disappear into a building on the opposite side. After a little while, three men emerged from this building. They glanced back and forth over the pavement and then raced into the first building. Mozelle stopped. She motioned to Trilochan to step into the shadows. Then she whispered to him, 'Triloch, dear, take off your turban.'

'I'll never take it off, never.'

Mozelle twitched with anger. 'Whatever. But don't you see what's happening?'

What was happening was easy to see—something fishy was going on. When Mozelle saw two men coming from the building on her right carrying gunnysacks on their backs, she quivered with fear—a thick liquid was dripping from the sacks. Mozelle bit her lips, thinking. When these two men disappeared into the alley's mouth, she told Trilochan, 'Okay, this is what we're going to do. I'm going to run to the corner building. You come after me like you're chasing me, okay? But we're going to have to do this fast.'

Mozelle didn't wait for Trilochan's answer but took off running for the corner building, and Trilochan ran after her. In a matter of seconds they were inside the building. Next to the stairs, Trilochan gasped for breath, but Mozelle was just fine.

'Which floor?' she asked.

Trilochan ran his tongue over his dry lips. 'The second.'

'Let's go.'

Then she clambered up the stairs, and Trilochan followed her. Blood stained the stairs, and seeing this, Trilochan went numb.

Once he reached the second floor, Trilochan went down the corridor, stopped in front of a door, and quietly knocked. Mozelle remained next to the stairs. He knocked again, put his mouth to the door. 'Mahanga Singhji! Mahanga Singhji!'

'Who is it?' a faint voice said from inside.

'Trilochan.'

The door opened slowly. Trilochan signalled to Mozelle. She came quickly, and both went inside. Mozelle found herself standing next to a skinny, terrified girl, and for a moment Mozelle stared at her. She was very slight and her nose was very beautiful, but she seemed to be suffering from a cold. Mozelle hugged her against her broad chest and wiped Kirpal Kaur's nose with the hem of her loose gown.

Trilochan blushed.

Mozelle spoke tenderly to Kirpal Kaur, 'Don't be scared. Trilochan's here.'

Kirpal Kaur looked at Trilochan with terrified eyes and then separated herself from Mozelle.

'Tell your father to get ready quickly, and your mother, too,' Trilochan instructed her.

Then, from the floor above they heard loud voices and someone crying out as though mixed up in a fracas.

Kirpal Kaur emitted a stifled cry from her throat, 'They took her.'

'Who?' Trilochan asked.

Kirpal Kaur was about to answer when Mozelle grabbed her by the arm and dragged her into a corner. 'Good for her,' she said. 'Now take off your clothes.'

Kirpal Kaur hadn't had time to react before Mozelle quickly pulled off the girl's blouse and put it aside. Mortified, Kirpal Kaur tried to hide herself behind her arms. Trilochan looked away. Mozelle took off her loose gown and put it on Kirpal Kaur. Now Mozelle was completely nude. Very quickly, she loosened the drawstring of Kirpal Kaur's pants, took them off, and then said to Trilochan, 'Go, get her out of here! No, wait!' She unfastened Kirpal Kaur's hair and then said, 'Go. Get out of here.'

'Come on,' Trilochan said. But then he suddenly stopped and turned toward Mozelle, who was standing shamelessly naked. The hairs on her arms were standing on end from the cold.

'Why aren't you going?' Mozelle asked with irritation.

'What about her parents?'

'To hell with them. Get her out of here.'

'And you?'

'I'm coming.'

Suddenly from the floor above them, a bunch of men clambered down the stairs. They came up to the door and began to pound on it as if they were going to break it down.

Kirpal Kaur's blind mother and paralysed father lay moaning in the next room.

Mozelle thought for a moment, gave her hair a light toss and said to Trilochan, 'Listen. I can think of only one thing. I'm going to open the door.'

A stifled cry fell from Kirpal Kaur's lips, 'Door!'

Mozelle instructed Trilochan, 'I'm going to open the door and go out. Run after me. I'm going to run up the stairs and you come too. Whoever's at the door will forget everything and follow us.'

'Then?'

'Your what's-her-name—this is her chance to escape. No one will say anything to her dressed like that.'

Trilochan quickly explained everything to Kirpal Kaur. Mozelle yelled loudly, opened the door, and rushed out.

She fell among the men outside. They were so startled they didn't react, and she immediately got up and climbed up the staircase. Trilochan ran after her, and the men gave way.

Mozelle blindly raced up the staircase. She was still wearing her wooden sandals. The men regained their composure and set off after them. Mozelle slipped. She fell down the staircase, hitting each hard stair and ramming against the iron railing. She landed in the corridor below.

Trilochan immediately came back down the stairs. He bent down and saw blood running from her nose, mouth, and ears. The men gathered around them, but none of them asked what had happened. Everyone was quiet, as they looked at Mozelle's pale, naked body, cut up everywhere.

Trilochan shook her arm. 'Mozelle! Mozelle!'

Mozelle opened her big Jewish eyes, red with blood, and smiled.

Trilochan took off his turban, unwrapped it, and covered her naked body. Mozelle smiled and winked at Trilochan as blood bubbled from her mouth.

'Go, find out whether my underwear is there, I mean . . .'

Trilochan understood, but he didn't want to get up. This angered Mozelle, and she said, 'You're a real Sikh! Go and see.'

Trilochan got up and returned to Kirpal Kaur's apartment. Through her dimming eyes, Mozelle looked at the crowd and said, 'He's a Muslim, but because he's so tough, I call him a Sikh.'

Trilochan came back, and his look told Mozelle that Kirpal Kaur had already left. Mozelle sighed in relief, and a tide of blood gushed from her mouth.

'Oh, damn it!' she said, and wiped her mouth with the back of her wrist. Then she turned to Trilochan. 'All right, darling—bye bye . . .'

Trilochan wanted to say something, but the words stuck in his throat.

Mozelle removed Trilochan's turban. 'Take it away—this religion of yours,' she said, and her arm fell dead across her powerful chest.

MAMMAD BHAI

IF you walked from Faras Road down what people called White Alley, you would find some restaurants at its end. Restaurants are everywhere in Bombay, but these ones were special because the area is known for prostitutes.

Times have changed. It was almost twenty years ago that I used to frequent those restaurants. If you went past White Alley, you would come to the Playhouse where movies were shown all day. Lively crowds swarmed outside its four theatres, and men rounded up customers by ringing bells in an ear-splitting fashion and yelling, 'Come in—come in—two annas—a first-class film—two annas!' Sometimes these bell ringers would even forcibly push people inside.

There were masseurs, too, who knocked their customers' heads around with what they claimed was a very scientific method. Getting a massage is all fine and well, but I don't understand why people in Bombay are so enamoured of it, why all day and night they feel the need for an oil massage. If you want, you can easily find a masseur at even three o'clock in the morning, and all night you can be sure to hear someone calling out from this or that street corner, '*Pi—pi—pi*', which is Bombay shorthand for 'massage'.

Faras Road was really a road's name but it was used for the entire neighbourhood where prostitutes lived. It was a large area. There were many alleys with their own names, and yet for the sake of convenience they were all called Faras Road or White Alley. There were hundreds of shops with cage façades in which women of all different ages and complexions sold themselves. They were available from eight annas to a hundred rupees and were of every sort—Jewish, Punjabi, Marathi, Kashmiri, Gujarati, Anglo-Indian, French, Chinese, Japanese; you could get whatever sort you wanted. Just don't ask me what they were like. All I know is that somehow they always had customers.

A lot of Chinese lived in the neighbourhood, and though I don't know what they all did for business some had restaurants with signboards covered in insect-like up-and-down script advertising God knows what. In fact all different sorts of people lived and did business there. There was one alley called Arab Sen although the people who lived there called it Arab Alley, and probably between twenty and twenty-five Arabs lived there working as pearl merchants. The rest of the alley's residents were Punjabis or were from Rampur.

I rented a room there for nine and a half rupees a month. The room got no natural light, and so I always had to keep a lamp on.

If you haven't been to Bombay, you might not believe that no one takes any interest in anyone else. But the truth is that if you are busy dying in your room, no one will interfere. Even if one of your neighbours is murdered, you can be assured you won't hear about it. In all of Arab Alley there was only one man who took an interest in everyone else, and that was Mammad Bhai.

Mammad Bhai was from Rampur. There wasn't anyone

better in the martial arts—fighting with clubs, wooden sticks, or swords. I often overheard his name mentioned in the restaurants of Arab Alley, but for the longest time I never got to meet him.

In those days I left my room at daybreak and didn't get back till very late, but I very much wanted to meet him. In the neighbourhood, he was a legend and there were countless stories about him. People said that when billy-club-carrying gangs, twenty or twenty-five strong, jumped him, he would dispose of the assailants in under a minute, then walk away without even one hair out of place. There were also stories about his unsurpassed skill with a knife. He was the quickest in all of Bombay, so quick in fact that his victim wouldn't realize he had just been stabbed but would walk ahead for a hundred steps before suddenly collapsing. People knew this could be the work of only Mammad Bhai.

I wasn't interested in witnessing his knife-wielding expertise so much, but I had heard so many stories about him that I couldn't help but want to see him up close. His presence overshadowed the entire neighbourhood. He was a gangster, and yet people said he was a resolute bachelor and never looked at anyone's wife or daughter. He sympathized with the poor and often gave a little money to the destitute prostitutes not just in Arab Alley but in all the alleys in the vicinity. Nonetheless, he never visited these women himself but sent a young apprentice to bring back whatever news they had.

I don't know how he made a living. He ate well and wore nice clothes, and he owned a small horse-drawn cart to which he yoked a strong pony. He drove the cart himself and was accompanied by two or three loyal apprentices. He would take the cart out for a tour of Bhindi Bazaar or go to a saint's shrine and then return to Arab Alley and go to an Iranian restaurant where he would sit with his apprentices and energetically discuss hand-to-hand combat.

A Marwari Muslim dancer lived next to me, and he told me hundreds of stories about Mammad Bhai, including how he was worth a 100,000 rupees. One time this man got cholera, and when Mammad Bhai found out, he called all the doctors of Arab Alley into his room and said, 'Look, if anything happens to Ashiq Husain, I'm going to kill every one of you.' In a reverential manner, Ashiq Husain told me, 'Manto Sahib, Mammad Bhai is an angel! An angel! When he threatened the doctors, they shook in fear. They looked after me so well that I was better in two days!'

In the dives of Arab Alley, I heard more stories about Mammad Bhai. One young man—an aspiring martial artist and so probably one of Mammad Bhai's apprentices—told me Mammad Bhai kept a dagger tucked in his waistband that was so sharp he could shave with it. He kept it without a scabbard, the knife's cold metal pressed against his belly, and the blade was so sharp that if he bent just a little wrong he would become old news fast.

You can imagine how each day my desire to meet him only increased. I don't remember what exactly he looked like, but after so many years I can still recall anticipating that he must be enormous, the kind of man Hercules bicycles would use as a model in their advertising.

Those days I left for work early in the morning and didn't return until ten at night, and when I got back I would quickly eat and go straight to bed. Living like this, how could I meet Mammad Bhai? I often resolved to skip work and stay in Arab Alley looking for him, but work heaped up and I couldn't carry out this plan.

I was thinking about how I might meet him when suddenly I got the flu so bad I began to fear for my health. One Arab Alley doctor told me there was a danger it would worsen into pneumonia. I was all alone. The man living next door had got a job in Pune and wasn't around. My fever was roasting me alive, and despite how I drank water continuously, my thirst never slackened.

I am a very tough person. Usually I don't need anyone to take care of me, but I didn't know what kind of fever it was—the flu, malaria, or something else. It crushed me flat. It was the first time in my life I wished for someone to comfort me, or if not that then just to show his face for a moment so that I would know that at least someone cared.

For two days I lay in bed tossing and turning, but no one came. And who could have? How many friends did I have? Just a handful, and they lived so far away that they wouldn't even know if I had died. Like I said, who in Bombay cares about anyone? No one gives a damn if you live or die.

I was in a very bad state. The hotel's tea boy told me Ashiq Husain's wife was sick and that he had left for home. Who could I call? I was very weak. While I was thinking about dragging myself down to a doctor's, there was a knock at the door. I thought it was the tea boy, the 'bahar vala' in Bombay slang. In a lifeless voice, I said, 'Come in.'

The door opened, and a thin man entered. I noticed his moustache first. In fact the moustache was what distinguished him, and without it no one was likely to notice him at all.

Adjusting his Kaiser Wilhelm adornment with one finger, he came up to my cot. Several men followed him in. I was stunned. I couldn't imagine who they were or why they were visiting me.

The skinny guy with the Kaiser Wilhelm addressed me in a tender voice, 'Vamato Sahib, what have you done? Hell, why didn't you tell me?' Changing Manto to Vamato was nothing new, and I wasn't in the mood to correct him. I weakly asked, 'Who are you?'

'Mammad Bhai.'

I shot up. 'Mammad Bhai . . . so you're Mammad Bhai . . . the notorious gangster!'

I immediately felt awkward and stopped. Mammad Bhai used his pinkie to press his stiff moustache hairs up and then smiled. 'Yes, Vamato Bhai. I'm Mammad, the famous gangster. I learned from the hotel's tea boy that you were sick. Hell, what were you trying to do by not telling me? It pisses Mammad Bhai off when people hide things.'

I was about to say something when Mammad Bhai addressed one of his companions, 'Hey, you there—what's your name? Go get that doctor, whatever-his-name-is, you know who I mean? Tell him Mammad Bhai needs him. Tell him to drop whatever he's doing and come at once. And tell the bastard to bring all the medicine he has.'

The apprentice left immediately. I was looking at Mammad Bhai, and all the stories I had heard about him were swirling around in my feverish mind, but each time I looked at him these images got confused and all I could see was his moustache. It was intimidating but also very beautiful, and it seemed to me that he had grown it out expressly to make his naturally soft and elegant features threatening. I came to the conclusion in my feverish mind that he really wasn't as tough as he made himself out to be.

As there wasn't a chair in the room, I invited Mammad Bhai to sit on my bed, but he refused curtly, 'We're fine. We'll stand.'

Then he began pacing, although there was hardly enough space in the room for that. He lifted his kurta's hem and drew out his dagger from his pyjama's waistband. The dagger must have been made of silver, and its dazzling blade was beyond description. He passed it over his wrist, cleanly shaving off the hairs there. He grunted with satisfaction and began to trim his fingernails.

His mere presence seemed to have reduced my fever by several degrees. Now with a steadier mind I said, 'Mammad Bhai, your dagger's so sharp. Aren't you scared to keep it tucked next to your stomach?'

Mammad Bhai neatly cut back one of his nails, 'Vamato Bhai, this knife's for others. It knows this. It's mine, for fuck's sake. How could it hurt me?'

He spoke about his knife just as a mother would talk about her son, 'How could he raise his hand against me?'

The doctor arrived. His name was Pinto, and mine was Vamato. He was Christian and greeted Mammad Bhai in keeping with his religion's way. He asked what the problem was. Mammad Bhai explained quickly, and his tone carried the threat that Dr Pinto should watch out if he couldn't manage to cure me.

Dr Pinto did his work like an obedient boy. He took my pulse and used his stethoscope to examine my chest and back. He took my blood pressure and asked all about my sickness. Then he turned to Mammad Bhai and said,

'There's nothing to worry about. He has malaria. I'll give him an injection.'

Mammad Bhai was standing nearby. He listened to what Dr Pinto had to say, and while shaving his wrist said, 'I don't want to know the details. If you have to give an injection, go ahead. But if anything happens to him . . .'

The doctor shook in fear. 'No, Mammad Bhai, everything will be fine.'

Mammad Bhai tucked his dagger back into his waistband. 'Okay, fine then.'

'So I'm giving the injection,' the doctor said, opening his bag and taking out a syringe.

'Wait, wait,' Mammad Bhai interrupted him. He was nervous. The doctor quickly replaced the syringe in the bag, and in a whiny voice asked, 'Yes?'

'It's just that I can't watch anyone getting stuck with a needle,' Mammad Bhai said and then left with his companions in tow.

Dr Pinto gave me a quinine injection. He did it very skilfully, as otherwise a malaria injection is very painful. When he was done, I asked how much it was.

'Ten rupees,' he replied.

I took my wallet out from underneath my pillow and was giving him a ten-rupee note when Mammad Bhai walked in. He looked at us with a furious expression. 'What's going on?' he thundered.

'I'm paying him.'

'What the hell! You're charging us?' Mammad Bhai asked the doctor.

Dr Pinto was terrified. 'When did I ask for any money? He was giving it to me.'

'Hell, you're charging us. Give it back.' Mammad Bhai's tone was as sharp as his dagger's blade.

Dr Pinto gave me back the note, packed his bag, apologized to Mammad Bhai and left.

Mammad Bhai twisted his thorny moustache with one finger and then smiled. 'Vamato Bhai, I can't believe that he was trying to charge you. I swear I would have shaved off my moustache if that bastard had taken your money. Everyone here is at your service.'

There was a moment of silence. Then I asked, 'Mammad Bhai, how do you know me?'

Mammad Bhai's moustache twitched. 'Who doesn't Mammad Bhai know? My boy, I'm the kingpin here. I keep track of my people. I have my own CID. They keep me informed—who's come, who's left, who's doing well, who's doing bad. I know everything about you.'

'Like what?' I asked, just for fun.

'Hell, what don't I know? You're from Amritsar. You're Kashmiri. You work in the newspapers here. You owe the Bismillah Hotel ten rupees and so never go by there. A paan seller in Bhindi Bazaar is after you because you still haven't paid him the twenty rupees and ten annas you owe him for some cigarettes.'

I could have died from shame.

Mammad Bhai stroked his bristly moustache again. 'Vamato Bhai, don't worry. Your debts have been cleared, and you can get a fresh start. I told those bastards to make sure never to mess with Vamato Bhai, so, God willing, no one will bother you again.'

I didn't know what to say. The quinine injection had given rise to a buzzing sensation in my ears. Moreover,

I was so overwhelmed by his kindness that it was hard to express my gratitude. I could only say, 'Mammad Bhai, may God look after you! Take care!'

Mammad Bhai pushed his moustache up a little and left.

Dr Pinto came by every morning and evening, and each time I mentioned the money, he put his hands over his ears and said, 'No, Mr Manto! It's Mammad Bhai's business. I can't take a single coin.'

I thought Mammad Bhai was incredible. I mean he was so intimidating that stingy Dr Pinto paid for the injections himself.

Mammad Bhai came to see me every day, either in the morning or the evening, and he would bring with him six or seven apprentices. He reassured me that it was an ordinary case of malaria, 'God willing, Dr Pinto's treatment will get you feeling right in no time.'

I was completely cured within fifteen days, and during my convalescence I learned everything about Mammad Bhai.

He must have been in his late twenties. He was very skinny and had surprisingly nimble hands. I heard from the people in Arab Alley that he could throw a pocketknife straight through a man's heart. And as I said earlier, he was an expert wielder of knives, clubs, and swords. Countless famous stories circulated about how he had committed hundreds of murders, and yet I am still not ready to believe this.

Nonetheless, I shivered in fright at the thought of his dagger. Why did he always keep this deadly weapon tucked unsheathed inside his waistband?

After my health recovered, we ran into each other in one of Arab Alley's run-down Chinese restaurants. He was trimming his fingernails with his dagger.

I asked him, 'Mammad Bhai, these days it's all about guns and pistols. Why do you still use a dagger?'

He adjusted his moustache. 'Vamato Bhai, I don't get any pleasure from guns. Even a child can use one. You squeeze the trigger and "bang!" What fun is there in that? This thing—this dagger—this knife—this pocketknife—there's pleasure in it, you know? Sure as hell there is! And it's that—what do you call it?—yeah—art. There's an art in it, okay? If you don't know how to use a dagger or a knife, you're nothing. A pistol's just a toy—a toy that can kill. But there's no enjoyment in it. Look at this dagger, look at its sharp blade.' He wet his thumb and ran it along the blade. 'With this, there's no bang at all. You can thrust it into someone's stomach just like this. It's so smooth that the bastard won't even know what's going on. Guns and pistols are nonsense.'

I fell into the habit of seeing Mammad Bhai every day. I felt obliged to him for what he had done for me, and yet whenever I tried to express my gratitude he would get angry and say, 'I didn't do you any favour. It was my duty.'

The neighbourhood was his. He looked after the people who lived there, and if someone was sick or having problems, Mammad Bhai would pay them a visit. His agents kept him constantly informed.

He was a gangster and such a dangerous criminal, and yet with God as my witness I still can't figure out what made him intimidating. That is, other than his moustache. Its every hair stood upright like the quills on a porcupine's back. Someone told me he greased it every day. When eating, he would dip his fingers into the food's gravy and then massage it, as ancient wisdom says that oil strengthens hair. His moustache gave him his name—that or maybe his dagger, secured in his shalwar's waistband.

We became good friends. Although he was illiterate, he treated me with so much respect that the rest of Arab Alley got jealous. One early morning on my way to the office, I overheard a man in a Chinese restaurant saying that Mammad Bhai had been arrested. This surprised me because he was friendly with all the area's police.

I asked the man why. He told me that a woman named Shirin Bai lived in Arab Alley and her young daughter had been raped the previous day. Shirin Bai had gone to Mammad Bhai and said, 'You're our protector. Some man did this horrible thing to my daughter. Damn you that you're still at home doing nothing!' Mammad Bhai unleashed a fierce insult at the old woman and then said, 'What do you want me to do?' Shirin Bai answered, 'I want you to slice the bastard's stomach open.'

Mammad Bhai had been at a restaurant eating dinner. When Shirin Bai stopped talking, he took out his dagger. He checked its sharpness against his thumb and said, 'Go, I'll finish your business.'

And he did. Within a half hour the man who had raped Shirin Bai's daughter was dead.

Mammad Bhai was arrested, but there were no witnesses. Even if there had been any, they would never have testified in court. He stayed for two days in police custody, but he was completely at home there as everyone from the street officers to the inspectors knew him. Nonetheless, when he got out on bail he knew he was in for it, and his spirits were low.

I saw him at a Chinese restaurant, and his usually clean clothes were dirty. I didn't mention anything about the murder, but he said, 'Vamato Sahib, I'm sorry it took the bastard so long to die. I made a mistake while stabbing him. My hand got twisted. But it was the bastard's fault too. He turned suddenly, and so everything turned ugly. He died, but I'm sorry for his pain.'

You can imagine how I reacted—he wasn't worried about having killed a man so much as having caused him a little pain!

The trial got underway. Mammad Bhai was worried because he had never faced a judge before. Like I've said, I really don't know how many people he'd killed, but he really didn't know anything about judges, lawyers, witnesses, and the rest.

The police presented the case and fixed a date for the trial. Mammad Bhai was distraught. Over and over he stroked his moustache and said, 'Vamato Sahib, I'd rather die than go into a courtroom. Hell, you don't know what it's like!'

His friends in Arab Alley assured him it wasn't serious since there were no witnesses. Only his moustache might cause the judge to turn against him.

He considered this. His court date had just about arrived when I found him in an Iranian restaurant. I could tell he was beside himself with worry. He couldn't figure out what to do about his moustache. He thought that if he showed up in court with it, there was a good chance he would get convicted. You will think that this is just a story, and yet I'm telling you he was truly distraught. His apprentices were worried too because usually nothing bothered him. But many of his close friends had advised him, 'Mammad

Bhai, if you have to go to court, shave off your moustache. Otherwise the judge will lock you up for sure.' He thought about it so much that he began to wonder whether he had killed the man or if his moustache had! He couldn't reach any decision. He took his dagger from his waistband and threw it into the alley outside. I couldn't believe what I was seeing.

'Mammad Bhai, what're you doing?'

'Nothing, Vamato Bhai. I've got a big problem. I have to go to court, and my friends are saying that if the judge sees my moustache, he's sure to convict me. What should I do?'

What could I say? I looked at his moustache and said, 'Mammad Bhai, they're right. Your moustache will influence the judge's decision. If you really want to know, a conviction won't be a judgment against you but against your moustache.'

'Should I shave it off, then?' Mammad Bhai asked, stroking his beloved moustache.

'What do you think?'

'It doesn't matter what I think—it's not for you to know. But everyone around here thinks I should shave it off. Should I, Vamato Bhai?'

'Yes. If you think it's right, shave it off. It's a question of the courtroom, and really your moustache is very intimidating.'

The next day, Mammad Bhai shaved off his moustache, and yet he did so only on the advice of others.

His case came before the bench of Mr F.H. Teague. I was there. There were no witnesses against him, but the judge declared him a dangerous criminal and ordered him to leave the state. He had just one day to put all his affairs in order before leaving Bombay.

After leaving the courtroom, he didn't say anything to me. Over and over he raised his fingers to his cleanly shaven face, but there wasn't anything there to stroke.

Just before he had to leave Bombay that evening, we met in an Iranian restaurant. Twenty or so apprentices surrounded him, and they were all drinking tea. When he saw me, he didn't say anything. Without his moustache, he looked entirely respectable. But I could tell he was sad.

I sat down next to him and asked, 'What's wrong, Mammad Bhai?'

He unleashed a directionless curse and then said, 'Hell, Mammad Bhai's dead.'

'Don't worry. If you can't live here, another place will do.'

He launched into an expletive-filled tirade against every other possible place to live. Then he said, 'It's not about where I'm going to live. Here or somewhere else, it's all the same. But why the hell did I have to shave off my moustache?'

He recited a litany of curses against those who had told him to shave it off. Then he asked, 'Hell, if I have to leave the city, then why not go with my moustache?'

I couldn't help but laugh. He flew into a rage. 'What kind of man are you, Vamato Sahib? Fuck, I swear they should've hanged me! But I'm to blame for this foolishness. I never feared anyone but, hell, then I got scared of my moustache.'

He slapped his face twice. 'Mammad Bhai, a curse on you! Asshole, you got scared of your moustache! Now get out of here, you mother . . .'

Tears welled in his eyes. How strange they looked against his clean-shaven face!

APPENDIX

WHY I DON'T GO TO THE MOVIES

FOR a long time I've wanted someone to ask me why I don't go to the movies. At home I'll get asked over and over why I don't eat okra, and my friends have long wanted to know why I don't wear Western trousers. Then both at home and elsewhere people have asked me why I don't keep my hair shorter. But no one has fulfilled my wish and gone to the trouble of asking me why I don't go to the movies. Those who know me know that for a long time I was completely enamoured of the cinema, that I would watch three films a day, and I would watch over and over those I really liked. I would travel from Amritsar to Lahore or Jalandhar or elsewhere to see them, and I remember that I went all the way to Delhi for one starring my favourite heroine. But then I stopped going to the movies altogether.

When friends used to ask me to go with them to a movie, I would say, 'I don't go to the movies any more,' and wait eagerly for them to ask why. But they never would. One friend slammed his car door saying, 'Oh, okay', and then drove away. Another smiled but instead of asking why, remarked that I was strange. Another said, just like a penny-pinching shop owner, 'Great, more money for me.'

But at long last today the awaited opportunity has come.

Once upon a time I knew all the actors' and actresses' names, their addresses, and how old they were—from Eddy Polo to John Gilbert, from Mary Pickford to Gloria Swanson. Lillian Gish had a sister named Dorothy, and I still remember how tall they were, and if someone mentions Paul Robeson, I start thinking about Robinson Crusoe and the taste of ginger spreads through my mouth. If my friends start talking about the acting of Shanta Veen, Shanta Hublikar, or Shanta Mazumdar, then I'll yell out, 'Shanti! Shanti!' But now I don't have any interest in the fairy-faced Naseem Banu, in the vixen Veena, in doe-eyed Ragni, in the bewitching Suraiya, or in the fair and statuesque Shameem. Maybe you'll think I've renounced the world and become an ascetic, that I've smeared ashes over my body and make a habit of tramping up to the mountains to meditate. But no, I'm still here in the very same world as you, that one full of colours and smells, although who knows what will happen tomorrow. I still eat, drink, sleep, get up, and appreciate good stories. Good poetry still thrills me. But, dear readers, I don't go to the movies.

Once upon a time, I decorated my room exclusively with posters of actors and actresses. I loved them so much that I made frames with my own hands, but these days all you'll see are cartoons drawn by Dasan, whose specialty is the psychology of monkeys. Just try to imagine how such a transformation took place.

It was as though I worshipped in a beautiful pavilion of the gods where each evening I attained inner peace by performing offerings before my favourite actors. But then something happened that ruptured my faith entirely, and

I blew out all the candles and stomped on all the flowers. Was I possessed by Ghaznavi? No, it was something quite different. Some don't go to the cinema because they have conjunctivitis; some don't because they fall asleep as soon as the film begins; some don't because they're too easily moved to tears and so love scenes make their hearts race out of control; and some don't because they think that films are the work of the devil. But none of these is my reason. While I do have poor vision, that's not it because I'm always wearing glasses. Then my heart's strong enough, knock on wood. (For proof, I have a cardiogram read-out.) Lastly, I think of films as something that people watch for fun. So why is it that I've stopped watching them?

If those people who know me as a film writer hear that I no longer watch movies, they'll be especially surprised. They'll wonder why a man who writes screenplays, writes dialogue, and almost even acted in one film (moreover who has spent about ten years in the film industry doing this and that), why this man no longer watches films. Without a doubt, they'll think I'm lying.

But, dear readers, God forbid that! If I'm lying, let some actress come on Judgement Day to seek amends. I'm telling you the truth. It was lies and only lies that made me sick of the movies. If this is a lie, let me go to hell. But it's not—I really don't watch movies any more.

This anecdote is from twelve years ago. I tried four times to break into the film studios (the very Somnath of Bombay) and at last I succeeded in getting in—an important day in my life. There was an intimidating Pathan guard standing in front of the gate, but I slipped by. As soon as I entered, I heard a voice resonating all around me, 'I smell human flesh! I smell human flesh!' A dark-skinned woman passed by, and I desperately wanted her to fall in love with me and, like the heroine in *Arabian Nights*, use some magic to turn me into a fly so that I could escape the upcoming calamity. But instead she walked away, thrusting her hips out sexily, unconscious of me. Suddenly a commotion arose, and I saw a large group of men appear from a corner, wearing armour and wielding drawn swords, then leap around chaotically before disappearing into a large stable. One dropped his sword in the process. Though scared, I wanted to pick it up, and as I slowly reached out my hand, I realized the sword was made of wood.

I wet my thumb and was running it along the sword's blade when an enormous mustachioed demon appeared in front of me. He was just about to set off for the gate when a voice broke over the scene, 'Hey, where're you going with our stuff?'

The demon froze in place, and in a trembling voice he asked, 'What's wrong, sir?'

'Whose moustache is that?' The other man, whom I mistook to be King Indra from some previous production, asked in a terrifying voice.

'Sir, well, it's mine,' said the demon in a humble voice, as he twisted his moustache.

This seemed to satisfy the other man. 'You can go now.'

The demon was free to go, meaning they didn't want him. The other man—the producer—turned to me and gave me work right on the spot. The next day I learned my name was no longer Saadat Hasan Manto but merely 'Writer', and that my job was to run to the store every five minutes to get the director some paan and otherwise not make a sound. Then, whenever I had a free moment, I was to write out whatever dialogue he recited in his broken Urdu and not make any suggestions.

In those days I didn't care much about Urdu, and so when the director made a mistake, I didn't really care. But, dear readers, one day it became rather serious. The producer came up to the director and shaking his hand said triumphantly that he had sold the rights for their thirteenth film. The director congratulated him and asked what it was called, and the producer smiled and said, 'You'll really like it . . . *Pharj-e-ada*.' The director turned to me and in trying to correct the producer's pronunciation said, 'Mr Writer, please start writing a film called *Farj-e-ada*. But before that get me some throat lozenges . . .'

I interrupted, 'Throat lozenges, betel nut, some chuna on my finger, one Pasang Soop cigarette . . . I'll bring you these right away, but the title *Farz-e-ada* is completely wrong.'

'What did you say?' the producer asked angrily.

'I said that what you said just now doesn't make any sense.'

'Why?' asked the director.

'Because it's completely wrong,' I said. 'You can say *Adaegi-e-farz*, or even *Farz-e-adaegi*, or I suppose you could stretch it to *Ada-e-farz*—people will be able to make some sense out of that too. But for God's sake please don't use *Farz-e-ada*.'

The producer stared at me. 'You're out of your mind. There's no way to change the title, we've already sold the film.'

This made me very upset, and so I upped and quit.

The story of how I quit my second film company is

similar. It was proposed that we name a new film *Ullu ke do pathe*. I objected, as the title should have been *Do ullu ke pathe*. But it stuck and they said to me, 'Who're you anyway? We're paying for it so if we want it call it *Pathe ke do ullu* then we'll go ahead and call it that.' So the shooting began and I quit.

From that time forward I began to have a bad feeling about films, and within several years it grew to an unbearable frustration.

After working in some small-time film companies, I finally found a job at a well-known studio that made accomplished films. I worked there as a writer for four years and in the process slowly laid to rest my interest in watching films. The entire story of this burial is long and drawn-out, but I have only several columns in which to recount a number of anecdotes:

1) There was an actress famous for her horsemanship. But when she was about to do her horse-riding scene, I saw that a wooden horse was being brought onto the set. The horse wasn't even a full one but only the part where she'd be sitting in the saddle. It didn't even have a face or tail. Three men hoisted the actress onto this strange-looking horse. Then the lights went on. The director shouted, 'Action!' Quickly, one of the stagehands put the reins in her hands and another gently manoeuvred this wooden horse to make it look as though it were galloping. The filming of this scene went on for a while. Then the next day was an outdoor shoot. A horse-riding master from the circus, dressed up in the actress's bra and sari, and mounted

a horse that reared so often and was so restless that others couldn't lay a hand on it. Various shots were filmed and afterwards everything was stitched together so well that when I saw the film it seemed to me as though the actress was really doing everything.

Then they needed a close-up of the actress's 'beautiful' hand, but in fact this knockout had extremely ugly fingers, and so the director immediately called for ten or twelve girls. One of them had nice hands. She got a little make-up work done to them, and then the director took his close-up and spliced this into the film. It reminded me of a line Ghalib wrote, 'Everyone has a complaint against God lodged in his heart.'

2) They wanted to make it seem like a tempest was raging, and so on the set men were making rain by sprinkling water from watering cans. Then to the side there was an aeroplane's rotors powered by a motor, and very close by two men were holding baskets of twigs and leaves and were tossing handfuls of these into the wind created by the enormous makeshift fan. The sky was a piece of cloth. One man switched the motor on and off, and another was rattling a huge sheet of aluminium. When I saw all this on the screen, I got goosebumps. It seemed like it was raining cats and dogs. The trees were bending under the storm's might and their branches were screeching beneath the ferocious lightning of the storm. And the hero was standing rowing a boat with a manly sangfroid.
3) Milk is boiling in a cauldron. But in fact it's whitewash.
4) It's snowing in the Valley of Kashmir. But it's only a

handful of workers scattering tiny slices of soap and pieces of paper from above some fake cypress trees.

5) A fantastic fog has descended, and the hero and heroine are wrapped up in each other saying sweet nothings. But smoke from the dry grass being burned on the set is suffocating them.
6) The heroine and the hero are joking around before shooting begins. The make-up man drops a little glycerin into the heroine's eyes, and behold, she's crying like an elephant!
7) Someone is singing. The actor is lip-synching.
8) A wooden phone rests on a table. A man stands close by holding a small bell. He shakes it, and the hero quickly picks up the receiver as though the call were real.
9) The heroine's hair is cut short, but on the screen she looks like an actress in a hair oil commercial.
10) It's a fight scene. No one makes any contact, but two or three men fall down and don't get up.
11) There's a bowl of fruit on a table. But only the banana that the hero's father will eat is real, and the rest are made of clay.
12) The sun is scorching hot but put a red filter on the camera and suddenly the scene is filled with the moon's cool light.
13) There aren't any zebras around but get a donkey and throw some black and white stripes on it and there you have your zebra.
14) A man pops a bit of flour into his mouth. He has poisoned himself, and everyone around is wailing and lamenting.

15) People are falling, but turn your camera upside down and it will seem like people are leaping upwards, as though they have springs in their legs. The audience will erupt in applause.

Dear readers, seeing all these tricks repeated time and again made me bitter. When I sat in the cinema hall and with the fellow members of the audience saw the heroine's fake eyelashes and the glycerin tears that fell from them, I thought of the English proverb, 'The straw that broke the camel's back.' The movies had made me cry once too often.

The cinema is such delusion and those in the film industry get sucked into it too—they can't tell any more that it's a delusion! Please God, let there not come a day when I return to watching movies.

WOMEN AND THE FILM WORLD

NOW that the Indian film industry has left its infancy, many people are talking about whether respectable women should be allowed to participate in it or not. Many believe that they should be strongly encouraged to join in order to cleanse the film world of 'impure' women, but there are also those who believe that to let such women participate for even one second would be an unpardonable sin.

The delightful irony is that the former—who with the best intentions want to purify the silver screen—are forgetting that while they can clean up the film world, the real world won't change at all. They can run prostitutes out of the studios, but this won't eliminate them from the world outside where they will still be seen working the streets. Then the latter are against letting honourable women experience the film studios' debauched atmosphere. But once they get worked up by thoughts of cleanliness and purity, they forget that actresses—whose acting they enjoy in the films they watch—were once respectable as well.

If a woman leaves a brothel and joins a film company and proves to be a wonderful actress, then no one has any right to complain. Society produces prostitutes, and its wide-reaching laws foster their existence. So why are they stigmatized, why is their collective death wished, when they, too, are part of society? If we want to transform them into something good, then we will have to work to improve society as a whole. As long as we don't think with new vigour about how our society operates, then in this so-called era of culture and civilization there will continue to be prostitutes everywhere and this 'impurity' will never disappear.

A factotum works all day in an office labouriously balancing accounts just so he can live, and another sells liquor for just the same ends. Although their means are different, they share the same purpose, and it's possible that if the peon could, he would start selling alcohol. Why is it then that prostitutes are viewed with such surprise and hatred when the fact of their existence isn't surprising and their lives aren't really despicable?

Respectable women owe their good name to the atmosphere in which they were raised—they pass from the affectionate protection of their fathers to the prosperous houses of their husbands and never know how complicated life can be. But women deprived of their father's love and concern, who grow up illiterate, and who have to feed themselves, are another matter. They are forced to face all of life's difficulties: some can't overcome them and they die; some take to begging; some fall ill and are admitted into hospitals; some do manual labour; and some encounter trials so severe that they become prostitutes, a fate that is itself an endless agonizing trial.

Women aren't born prostitutes but are either forced to become them or choose to be them on their own. Demand always spurs supply—because men lust after women without regard to who they are, you'll find prostitutes everywhere. If men stopped desiring women, then prostitution would disappear by itself.

Our so-called honourable citizens hold fundamentally flawed opinions about prostitutes in that their posturing is essentially no more than a way for them to insist upon their respectability and dignity. Men control society and take advantage of their power. Society says that men always remain men, regardless of whether they commit sins at each and every step of their way, but a woman no longer remains a woman if she succumbs even once to a youthful desire or some other impulse, or if she loses her way for a moment due to a man's forceful demands. She's viewed with contempt and hatred, and doors close for her that would remain open for men.

I wonder, if women can be chaste, can't men be too? If women can be promiscuous, can't men be too? Then why do we direct our wrath only at women?

It is said that studios should refuse to hire prostitutes, but doesn't this imply that men can't control themselves and so this serves as an admission that compared to women, men are in fact much weaker and liable to err?

The film industry has to have both men and women, and disagreements between them are often fruitful. If people didn't think that acting lasciviously was part and parcel of being in the film world, and if men were able to control themselves, then women couldn't ruin things even if they tried.

I want to ask those men who plan to invite respectable women into the film industry what they mean by 'respectable.' Aren't prostitutes who don't cheat anyone also respectable? If they mean 'chaste', then I want to ask whether they think that acting requires this. Does it seem likely that in order to act you must be chaste? If they really believe this, they're completely wrong and their reasoning is suspect.

In order to act well, actors and actresses must know life's ups and downs. It's impossible for an actress to portray a woman separated from her lover if she hasn't already experienced this several times, because how can a woman portray grief if she has never known it? If actresses want to succeed, they should know about more than love. They need worldly experience if they want to be able to act in character.

Reality is right before us and we cannot cover it up. If we want to make better and more artistic films (ones that really sparkle), and if we want to avoid going down the wrong path, then we should demand more of ourselves. Humans are capable of both behaving with great character and with great error, but this has nothing to do with art. Whether the film world has respectable women or dissolute ones, the only thing that matters is that films mirror reality.

I'm not saying that prostitution is good, and I'm not advocating that film companies should hire prostitutes in droves. What I want to say and have said is clear: to be a good actress, a woman must be experienced in the ways of the world—in both its pleasant aspects and its unpleasant ones—because if she can't call up a painful memory when it's needed, she won't be convincing. Really, I just can't stress enough how important it is for an actress to be widely experienced.

Whether an actress is a prostitute or an exemplar of chastity, in my eyes she is only an actress. I don't care about her 'honour' because it doesn't impact her ability to act. Similarly, a prostitute can become a writer of the first calibre and society can benefit from her thoughts and perspective, but untold harm can come from listening to an educated married woman. A Parisian prostitute was the first to be shot in the French Revolution, and at Jallianwala Bagh, a prostitute's son was the first to die.

Don't look down upon the wayside vagabonds.
Who are you to know if there isn't a nobleman among them?

LECTURE AT JOGESHWARI COLLEGE, BOMBAY

THE title of my talk is 'Modern Literature'. The funny thing is I don't know what that means. Then again, it seems like we live in a day and age where people self-consciously choose to talk about just those things they don't understand. Recently Gandhiji lay half dead in Agha Khan's mansion. When people feared he was a goner, a tangerine was proffered. After several days, this tangerine became a matter of curiosity. Some said it wasn't a tangerine but a mandarin orange. Some said, no, no, it was neither a tangerine nor a mandarin but a clementine. No one could agree on which type of fruit it was. Tangerine, orange, mandarin, clementine, grapefruit, sweet lime, bitter lemon, sweet lemon, so on and so forth. The doctors elaborated on how many vitamins each had and they calculated calories too. How many calories does a Seventy-five-year-old man need each year? They started discussing that, and, gentlemen, Gandhiji's tangerine or orange or whatever soon became Saadat Hasan Manto. That's me. But some call modern literature, or 'new' literature, or progressive literature, by my name too, and they disapprove of it completely. (Ismat Chughtai gets mistreated the same.)

In the same way that I—meaning Saadat Hasan Manto—don't understand myself, I also don't understand modern literature, or 'new' literature, or progressive literature, and, as I've already said, neither do those who pretend to. I mean, those who in a handful of essays have attached ever yet newer names to this literature of many names, calling it socialist and smut.

I'm not against calling things by their names. If I didn't have a name, how would the critics address me, those who have excoriated me hundreds of thousands of times? Names make praising or insulting someone much easier, but if you use a lot of names to identify one thing, then confusion sets in.

The biggest confusion is about progressive literature, and yet this is unnecessary. Literature is just literature or it's not. A man is just a man or he's not. The same is true of a donkey, a house, a table, or anything else. You could say that Saadat Hasan Manto is a progressive human. There's nothing nonsensical about that. Saadat Hasan Manto is a human, and every human should be progressive. When people refer to me as progressive, they don't implicate my style but rather prove their faults. I mean that they themselves aren't progressive—they don't want to change. I want to see improvements in each aspect of life, and I hope you all do too. Now you are students, and by improving each day, hopefully you'll be able to give life to your ideals.

Everyone is progressive. Even people who are nihilistic or supremely conservative think of themselves as progressive. Each era thinks itself more intelligent, perspicacious and modern than those before. This is true for literature too. Many writers today can't be bothered with Sharar's [Abdul Halim Sharar] novels and Rashid ul-Khairi's stories. Readers too. Go shopping and you'll see that books written even a decade or two ago are hard to find. The books of Krishan Chander, Rajender Singh Bedi, Ismat Chughtai and Saadat Hasan Manto are read more than those of M. Islam, Teerath Ram Ferozpuri, Syed Imtiaz Ali Taj, and Abd Ali Abd—and the reason is that Krishan Chander and his peers write about life's new experiences.

Our country's political and social conditions were very different twenty or twenty-five years ago, so you can well imagine how different things must have been fifty or sixty years ago. If we were living in the Mughal Age, it's very likely I'd have a harem, and if not that then at least several courtesans as well as my wife. I'd fight pheasants as my hobby, and instead of reading an essay, I'd recite a fabulous poetic tale in honour of Principal Balaqa that would please him so much he'd fill my mouth with pearls, or Jogeshwari College would give me a fellowship so that I could build up my horse stable. But, as you know, things are very different now. From here I'll have to walk to the train station, and when I get back to Filmistan I'll have to tell my bosses what I was doing for so long at the doctor's. I lied—I told them I was going to the doctor's and then came here!

Yes, things are different, and this difference is just what appears in literature. In the Enlightenment, people liked to enjoy themselves and take it easy. In their literature you read about luxuries and can sense how a sort of drowsiness had overcome writers. Their poetry was about the untimely death of their pure-breed cocks, and everyone thought it was great stuff. But today's poets write about their own approaching untimely deaths. Back then, writers wrote about djinns and fairies and became famous. Today people write about men and women—a subject matter many times more interesting than djinns and fairies. Writers then were happy. Writers today are dissatisfied. They are unhappy about their living conditions, their society, their literature, and they are especially critical of themselves. But people have given this mentality the wrong name. Some call it progressive, some call it smut and some call it socialist. Some even say that these writers are obsessed with women. The truth of the matter is that men have been obsessed with women since Adam and Eve, and why not? What—should men be obsessed with elephants or horses?

A male pigeon coos when he sees a female pigeon, so why shouldn't men write a ghazal or a story when inspired by a woman? Women are much more interesting, pretty and intelligent than pigeons. That goes without saying.

It used to be that poetry used handsome boys to signify women. Obviously, the poets must have seen some advantage in this, and yet today poets stand firmly against this tradition. Today's poets find it disgusting and unnatural that a woman's face should have a fuzzy moustache and the beginnings of a downy beard, and they want readers to appreciate women for who they really are. Honestly, tell me, with God as our witness, would you like your lover to have a beard?

My point is that literature changes with the times. The editorials in the newspapers and the poisonous demonstrations in the streets that challenge this are worthless. Those who want to bring down progressive literature, obscene literature, or whatever you want to call it, what they should really do is change the conditions that motivate such writing.

Whether the bill to ban this literature was penned by the King of Mahmudabad, Mahirul Qadri (the poet from Hyderabad) or Bombay's Dr Mirza Haider Baig doesn't matter—it's still worthless. As long as there is a wall that separates men and women, Ismat Chughtai will pick at its mortar with her sharp fingernails. As long as cities dump their trash in Kashmir's beautiful countryside, poor Krishan Chander will cry heavy, silent tears. So long as there is human weakness (and especially so long as it exists in me), I will search it out and expose it to others. The King of Mahmudabad and his like-minded cast think this is the very height of nonsense. They say that whatever I write is smut. And I say, that's exactly right: I write exclusively about human nonsense and filth. If the King of Mahmudabad becomes a Congress Party leader or Dr Haider Baig invents a concoction that cures a cough, I couldn't care less. But when I'm sitting in the train and take out my new expensive pen just so everyone will look over in awe, I get interested in my crassness. When my next-door neighbour beats his wife but she still cleans his shoes, I hardly feel any sympathy for her. But when she gets beaten up, threatens suicide, leaves the house to watch a movie so her husband must suffer through the next two hours' of uncertainty, then I feel a strange sort of sympathy for both. A boy falling in love with a girl isn't even as interesting as a head cold, but I'll be interested if I learn that hundreds of girls have fallen in love with him, and yet he remains as starved for love as a poor Bengali is for food. He unwittingly gets me to listen to his love talk—and whatever tear-jerking tragedy it contains—and I end up telling his story to others. The woman who labours all day grinding spices and who sleeps soundly at night will never be the heroine in any of my stories. My heroine is the cheapest of whores who works at night and sleeps fitfully during the day, persecuted by nightmares that she's getting old, and whose heavy eyelids are weighed down by years of missed sleep. That's what I write about. *Her* desperation, *her* illnesses, *her* anxieties, *her* insults—that's what I like, that's what I write about, not the housewife's pleasant banter, good health, and high-mindedness.

People object that the only thing new writers write about is sex. For myself, all I'll say is that the subject interests me. Why? Just because. Ascribe it to perversion. But if you're smart you'll be able to trace out its causes. That is, the age we live in. If you're still unaware of the times, please read my stories. If you can't stand my stories, the reason is that the times are insufferable. Whatever faults I have are those of the times. My stories aren't fake, even though they're accused of being so. It's the establishment that's fake.

I don't like to raise a stir. I don't want to get people riled up. How can I be said to lay bare our culture's, our society's, deep dark secrets when they're already easily visible? But I also don't try to cover anything up. That's a tailor's job, not mine. People say I have dark intentions, but I don't use black chalk on a blackboard: I use white chalk so that the blackboard's black becomes even more noticeable. This is my special style, my special way, which is called obscene, progressive, and God knows what all else. Curse that Saadat Hasan Manto who doesn't even swear as you're supposed to!

When I started writing, my family was less than pleased, and accordingly, everyone else became interested. They started in on me, 'Hey, you should find a job. When are you going to give up writing your awful stories?' Ten years ago an awful story had a different name; now it's called modern literature, by which people mean they've already improved enough to please themselves. The time will come when people understand modern literature, and Dr Haider Baig won't have to bother leaving his hospital in order to diagnose the disease plaguing young writers.

Since the beginning of the war, modern literature has had a new angle to deal with. It's said that with the world on fire, the earth soaks in the blood of thousands every day. People have lost their minds in death and destruction. But like other animals, people have two ears. Why is the new generation of writers silent? Do they write only about sex? The world's balance of power is changing. Every moment, every second, a new order is emerging, and yet they're stricken by a strange silence.

I won't try to answer for others. For me, I know that the world really is changing, and yet if I started to write different things, I would no longer be myself. I'm timid by nature. I'm very afraid of going to jail. My life isn't harder than prison, but if there were a jail within the jail and I were thrown in there, I'd surely be a goner. I love life. I like being free to do what I like. If I were on the open road, a bullet in the chest wouldn't be a big deal, but I don't want to die like a fly in some jail. I stand before you on this stage reading my essay and if you start abusing me, you won't get so much as a beep out of me. But if someone bashes in my head during Hindu–Muslim riots, each and every drop of my blood will cry till eternity. I'm an artist. I can't stomach blood and guts. If I write about the war, and in my heart some evil springs up that leads me to buy a gun to use in some dark alley, that's a worse death than even giving up writing, buying a dairy farm and peddling diluted milk. Guns and torpedoes aren't for me. Neither is anti-aircraft gunnery.

When I was a boy, a police officer lived in the neighbourhood. He kept a pistol in a box. When he brought the box down, the kids yelled, 'Look, don't go in there. There's a pistol in there.' Sometimes we dared go into his room. Standing far away, we looked at the gun with our hearts beating madly. We thought it would go off by itself.

So tell me, what am I supposed to say about howitzers and tanks? I'm not going to write about the war, and yet when and if I hold a gun without fearing it will go off by itself, I'll probably take it outside to wave it around. Then I'll know who my true enemies are. Then I'll either empty its bullets into his chest or do the same to myself. Upon my death, some critic of mine will call me crazy, which my soul will take as the highest honour. Then it will rise and pin this medal proudly on my chest.

1 January 1944 Saadat Hasan Manto
Bombay

GLOSSARY

Here, the in-text transliteration precedes a more rigorous rendering of the Urdu vowels and nasalization: *hamzah* is indicated with a single closed quotation mark (') and *ain*, with a single open quotation mark (‘).

Adana	*raag* name
babu	respectful title for a man older than the speaker and of higher socio-economic status
bahar vala	literally ‘outside person’ but in Bombay slang, ‘tea boy’
beora	local Indian alcohol
bhangan	a woman of the sweeper caste
bhapa	dad
bismillah	phrase that means ‘in the name of God’ that is used before you begin anything new and colloquially can be used to express surprise
changli	‘good’ in Marathi
chane	‘fish scales’ in Punjabi
chikku	the sapodilla fruit
chuna	lime, or the white acidic paste from the berries of the evergreen tree *Citrus aurantifolia* used in preparing *paan*

dalal	pimp
dhani	Indian dance step
dhrupad	genre of north Indian music thought to be the oldest extant classical music tradition in India
ghatin	a woman of a low caste in Bombay who does menial labour
kaserail ki peti	type of *peti*
kashta	*sari* that at nine yards is longer than average and that is wrapped in a special way—passed from the front between a woman's legs and tucked into the waist from behind—and associated with the underclasses and with coarse eroticism
lahaul wala quwat	the phrase 'there is no sway or strength but that of God' can be said to repel Satan or when you want to express something along the lines of 'shit' or 'to hell with it'
Malkos	*raag* name
Mian ki todi	*raag* name
paan/pan	digestive concoction that usually includes grated betel nut and tobacco
Patdeep	*raag* name
peti	small instrument used to accompany singing
sang-e-aswad	the Black Stone in the Ka'aba in Mecca
sayyan/sa'ī	wandering Muslim holy man, fakir
seth	a banking caste, or colloquially, a rich man

shalwar kameez/ qamiz	pants and blouse set
shervani	long coat for men that extends several inches below the knees
Tandau	Shiva's angry dance

BIBLIOGRAPHY

Adarkar, Neera and Meena Menon. *One Hundred Years, One Hundred Voices: The Millworkers of Girangaon: An Oral History*. Intro. Rajnarayan Chandavarkar. Calcutta: Seagull, 2004.

Akhtar, Salim. 'Is Manto Necessary Today?' Trans. Leslie Flemming. *Journal of South Asian Literature*, 20:2 (Summer, Fall 1985): 1–3.

Alter, Stephen. 'A Few Thoughts on Indian Fiction, 1947–1997.' *Alif: Journal of Comparative Poetics*, 18 (1998): 14–28.

——. 'Madness and Partition: The Short Stories of Saadat Hasan Manto.' *Alif: Journal of Comparative Poetics*, 14 (1994): 91–9.

Asaduddin, M. 'Manto Flattened: An Assessment of Khalid Hasan's Translations.' *Annual of Urdu Studies*, 11 (1996): 129–39.

Azmi, Khalil ur-Rahman. *Urdu men taraqqi pasand adabi tahrik*. Aligarh: Anjuman Taraqqi Urdu (Hind), 1972.

Bismillah, Abdul. 'A Letter from Manto.' *Annual of Urdu Studies*, 11 (1996): 167–74.

Biswas, Ranjita. 'Little China Stays Alive in Eastern India.' Inter Press Service News Agency, August 3, 2006.

Bhalla, Alok. 'Dance of Grotesque Masks: A Critical Reading of Manto's "1919 ki Ek Bat."' *Annual of Urdu Studies*, 11 (1996): 175–96.

Chandavarkar, Rajnarayan. *Imperial Power and Popular*

Politics: Class, Resistance and the State in India, c. 1850–1950. Cambridge: Cambridge University Press, 1998.

——. *The Origins of Industrial Capitalism in India: Business strategies and the working classes in Bombay, 1900–1940*. Cambridge: Cambridge University Press, 1994.

Cohen, Ralph. 'Do Postmodern Genres Exist?' *Postmodern Literary Theory*. Niall Lucy, ed. Oxford: Blackwell, 2000. 293–309.

Daruwalla, Keki N. 'The Craft of Manto: Warts and All.' *Annual of Urdu Studies*, 11 (1996): 117–28.

David, M.D. *Bombay: The City of Dreams*. Mumbai: Himalaya, 1995.

Delacy, Richard. 'Sa'adat Hasan Manto: The Making of an Urdu Literary Icon.' MA Thesis. Monash University (Clayton, Australia), 1998.

Desai, W.S. *Bombay and the Marathas up to 1774*. New Delhi: Munshiram Manoharlal, 1970.

Désoulières, Alain. 'Vie et œuvre de Saadat Hasan Manto.' *Toba Tek Singh et autres nouvelles*. By Saadat Hasan Manto. Trans. Alain Désoulières. Paris: Buchet-Chastel, 2008.

Evenson, Norma. *The Indian Metropolis: A View Toward the West*. New Haven: Yale UP, 1989.

Flemming, Leslie A. *Another Lonely Voice*. Berkeley: Center for South and Southeast Asia Studies, UC at Berkeley, 1979.

Hansen, Thomas Blom. *The Saffron Wave*. New Delhi: Oxford University Press, 1999.

——. *The Wages of Violence: Naming and Identity in Postcolonial Bombay*. Princeton: Princeton University Press, 2001.

Hasan, Khalid. 'Saadat Hasan Manto: Not of Blessed Memory.' *Annual of Urdu Studies*, 4 (1984): 85–95.

Heathcote, T.A. *The Military in British India: The Development of British Land Forces in South Asia, 1600–1947*. Manchester: Manchester University Press, 1995.

Hodgson, Marshall G.S. *The Venture of Islam: Conscience and*

History in a World Civilization, Volume 1, The Classical Age of Islam. 1958. Chicago: Chicago University Press, 1977.

Isenberg, Shirley Berry. *India's Bene Israel: A Comprehensive Inquiry and Sourcebook*. Berkeley, CA: Judah L. Magnes Museum, 1988.

Joshi, Lalit Mohan, ed. *Popular Indian Cinema: Bollywood*. London: Dakini, 2002.

Joshi, Shashi. 'The World of Saadat Hasan Manto.' *Annual of Urdu Studies*, 11 (1996): 141–53.

Kumar, Sukrita Paul. 'Surfacing from Within: Fallen Women in Manto's Fiction.' *Annual of Urdu Studies*, 11 (1996): 155–62.

Malhotra, Rahul and Savita Divedi. *Bombay: The Cities Within*. Bombay: India Book House, 1995.

Manto, Saadat Hasan. *Mantonamah*. Lahore: Sang-e-Meel, 2003.

——. *Mantonuma*. Lahore: Sang-e-Meel, 2003.

——. *Mantorama*. Lahore: Sang-e-Meel, 2004.

——. *Manto Baqiyat*. Lahore: Sang-e-Meel, 2004.

——. *Manto Drame*. Lahore: Sang-e-Meel, 2003.

——. *Manto Kahaniyan*. Lahore: Sang-e-Meel, 2004.

Naqvi, Tahira. '*Ajeeb Aadmi*—An Introduction.' *Annual of Urdu Studies*, 18 (2003): 431–34.

Pearson, M.N. *The Portuguese in India*. Cambridge: Cambridge University Press, 1987.

Prakash, Gyan. *Mumbai Fables*. Princeton, NJ: Princeton University Press, 2010.

Rajadhyaskha, Ashish. 'Indian Cinema: Origins to Independence.' *The Oxford History of World Cinema*. Geoffrey Nowell-Smith, ed. Oxford: Oxford Univeristy Press, 1996, 398–409.

—— and Paul Willemen, ed. *Encyclopedia of Indian Cinema*. Oxford: Oxford University Press, 1999.

Rangoonwalla, Firoze. *A Pictorial History of Indian Cinema*. London: Hamlyn, 1979.

Rushdie, Salman. 'Damme, This is the Oriental Scene for you!' *The New Yorker,* June 23–30, 1997: 50–61.

Sen, Sailendra Nath. *Anglo-Maratha Relations 1785–96*. Delhi: Macmillan, 1974.

Spear, Percival. *India: A Modern History*. Ann Arbor: University of Michigan Press, 1961.

——. *The Nabobs: A Study of the Social Life of the English in Eighteenth Century India*. London: Oxford Univeristy Press, 1963.

Time, February 18, 1929.

Wadhawan, Jagdish Chander. *Manto Naama: The Life of Saadat Hasan Manto*. Trans. Jai Ratan. New Delhi: Roli, 1998.

ACKNOWLEDGEMENTS

WE'D LIKE to thank the editors of the following magazines for publishing some of these stories, essays, and condensed versions of my introduction: Harold Jaffe, *Fiction International*, for publishing 'The Insult'; Donald Breckenridge and Jen Zoble, *In Translation*, for publishing 'Hamid's Baby', 'Mozelle', and 'Ten Rupees' and for including 'Hamid's Baby' in *The Brooklyn Rail's* best fiction anthology; Giriraj Kiradoo, *Pratilipi*, for publishing 'Janaki', 'Peerun', 'Why I Don't Go to the Movies', and 'Women and the Film World'; Brigid Hughes, *A Public Space*, for publishing 'Barren', 'Khushiya', 'Rude', and 'Siraj'; and Olivia Sears, Natasha Wimmer, and Jeffrey Yang, *Two Lines*, for publishing 'Smell'.

A NOTE ON THE TRANSLATORS

Matt Reeck is a writer and translator. His poetry has been published in many national magazines, as have his translations. He won a Fulbright Scholarship to travel to India, and he has received PEN and NEA translation grants for upcoming work from the Urdu. He is married and lives in Brooklyn, NY.

Aftab Ahmad earned his PhD in Urdu literature from Jawaharlal Nehru University. Recipient of a PEN translation grant, he has taught at AIIS Lucknow and UC Berkeley. He now teaches at Columbia University.